THE RUNAWAY

*"Claire Wong's beautifully crafted debut both moved me and
brought to life once again the power of storytelling."*

Susan Lewis, *Sunday Times* bestselling author

Published by Lion Fiction
an imprint of
Lion Hudson plc
Wilkinson House, Jordan Hill Road
Oxford OX2 8DR, England
www.lionhudson.com/fiction

ISBN 978 1 78264 242 8
e-ISBN 978 1 78264 243 5

First edition 2017

A catalogue record for this book is available from the British Library

Printed and bound in the UK, January 2017, LH26

THE
RUN
AWAY

Claire Wong

LION FICTION

to my grandma,
for teaching me the magic of stories

and the beauty of words

ACKNOWLEDGMENTS

Huge thanks to Jess Tinker, who has been brilliant to work with during this whole process, to Julie Frederick for her editorial wisdom and insights, and to everyone at Lion Fiction.

Thank you to my mum for proofreading early drafts, to my dad for sharing his wealth of knowledge about Welsh rural communities, and to Emma for being the first person to read *The Runaway* all the way through!

There are two friends without whom this book would probably still be hiding on my laptop: thank you to Hugh for your well-timed encouragement, and to Lois for pointing me in the right direction. And thank you to Mari for letting me ask Welsh language questions.

Thank you to all the friends, family, and colleagues who have been so enthusiastic about this project. Writing can be a solitary pursuit, but it's great to share this with you.

And finally, thank you to Dave for your encouragement and constant optimism.

PART ONE

KEY

CHAPTER ONE

RHIANNON

I never meant for this to happen.

I could still turn back before I pass the last houses and really have to commit to this. I could make the walk home along Church Road and onto Heol-y-Nant, where the window ledges are bright with marigolds at this time of year. But this is not how it was supposed to be.

I'd expected a shout to follow me down the road. I scripted the whole apology, and prepared how I would react on receiving it. I'd pictured it so perfectly: Aunty Di running after me, my cousins hugging me so that we look like a real family. People would have stopped what they were doing and turned to watch as we made our way back through the village. The twitch of net curtains would have betrayed the nosiness of our elderly neighbours. But I would have smiled reassuringly to all the families I know on these roads, as if to say *don't worry, I'm not going anywhere after all*, and I would have seen the relief in their eyes. I'd be known after today as "Rhiannon, who we almost lost forever". And I would have been far too gracious and sensitive to tell them it should be "whom".

I would have let them persuade me to come home, if anyone had followed me. But nobody came. Instead, here I am, already at the edge of the village, with Dyrys Wood spread out across the hills before me.

I don't understand how no one has noticed, but I won't go back, not after everything that has happened. I grit my teeth and walk

11

on. The road slopes down towards the farmhouse where the Evanses live, and after that the river snakes southward, and the green valley rises back up, and then there's nothing but Dyrys Wood as far as the eye can see. If we'd grown up in another age, we'd have probably been allowed to play there as children, but these days no one thinks they are safe, and Aunty Di worries more than anyone I've ever met – not that she would ever admit it. So of course I was never allowed there without an adult to walk with me and call me back to the path when I ran off. Maybe that is why I find myself heading straight for the woods now.

Shifting the shoulder straps of my rucksack, which is already uncomfortable, I keep walking down the road, though it is becoming more of a muddy track now, and my feet are sinking deeper with every step. Not many cars come this way – just the occasional farm vehicle or some lost hikers looking for their campsite. Most turn back before the bridge anyway, because it's so narrow. People like to say that our village, Llandymna, was never built for an age like this: nothing seems to cope well with cars or technology round here. Visitors call it quaint; everyone at school calls it boring.

I stop on the bridge for a moment and look around the valley. It's peaceful here. The only sounds are birdsong and farm animals in the distance. I breathe in the clear air deeply and lean forward over the low wall. Blood rushes to my head as I tilt my weight down to get a better look at the waters ambling below. They say the basin this river runs through was first hewn out by ice millions of years ago, carved from its slow crawl across our land. The stones that make this bridge might be that old. They might remember the years when everything was frozen white, before sheep and humans and green grass came to cover the slopes.

Thinking about the oldness of everything calms me, and suddenly this afternoon's row with my aunt seems less important. Not so unimportant that I will forget it, mind. She treats me like a child, and it's time she learned to take my threats seriously. If I go back, she will think I didn't mean it when I warned her I'd run away from home. I thought I meant it at the time, but standing here on the bridge I feel so unprepared for whatever follows next that I wonder how sincere I really was. I will never let anyone else ask that question, though. I have made up my mind: I am never going back.

I might still be visible from the village here. Someone walking down the west side of Llandymna, by the White Lion pub, could see me if they looked out towards the hills. I need to get out of sight if I'm to properly disappear. The dark green of Dyrys Wood stretches, rich and inviting, up to the horizon, and I am drawn to it.

I run up to the forest that unfolds ahead, climbing over the stile in the low fence that keeps sheep from straying there, passing through the gateway of those first few tree trunks, and overhead the sky is suddenly gone. The forest is cool, the air rich with the smell of earth.

There's a rough pathway, which I follow between the trees. Everyone knows that Dyrys Wood stretches for miles ahead and that you can walk and walk for ages here, and that's even if you manage not to get lost from the path. Even its name, *Dyrys*, means something wild and entangling. I picture briers and thorns gathering around me, like the enchanted forest in Sleeping Beauty. Not that I look like anything out of a fairy tale, with my rucksack on my shoulders, and my phone sticking out of the pocket of my jeans. I have always loved fairy tales, even now at the age when I am supposed to be too grown up and cynical for them. I love how the characters get to be heroes, no matter what they are working with: whether it's because they are clever, or kind, or brave, things work out for them. Whereas in real life, you can be as clever or brave as you like, and you might still live with a guardian who sees you as nothing but a nuisance and punishes you every time you disagree with her. Or you might be stuck in a tiny, inward-looking village where people gossip and interfere and your so-called friends are fickle with their support, and life never hands you the adventure or rewards that you hear about in stories.

I put my hand to my throat, and find the familiar shape of the pendant I always wear – a chain with three charms on it: a key, a rose, and a book. Each one is an emblem from a fairy tale. I wear it because it feels like carrying a little bit of another world, a better world, with me wherever I go.

The path through the wood hasn't been cleared for some time, and thorny stems have crept out to tear at my clothes. It seems to make little difference whether I walk along the path or over the forest floor, so I turn away from the narrow road and choose my own route. A startled blackbird flies away with a trilling alarm call.

My pocket buzzes. I take out my phone and see it's Aunty Di calling. She must have finally realized I have gone. This is quite slow to start worrying, by her standards. I know what she'll say. I can already imagine her voice, telling me off for making such a fuss, demanding I come home at once. As I stare at the screen, I know that if I answer this call I will inevitably end up going back. And if I ignore it? Others will worry too. They will finally pay for how they treated me. They will no longer be able to laugh at me, or ignore me. All the peacefulness I felt standing on the bridge minutes ago ebbs away and I am only angry now as I think of the people I have just left behind. I want them to miss me. I won't let them mock me by going back and being accused of melodramatic empty threats. I let the phone keep ringing.

LLANDYMNA

Tom Davies knows his sergeant would advise against this, but he knocks on the next door all the same. Either you are on duty, or you are not. Taking on unofficial search parties confuses things: it blurs the boundaries, which a young police officer at the start of his career cannot afford to do. But Diana seems worried. It can do no harm for him to ask some questions this afternoon. Besides, it is a quiet day in the village; in Llandymna, Tom reflects, every day is a quiet day.

It takes a while for this door to be answered, but eventually it opens, and a small white-haired woman invites him inside. Maebh O'Donnell has wrapped herself in a plaid shawl though it is the height of summer, for Llandymna's old stone cottages never really lose the chill that clings to their walls. Tom has to duck under the doorway as he enters the house. He always feels just a little too tall and gangly to be properly comfortable in his surroundings. Maebh offers him a cup of tea, which he declines. She returns to her armchair by the fireplace, lowering herself with knees that groan in protest at the strain put on them. Movement is something Maebh often views as an unnecessary luxury these days.

"Well then, what can I do for you, Thomas Davies?" she asks in the song-like Irish accent she has never lost, though she has spent most of her life in this little village on the side of a hill in Wales. Her eyes are sharp and searching, and Tom wonders if she already guesses the answer to her own question. She has known him since he was a child, and even though Tom has finished his two-year probation with the police force now, he knows Maebh still sees the boy who once crashed his bike, stabilizers and all, into her doorstep.

"I came to ask if you have seen Rhiannon today."

Maebh sits back slowly and clicks her teeth. "She is missing, then?"

"She isn't at home, and Diana is worrying. I hoped she'd be here."

"Rhiannon hasn't been to visit me lately. I take it there's been another row, then?"

"You know Diana. She isn't going to admit that in front of me," Tom answers, and Maebh nods. Diana is a self-possessed woman with a lot of influence in the village, but her relationship with her niece shows cracks in her polished image. Nobody would dare suggest that she actually resents caring for her late sister's daughter, but Rhiannon's behaviour gives gossips something to chew on as they imagine what shouts and insults must be exchanged in that house.

"But if they *have* argued," Tom continues, "Rhiannon may have just gone to get some space, and she could be back home in an hour or two."

"And yet here you are, on your day off, asking me if I've seen her, and wearing that look of concern on your face."

Tom sighs. Maebh has a particular way of seeing through people with her steely blue eyes, and getting to the hidden heart of a matter with a single incisive comment.

"You know what she can be like," he replies. "She's a teenager with a fiery temper, and apparently a grudge to carry against almost everyone she knows. I don't know what she might do to prove a point."

"I imagine she'd do a great deal," Maebh muses. "I believe she's threatened to run away from home before now?"

"There wasn't much she didn't threaten at the school fundraiser last week."

"Ay, I heard about that."

"Could she be avoiding everyone out of embarrassment over that? She did verbally abuse most of the people there, after all. And significantly damaged one of the school's display cabinets. I had to attend the scene after that, in an official capacity. The headteacher considered pressing charges for vandalism."

Maebh barks out a laugh. "As if that would help! Besides, I can't say I really blame her."

Tom does not react to this last part. He has grown used to the fact that, at unexpected moments, Maebh will utter a sudden attack on the people of the village. He does not know why exactly, and nothing has ever come of it. When he compares her to Rhiannon, he wonders if there might not be the same rebellious streak in both of them.

"Do you have any idea where she might be?"

"She never spoke to me of planning to go somewhere, if that's what you mean, and she talked to me about most things. I have enjoyed her visits. We always have so much to talk about, she and I. Rhiannon understands the importance of stories, and you know how I do like storytelling!"

Maebh speaks lightly, but her bony fingers twist themselves up in the folds of her shawl, as if another, deeper worry is gnawing its way to the surface.

RHIANNON

If I'd been born into this community a thousand years ago, they would probably have decided I was a changeling. Even when you account for the fact that I was brought up by my aunt, even when you consider my mother's wild spirit, it would still be easier to explain away my inability to fit in here by saying the fairies swapped me for the real Rhiannon early on, during that stage when all babies look pretty much the same, even if no one will admit it. We could have imagined her: the real Rhiannon, out there somewhere, dutifully fitting in with her surroundings, doing her homework on time and asking no difficult questions while I, the imposter, use my fairy-magic to dream much too dangerously, and to see far too much of what is rotten in the very fabric of the village, while others go on blindly.

Nobody believes in changelings any more, though we do still like to be able to explain things simply. I wonder if knowing my mother better would explain me.

I like to think she had something of the fey spirit in her. When people who remember her better than I do talk of her, she is always described as headstrong and irresponsible, which, if you think about it, are just different words for untameable. The wind is untameable, and so are rivers, and there is something poetic in that. But in my mother, I am told, there was more trouble than poetry.

She was Aunty Di's sister. She loved being outdoors, and never walked anywhere if she could run or skip, even after she outgrew the age when people allow you such indulgences. I like to picture her racing along the hedge-lined track to the church on Sundays, with Diana walking all the slower and more stately to indicate that she was not participating in this behaviour. Di worries about what people think. She wants me to worry too. *"Brush your hair, Rhiannon. Don't you know you'll look a state to your school friends if you go like that?"* I don't think my mother spent hours untangling and rearranging her chestnut curls, even after she met my father.

I forgot where I was for a moment there. I do that sometimes. Normally, it's hard to come back to the real world when my thoughts have taken me away, but today the fresh air and the birdsong make a more refreshing setting than my tiny bedroom. I am sitting in a clearing in the forest. Opposite me, two trees grow a few paces from one another and a dead branch has come to stretch from one to the other, caught in the boughs. I wonder if I could use them to build a shelter. If I had some kind of blanket, I would hang it over the branch, like a child's den.

Going home is out of the question, obviously, but I don't exactly know what I'm going to do instead. I didn't technically plan or pack for this outcome. As I left, I grabbed the bag on the landing because I figured that if you storm out without taking anything with you, you're just an angry person going for a walk; but if you're carrying some kind of luggage, then you're someone who is leaving for good. It's my old camping bag – not the full-size one with all the really useful stuff, but the smaller one Diana pulled out of the loft, saying that since I never did get around to doing the Duke of Edinburgh award with the rest of my class, we would have to get rid of all this clutter. It was taking up valuable space for my cousins' finger paintings or something, and besides, no one from Llandymna would be mad enough to choose to go camping. The farmers around here tend not to take holidays: they can't afford to leave their animals alone, and those who can leave for a week in the summer usually make the three-hour drive to the coast for a picnic where everything tastes of sand. Mind you, Hannah Bromley from my English lit class went to the Caribbean with her parents last summer, and she came back all tanned and told the rest of us we hadn't seen real beaches if we'd never been to the Bahamas.

Now that I think about it, I wish I'd brought my other bag: the brown one I take to school. That one has my purse in it. I could have bought a bus ticket to a nearby town – one with its own train station. Then I could have gone just about anywhere, although still not the Caribbean beaches, because Hannah Bromley says tickets cost hundreds of pounds, and that's a lot more than I have. I suppose this makes me sort of homeless, but not like people in big towns and cities, who sit in the doorways of disused shops. I would be scared to be homeless in a city, where anyone could get to you, but if I live out here in the woods, that will feel safer. If I have to sleep outside, I would much rather it be somewhere remote. In big towns you have to deal with muggers and weirdos, and all the homeless women I've ever seen have had dogs, which have probably been trained to protect them. Here, your worst enemies are the cold and the rain, and any Llandymna native can handle them.

I am almost an hour's walk from home here. The clock on my phone tells me this, which is about all it's useful for now, as the bars of signal have disappeared. You never quite know whether your phone is going to work in Llandymna. There are a couple of hills north of the village where reception is strong: people sometimes go up there for calls if they don't have a landline, like when Elsie Jones speaks to her brother in Canada. Jenny Adams, who joined my history class after her parents moved from Bristol to Bryndu, which is about ten miles away from Llandymna and where my school is, said she couldn't believe people still lived in these conditions. I told her she was narrow-minded and stuck up for thinking her life experience was the only normal and right one. She hasn't spoken a word to me since.

It's grown cooler while I've been sitting here. I need to work out what on earth I'm going to do for shelter, and what I'm going to eat tonight, or my new adventure is going to be cut short very abruptly.

I open up my rucksack, my stage prop that was meant to convince people they had nearly lost me, and empty out its contents, hoping there will be something useful in there. Most of the space is taken up with my sleeping bag. After that, out falls Uncle Ed's folding knife, and a lighter that was for starting up the gas stove, except the stove isn't here. It must still be in the attic. There's a small and flimsy saucepan, the sort where the handle folds in to save space. Finally, some crushed remains of rations from my last school hike fall out: an empty water bottle I forgot to throw away and several crumpled packets of dried couscous, which our teachers recommended as good outdoor food. No tent, of course; no waterproof clothes except for the jacket I am wearing, no torch: I could kick myself for not having planned this better. But of course, I had no choice. It was other people who goaded me into leaving so abruptly. This is not my fault. I wrap up the food again. If I can't see it, I will feel less hungry and then it will last longer. Instead I focus on the empty bottle, which I press and remould in my hands until it has just about returned to its original shape. If I could find a stream, I could collect water, and that would be a good step towards surviving my first day in Dyrys.

Standing up, I listen for any sound resembling running water. For a moment I think I hear it, but then a magpie drops from a tree nearby in a cackling bundle of black and white feathers. He hops away, squawking indignantly, and now all I can hear is the birds talking to one another, oblivious to my silence. Focusing again, I concentrate on searching through every level of sound about me, and eventually I pick it out again: something faint and light, like a shiver running over the stones of the earth. I gather my belongings and run towards the sound.

I run because it feels good to have a direction. There's no one else around except the birds and chattering squirrels. As I move swiftly between trees, it's as though everything here is enchanted, and I am part of the spell. The earth that is dislodged by my feet and kicked up as I run starts to shimmer like bronze dust in my wake. Then suddenly, *thud!* I'm on the ground, tripped by a tree root.

I clamber back to my feet and brush the dirt from my hands. As soon as I find this stream, I'll wash them properly. I walk slowly now, taking care to keep my footing where the ground slopes down, where it's riddled with tree roots or concealed by brambles. The sound of the stream is growing clearer with every step, and as I gingerly sidestep a tangle of holly that blocks my path, I finally see it before me.

It glints silver in the sunlight. Trees bend over it, as if trying to catch a vain glimpse of their reflection. The stream arcs in either direction away from me, gently drawing itself into a broad crescent and disappearing into the depths of the forest. Triumphant at having found it using only my keen sense of hearing, I bathe my arms up to the elbows in its cool waters, and then take a first well-earned drink, scooping up the water in my hands and lapping it up quickly before it can trickle away.

I look up from the stream and see at once that on the other bank, partially concealed by greenery, there is a little house, or rather the ruins of a house. A tangle of moss and ivy hangs off its stone walls, and the few weathered fragments of a wooden wheel lying nearby tell me that this was once the watermill. It must have been abandoned for over a hundred years, after the river shrank to a stream and no longer carried enough strength to turn the mill wheel.

I inspect it thoroughly, searching for breaks in the stones or gaps in the roof. There are plenty. I pluck an ivy leaf from its tendril clinging to the north side, and hold it in the palm of my hand. From a distance, it looks deep green and perfect, but bringing it closer I can now see the tiny veins that crack across its surface and the brown marks around the edge. Disappointed, I allow it to fall to the ground and do not watch to see where it lands. I suppose this place will do, for now.

CHAPTER TWO

LLANDYMNA

Diana rearranges the pans on the draining board a third time, and the kitchen rings with metallic slams. Next, she will tidy the cupboards. She has been meaning to do this for a month now. Everything must be taken out, sorted and wedged back into the available space. It is the only piece of housework left that is likely to hold her attention today. Quickly and expertly, she twists her dark hair into a knot that she pins to the back of her head with a silver clip. She has mastered the art of sweeping it all up in one motion so that not a single strand can get in her way while she works.

The other side of the back door, Owen, her youngest, sits on the patio and plays with the snails that crawl within reach. Occasionally he grinds his unfamiliar new teeth, somehow sensing that all is not right in his little world today.

Diana props open the kitchen door so that she can watch her son while listening for the doorbell. Normally, she insists on having all the doors in the house closed, so it takes her a while to find anything heavy enough to hold it open. From here she thinks she can hear a knock or approaching footsteps, but the sound doesn't turn into anything material. She goes back to her work, deliberately drowning out any noise that she might mistake for Tom Davies' return. She sets the jam jars in sensible rows on the counter, takes inventory of her supply of flours, and discovers that she will need more soon, as there is no question of her not baking something for Joan Perry's cake sale. Governments might fail, fire might rain down

23

from the sky, but Diana's coffee and walnut sponge is something you can count on.

The doorbell rings, and Diana throws a bag of caster sugar down onto the table, scoops up little Owen into his highchair, and answers it. Tom Davies stands on the step, next to his friend Callum Rees. Their faces tell her everything. Her heart seems to plummet into her stomach.

"Nothing?" she asks, losing her usual commanding tone in this simple question.

"Diana, I'm sorry," says Tom. "Nobody has seen anything. I take it you haven't heard from her?"

"No, I've been calling her but she isn't – I haven't managed to get through." Diana stops herself short of admitting that her niece is probably choosing not to answer her calls.

"If you're concerned for her safety, we could… I could investigate in a more formal capacity, if you want to report her as missing."

"Report her?" Diana repeats, with an incredulous laugh. "You make it sound as though my niece is a criminal, or an interesting piece of journalism! She could be on her way home from the library right now. She likes to go there. Perhaps she simply forgot the time while she was immersed in one of her books." She starts to speak faster as she weaves together this picture: a scenario that does not involve Rhiannon having stormed off after yet another shouting match.

"That's probably right," says Callum, even though they have already checked the library and found no sign of Rhiannon. He fears he will get dragged into an all-night search party for a teenager having a tantrum if he does not act quickly. "Once she realizes she's missing teatime, she'll come back."

He had been on his way to the pub to watch the match this afternoon when he met Tom on Church Road and somehow agreed to help him in his inquiries. He is still in his red shirt, despite having missed the entire game.

"But if she isn't answering her phone, it will be difficult to know that," Tom presses, knowing full well why Callum wants to stop the search as soon as possible, but feeling less sure that he understands Diana's reaction. "I'm sure everything's fine, Diana, but if you are concerned, I can call the station right now."

"No need, Tom. I know it's your day off. As you say, everything is most likely fine. It's just that you can't be too careful where young people are involved. And I just want to know that Rhiannon is safe."

Her words sound measured, careful, almost rehearsed, but in her eyes is a flicker of a growing panic that she hopes the evening shadows will hide. Tom relents with a compromise.

"All right, but I think we should check by the gorge before we call it a day. It's the only steep enough drop around here for anyone to fall and hurt themselves. And we can search it before it gets dark. If she doesn't come home tonight, I strongly advise you to call the police. But you may have managed to speak to her before then."

No one looks fully appeased by this suggestion. Diana looks conflicted; Callum realizes he has been volunteered to go with Tom to the gorge, which means more walking. Neither can think of a more reasonable suggestion, though, so they all agree to this.

RHIANNON

It's getting late. I've moved all my belongings into the old mill house and unrolled my sleeping bag where the ground is flattest and least stony. Next I need to build a fire. It will keep me warm and scare away any animals that come creeping around at night. Not that I think there will be anything that dangerous in these woods. There used to be rumours of an enormous wildcat living in Dyrys, but no one really believes that unless a visitor is asking, in which case we say it's all true! Callum Rees told me he saw it once, and that it was the size of a panther, but I never believe anything he says. He just does whatever he thinks will make people like him. I think he would grow out of it much faster if his strategy was less successful, but he seems to have a lot of friends.

As the shadows grow longer, I start to think more about my safety. I know it's unlikely that I'll see anyone else out here, but what if I do? I'm a long way from the nearest house. Suppose someone wanted to rob me of the few possessions I have here? There would be no witnesses to stop them. I suddenly wonder how much of the feeling of safety most people have, day to day, comes from being near others, neighbours and friends, and knowing that if we stay within close range of just enough of them, chances are at least one will want to uphold the law rather than break it.

I pull a few stray branches and twigs together into a pile near the doorway of the mill house. Whatever door once stood there has long since rotted away. When the pile of wood looks about the right size, I take out the lighter and press my thumb down on the button. A yellow flame jumps out of the casing and I press it to the middle of the wood. Nothing happens at first, and then a thin twig catches fire. The flame runs the length of the twig, blackening its bark, and then fizzles out. I try again, holding the lighter to another twig this time, which just smokes feebly for a few seconds. On the third attempt, even less happens. The wood must be too rain-soaked to burn.

I can't believe I am struggling at the first hurdle. I should be able to build a fire! I went on one of those survival skills weekends they send youth groups on, and I was far better than anyone else on my team. Of course, it turned out everyone else thought that the point of the weekend was to "bond" and "build relationships", so from their perspective I was bottom of the class, but only because their criteria were stupid.

It must be the wrong sort of wood. The branches are probably too young and green or too old and rotten, or from a tree that does not burn so well. I will have to test different types of wood to find what burns best. Then I'll be able to heat water over the fire and use that to cook the food I've brought. Not tonight though. I am exhausted, and can go without eating if it means getting to rest sooner. I wrap myself up in the sleeping bag and for a split second am struck by the sickening enormity of the decision I have made in leaving home, before tiredness overwhelms me and I curl up inside my sleeping bag.

The sun has set now. Between the dimly silhouetted trees are gaping spaces of darkness so black that it might almost be solid and heavy – something one could claw at in a moment of madness and force away to bring back the light. But this is stupid, I tell myself; just my imagination getting carried away. It's been a strange day, and I am tired. Yes, that's it. This uneasiness, this fear, is simply because I am half asleep already, almost in a dreamland, where everything is felt so much more intensely. I wriggle deeper into the sleeping bag and close my eyes.

LLANDYMNA

Tom and Callum walk into the White Lion just as the barman calls for last orders. Callum groans: for him, this is another cruel reminder of how much of his day has been taken up with a wild goose chase. He marches up to the bar with the look of a man who knows he has earned this drink. Tom does not follow; he has spotted Ifan and Nia Evans sitting at a nearby table, saving two seats for the search party.

"Evening," he says as he joins their table. "Thanks for waiting so late for us."

"Not at all," Nia says, though Tom has to strain to hear her voice over the background noise. "We've been worried about Rhiannon, haven't we?"

Ifan realizes a moment too late that this last part was addressed to him, and grunts an unconvincing agreement.

"I don't suppose you had any luck looking for her?" Nia continues.

"None," Tom replies. "We asked around the whole village, and then we went up to the gorge, just in case she'd gone for a walk and fallen somewhere. But there's no sign of her."

"Poor girl." Nia shakes her head sadly. "And poor Diana."

The Evanses have lived in Llandymna their whole lives, and own the nearest farm to the village. As is the way in Llandymna, Ifan and Nia have become friends with Tom and Callum, not out of any real shared interests, but because they are close enough in age and they are simply here. That tends to be enough to build a bond of loyalty in this small village. Nia was in the same school year as Tom, and they used to take the bus to Bryndu High School together. She was generous and well liked back then, but Tom thinks she has become quieter since marrying Ifan. She has placed herself in the corner seat this evening, and sits with the perfect poise of someone tightly holding in their limbs, barely breathing for fear of trespassing onto someone else's territory. You can tell, if you watch her for long enough, that Nia has resolved to squeeze her life into the smallest possible space, ever minimizing any trouble she might cause to others.

Ifan, by contrast, has planted himself squarely on an armed chair, and keeps one hand resting on the pint glass in front of him, his legs stretched out under the table. In another part of the world, Ifan Evans might be laughed at for his name, Tom reflects, though he is hardly a man to let others mock him. Yet Llandymna has already weathered the naming of Billy Williams after his father William Williams, who used to run the corner shop next to the church before Callum's family took it over, so its inhabitants have accepted Ifan's name without question.

"Poor Diana?" Callum joins them, setting a pint glass down emphatically. "She's not the one who's been traipsing round the fields all evening. I've been out there with a torch for more than an hour."

He takes out his penknife, a recent birthday present, which he has taken to flicking open and shut distractedly in moments like this. It seems to fit with the image he is trying to achieve.

"If you ask me," Ifan says, "Diana should've expected this to happen one day. That Rhiannon's her mother's daughter after all."

Ifan eyes each of the others to check that they agree with him. No contradiction is forthcoming, and this is encouragement enough for him to continue. In the corner of the pub, against the background murmur of last orders and other people's conversations, Ifan reminds them of the stories of Elin Morgan, whose name has become a byword for losing touch with reality and your roots, living wildly and understanding nothing of consequences.

"Disappeared for years, she did, and then shows up back here, pregnant and unmarried. And then one night she leaves her child at home all alone, and goes out no one knows exactly where, except that she goes at such a speed that she overturns her car on the way and leaves her family to pick up the pieces."

With such a mother, Ifan argues, and no father to speak of, how could anyone be surprised at how Rhiannon has turned out? Nia, who has helped Diana with babysitting ever since she became her niece's legal guardian ten years ago, looks pained at the way her husband tells the story.

"But we don't know for certain what has happened," says Tom, when Ifan's clear-cut assessment of the situation has finished unfolding.

"Well, I expect we'll know tomorrow, when she's come back to her nice warm home and a guaranteed hot meal."

"I hope you're right."

"You don't suppose," Nia asks, "that she might have gone off to look for her father?"

"I think it's one of the options we'll have to start considering if there's no sign of her tomorrow."

"She's a good girl really," Nia says with a sigh, "but things have been very hard for her. She's been through such a lot for someone so young."

"Haven't we all?" says Callum. Being the member of the group who believes he has ostensibly suffered least in life so far, he is the most defensive on this subject. He kicks absent-mindedly at the chair legs and tries to look solemn.

Tom considers reminding Callum of how much more tragedy that family has experienced over the last ten years, first with Elin's death, then the death of Diana's husband Edwin two years ago, but thinks better of it. With both Callum and Ifan, it is worth choosing your battles wisely. Callum may be young and hotheaded, quick to see accusations at every turn, while Ifan is a little older and requires a certain level of respect from even his closest friends, but the end result is much the same. They do not like to be challenged when they have articulated an opinion. Tom glances at Ifan, and sees with relief that he is still relatively sober. Tonight will not be a night for helping him stagger back to the farm, or intervening in the arguments Ifan likes to search out after too many drinks.

The barman, having called for closing time ten minutes ago, is now tidying up as noisily as possible.

"Best drink up," Tom says.

CHAPTER THREE

RHIANNON

I know something is different even before I am fully awake. The sunlight falls warm on my eyelids, and the birds warble somewhere outside. But the surface under my shoulder blades is hard and uncomfortable; my bones ache with each shift and turn. The air is cold, too. I open my eyes and take it all in: the walls of moss and stone, the broken roof overhead, the leaf-strewn floor. So it wasn't a dream.

Drowsily, I stand up in this strange new space where every breath tastes of dew and smells of rich earth. The ruins of the old mill look strangely bare in the daylight, my belongings occupying one small corner of the space. Then, as if I've done this every morning of my life, I go down to the stream and wash my face in the glittering water.

Something in the clear morning light and the cool running water makes me hopeful about today. I feel as if here in Dyrys I might have a chance at the life I've wanted for so long. I will not be afraid. That's exactly what they would want, for me to be scared so I would go home and apologize. I shall live wonderfully instead. I shall do whatever I want, with no one to give me orders, and I shall depend on nobody.

With renewed determination, I look to the pile of twigs that I tried to turn into a campfire last night. This time I won't be beaten. I discard any bits of wood that feel damp, and pull together some new timber from the forest floor. I pile the thinnest twigs together in the centre, surrounded by bigger branches. Then I hold the lighter in the middle of this pile until the twigs catch light. Quickly, I push the branches over them and watch as the flames lick around the bark, blackening it so that it curls away. The fire starts to take hold, and I stand with my hands on my hips and survey my work, not needing to hide the grin that is spreading over my face.

I take the little pan down to the stream and dip it into the water, then inspect the contents to make sure no leaves or bugs have been captured along with it. I carry the pan back up to the fire and realize I have nothing to balance it on. I could make some sort of tripod from a few branches, but that would catch fire before long and throw hot water over the flames. I resign myself to holding the pan over the fire until the water boils, and I sit on one of the larger pieces of the broken mill wheel, which lies on its side and has become home to moss and ferns over the years.

While I wait, swapping the pan from one hand to the other as my arms start to ache, my thoughts drift off again and I see myself as I might one day be: gathering my own food, keeping a look out from high up in the trees, living out here like some kind of Robin Hood figure. I picture travellers getting lost in these woods one day, until I appear out of nowhere to help them find their way, and the look of wonder on their faces will be enough to sustain my confidence that I have made the right choice. And so the stories will filter back to the neighbouring villages and towns, rumours of the girl who lives in the woods. Legends start with a kernel of truth, and mine will begin here.

I love the feeling of timelessness about this place. It feels as if Dyrys could easily be straight out of my imaginary world. I have my own place that I go to when I'm gazing out of a window or when I can't sleep for rage at how the day played out with all its ignorant people. When I'm there, I am not Rhiannon any more. I am not in Year 12 and thinking about university, or expected to cook fish fingers for my cousins while Diana goes to another community council meeting so she can tell other people what to do and hope they will reward her by electing her as the next Chair. And, since I get to make the decisions in this world, I choose a version of me whose hair never frizzes after rain, and who dances amazingly and who knows how to speak in a way that makes people take her seriously.

While I inhabit this other world, I can cope with anything. Who cares what people say behind your back if you can go on adventures whenever you like? When Ellie Williams told everyone I had called her some names that were definitely outside my usual vocabulary, and petitioned the class to stop talking to me as a suitable punishment, I just ignored their silent stares by thinking about the book I was reading that week. It had glorious mountain ranges that needed scaling, and horrifying mysteries to solve along the way. I had no time for their childish concerns. I have lived out epic sagas in the time it takes Ellie Williams to decide what colour nail varnish best matches her shoes.

The water starts to bubble and boil, at last. As I tear open a packet of couscous and pour the contents in, I can't help but wonder how they make kettles heat water so fast, compared to this. I have no fork to eat it with, but I remember reading once that in Morocco they eat couscous without cutlery, rolling it together with their hands. I am so hungry this morning, I barely have the patience for my meal to cool down before I start scooping it up. In minutes, I have wolfed down the whole portion. As I swallow the last mouthful, I realize that I only have a couple more of these, and some cereal bars in the pocket of my coat. How long will that last? I have just gone through about a quarter of my food supplies on my second day in Dyrys.

Stop and think. I remember what I learned from Uncle Ed, and from books at the library. *The average human can last three minutes without oxygen, three days without water and three weeks without food.* Air and water will be no problem here, so that just leaves food. Of course, if you leave it the full three weeks without eating, you'll be too weak to go and find yourself anything. But the point is that it should be possible to ration things out and make them last, if I can just get used to ignoring the feeling of being hungry. And I can add to my supplies by foraging in the woods.

It's a good time of year for gathering food – there are fruit trees already covered in cherries and damsons around the edge of the village, and later on there will be blackberries on every thorny clump of brambles in these woods. When I was younger, I used to go blackberry picking with Nia Evans on September weekends, and then we would bake a pie together back at the farmhouse. Just remembering the smell of it makes me hungry. I wish I could remember more about which plants are edible so that I don't poison myself by accident. Uncle Ed had a book on foraging, which is still on the shelves in the hallway, but I haven't picked it up in years. I don't imagine Di reads it either. She kept most of Uncle Ed's things after he died, but they all just sat around the house in boxes, like we were collecting for a museum exhibit on his life. I kept his pocket knife though. I figured no one else was going to need it, and it made sense to keep it somewhere out of Owen and Eira's reach. They are too young: Eira is in her second year of school and Owen is just learning to put sentences together. I think, out of all the people in Llandymna, they are the ones I will miss. Them and Maebh, of course.

If Aunty Di were here, she'd make a plan for the day. She would write me a list, and it would say: *"Go to that overgrown hedgerow that leads out of the village where you know there will be damsons ready for picking, and then come back here and think about how you are going to fix the roof of this old house before it rains next, and for goodness' sake remember to boil any water before you drink it, or you'll get ill and have no one to blame but yourself."* Since she isn't here, I am free to do whatever I want, whenever I want, so I start to gather more firewood instead. Fallen twigs and branches lie scattered all around, but anything sturdier, like a proper lump of wood, is harder to find. I gather up an armful of what I can see, and the twigs scratch at my skin where I hold them. I take the wood and put it just inside the house by the doorway. Now, if it rains, I will still have a supply of dry wood to make a fire. But I still need to fix that hole in the roof somehow. I need something waterproof, like a tarpaulin, only smaller. Standing in the doorway of the house, my eyes fall on the drawstring bag my sleeping bag was previously rolled up in. I won't need that any more, and it is probably waterproof.

I take out Uncle Ed's pocket knife and flip out the blade, using it to cut through the drawstring and down one seam of the bag, opening it out as a flat piece of material. Now it is wide enough to cover the hole. I just need to find a way to get up to the roof. There is no chair or ladder to stand on here. I may have to climb up the outside of the building somehow. And how will I attach it, without nails or pegs? I need more time to think about this.

LLANDYMNA

At nine o'clock exactly, the doorbell rings three times. Maebh opens the door to Diana and her two young children. Diana's face is taut, all the muscles in it clenched with sharpness and urgency.

"Thank you so much for doing this, Maebh dear," she says as she ushers Eira into the house. "I really do appreciate it so much. Now, Eira, you're going to be good for Maebh, aren't you? I want to hear nice stories about what a lovely little girl you've been. Understand?" She lowers her voice as she turns back to Maebh. "I don't know how long I'll be – the police are on their way over to the house now. Owen won't understand what's going on, but I don't want Eira to be upset by any of this. Here, I brought you one of my marmalade cakes to say thank you for being so helpful to us all. It's still warm – no please, keep the tin it's in, I have plenty. I'll telephone to let you know when I can pick her up."

Though her tone is bright, all the words come out a little too fast and clipped. Maebh thanks her for the cake and reassures her that they will be fine spending the day together.

"Will it be our Tom who comes to speak to you, do you think?"

"Oh no, I shouldn't think so," Diana replies. "I'd hope they'd send a proper policeman for a matter like this – one with a bit more experience."

Eira asks if she can do some colouring, as she has brought her best pencils with her today, and Diana leaves quickly, with Owen gurgling as he is carried out. Maebh sighs as she closes the front door behind them and feels peace return to her house.

"Now then, Eira, my lovely, have you had any breakfast yet? How about some toast and jam?"

Eira is five years old, with fair hair so light that her parents chose to give her a name that means snow. She is everything one might expect a daughter of Diana to be: well behaved, polite, and very articulate, though she has inherited her father's complexion. She skips ahead of Maebh into the kitchen and clambers up onto the chair where she always sits, while Maebh takes out a jar of raspberry jam and puts a slice of bread into the toaster. Today must be a day of normal, familiar things for Eira. She will have enough uncertainty to deal with when she understands what has happened.

"Look, here's the crust of the loaf," says Maebh. "You don't like to eat that part, do you? But do you know who does like it?"

Eira thinks for a moment, and then her face lights up. "Mr Blackbird!"

"Yes. Shall we take him some breakfast too?"

They go out into the garden and Maebh tears the slice of bread in two, handing one half to Eira, who carefully and methodically breaks off small pieces and scatters them on the grass.

"Food for you, Mr Blackbird, and all of your friends," she sings to a made-up tune as she distributes the bread. When they have finished, they retreat back inside, where the toaster has popped, and so Eira is distracted by eating for a few minutes. By the time she remembers to look up through the window, a pair of blackbirds and a house sparrow have appeared in the garden. Eira squeals with delight and watches them avidly.

When the birds finally leave, startled by the arrival of a neighbour's cat, Eira remembers that she had planned to draw pictures with her favourite colouring pencils today.

"Can we go to the living room now, please?" she asks.

"Yes, but you'll have to be patient with poor old Maebh. I can't walk as quickly as you these days, with my ancient bones!"

They make their way from the kitchen to the front room of the little house, one bounding ahead full of energy, the other taking it more slowly. It is a small room, sparsely furnished with some comfortable chairs for guests and Maebh's own chair next to the fireplace. Over the mantelpiece hangs a painting of a boat crossing the Irish sea, with the misty blue form of land just visible on the horizon.

As she sits herself down on the rug and opens her pencil case, Eira suddenly says, "Rhiannon's gone, hasn't she?"

Maebh sighs. She had known Eira was a clever girl and would figure out the truth before long. "What makes you say that, Eira-wen?"

"She and Mummy were shouting at each other again yesterday, and then Rhiannon said she was going to run away. And then I heard her slam the door, and she didn't come home even after bedtime."

So, Maebh thinks, *Eira has known all along what others only suspected: that Rhiannon has run away. It won't come as much of a surprise to anyone.*

"Well, today your mummy is talking to some people who are going to help find her. So don't you worry."

"It was very quiet without her. She shouts a lot, mostly at Mummy, but sometimes at other people too. She used to tell me stories though, before she started being cross all the time. I liked that a lot more." Eira does not look up as she says this, so that she can focus on counting out her pencils.

"I'm sure you did, my lovely. Tell me, what is your favourite story?"

"I like the ones with talking animals."

"I see, and do you know the story of the white fox who could talk?"

Eira shakes her head, and Maebh smiles, because this is a story she is about to make up. She asks Eira if she would like to hear it, and of course she says yes.

With the four age-old words, Maebh begins, "Once upon a time, there was a little white fox cub that lived in a land covered in snow. All the trees and fields and hills were covered in it, and all the lakes and rivers were ice. Can you picture that much snow everywhere? The little fox cub loved to slip and slide around on the ice lakes, and he would spend hours every day playing outside, building snow mice and snow badgers with his brothers and sisters, because in that land the schools could never open because it was so snowy, so they stayed closed and none of the animals ever had to go to classes.

"One day, the little fox stayed out playing extra late, and kept on rolling in the snow until he was much further from home than he had ever been before. When it was time to go home, he looked around to see no sign of his family, and realized he was lost.

"The little fox felt scared to be on his own, and began to cry. But as he was crying, he heard a voice say, 'Are you all right, little fox?' He looked up, and what do you think he saw there? A talking fawn, with big kind eyes and a black shiny nose!"

Eira stops arranging her pencils from red through to violet and her eyes grow wide as Maebh continues.

"'I'm lost and can't find my way home,' the fox told the fawn sadly.

"'I'll help you find your way back!' said the fawn. 'We should go and ask the king of the owls. He flies all over this land and knows where everything is. He can tell you which way to go.'

"So the little fox and his new friend went to speak to the king of the owls. He lived in a hollow in a tall pine tree on the edge of the forest, the tallest tree you can imagine. And when he heard the sound of a fox and a fawn coming towards his home, he flapped down to a low branch to see them, and all the other owls came and perched nearby too. There were tawny owls and barn owls and eagle owls, all peering down from their branches to see these new visitors.

"'Whooooo are you?' asked the king of the owls, with a frown that was very stern." Maebh pulls a face that might resemble a gruff owl, and Eira giggles. "The brave little fox was not afraid, though; he explained why he was there, and the owls all looked at him curiously. The king of the owls seemed thoughtful at this, and said, 'Hmmm, how interesting. I believe we received a message not long ago about a white fox cub just like you. It was delivered by one of our messenger owls, who fly all around the land bringing me news. Fetch me that letter!'

"A tawny owl flew up to the hollow tree and returned a few moments later with a letter in his beak. The king of the owls read it carefully.

"'Well, little fox, this letter appears to be from your family. It seems you are very important to them, and they want you to be safely with them again. They ask that if I see you, I show you which way to go home, and they sent you this.' The owl held up in his taloned foot a collar as blue as the evening sky. 'Apparently it will help you get home. I believe it may have magical powers.'

"And so the owls gave the fox the blue collar and pointed him in the right direction to go home. The little fox thanked them and the fawn for their help and set off.

"'Wait for me!' cried the fawn. 'I'd like to come with you and help you get back to your family!' The little fox smiled, because he knew he had made a new friend. They walked and walked together, trudging through the deep snow drifts. Overhead, the moon was bright, and lit their way.

"'What do you think the collar does?' asked the fawn.

"'I don't know,' replied the fox. 'It's from my family, but I've never seen it before.'

"'Maybe it makes us invisible, so no big scary animals see us. Or maybe it will help you to fly home. Do you think it can make you fly? Try jumping and see what happens!'

"The fox jumped up into the air, but quickly hit the snowy ground again with a bump.

"'Ouch! I don't think it's a collar that makes you fly.'

"They kept on walking, and after a while more snow began to fall. Soon the snow turned into a whirling blizzard, and it became hard to see ahead.

"'Have you noticed,' said the fawn, 'that it isn't cold, even in this storm? How strange!'

"The fawn was right. Even as it grew darker and more snowy, the fox and the fawn felt none of the bitter chill.

"'That's it!' said the fox. 'Somehow the magic in the collar must be keeping us warm so that we can keep walking!'

"At last, the blizzard cleared, and it became easier to see the way ahead. Two tall hills loomed on the horizon, and the little fox recognized them. Those were the two hills he could see from his home. They were nearly there! But between them and their destination, there was a wide rushing river. And over the river was a long narrow bridge. And in front of the bridge stood a wizard dressed all in grey."

Maebh picks up her shawl from the arm of the chair and throws it over her head and shoulders like a hooded cloak.

"'Hello there, little ones,' the wizard said. 'Have you come to cross the river?'

"'Yes,' said the fox, answering honestly because he knew that wizards were kind and clever. 'What must we do to cross it?'

"'This bridge, my friend, is a Fearless Bridge. Only those with no secret worries can cross it. So, for example, if I wished to cross the river, I would first have to tell you that I am terrified of spiders, and a little anxious that I may have left the kettle on when I left the house this morning. Now, see! I can stand on the bridge without a problem. But if I had not told somebody that before stepping on, I would have been thrown into the river.'

"The little fox and the fawn thought very carefully about this. The fawn spoke first: 'I'm a bit afraid of bears, and eagles, and things that eat deer, but not of you – ' he turned to the fox, 'because you're my friend!'

"'I'm a bit scared of this bridge now,' said the fox, 'and also of not seeing my family again. But actually, now that I've told you about it, I feel a bit better already.'

"'That is the magic of the Fearless Bridge at work,' said the wizard. 'Now you are ready to cross it.'

"The fox and the fawn stepped onto the bridge and, to their relief, it did not throw them into the water. They scampered across and there, on the other side, was the fox's family, all waiting for him. He had made it back! They were all so happy to see each other again, and they thanked the fawn for helping him come home. And they all played together for the rest of that day and the next, making snow angels in the deep drifts by the little fox's home."

The story ends, and Maebh is about to ask Eira what she thought of it, and which animal she liked best, when the phone rings.

"Was that Mummy?" asks Eira, when Maebh returns.

"Yes, my lovely, it was. She says you are allowed to stay and play here for a bit longer."

"Oh good. I'm going to draw a picture of a fox for you."

Maebh says nothing of the rest of Diana's news: of the interview with the police officers, or of how even now a search party is setting out to search the surrounding countryside. She shudders at the thought of it all.

*

Diana sits opposite the two police officers who occupy her sofa. The room smells of fresh coffee, which she had anticipated would be appreciated today. Owen is sleeping upstairs, affording them some peace to talk. Light streams in through the window, and she smooths out a wrinkle in her navy blue skirt.

"Can you describe for me the circumstances of Rhiannon's disappearance, Mrs Griffin?" The officer's voice cuts through the serenity of the picture Diana has been enjoying. He is a tall, slightly rotund man, with a musical Welsh accent. His colleague is a woman who eyes Diana with detached suspicion.

"I last saw her yesterday, at quarter past four," she says. She listens to her voice as she speaks, critiquing herself for any sign of unsteadiness. "She left the house then, and has not come home since."

"And did she say where she was going at the time?"

"She did not. I had assumed she would be at the library, or out for a walk. When I had fed the children, and Rhiannon still hadn't come home, I tried to call her, but there was no answer. I was unable to go out and look for her myself, as that would have meant leaving Eira and Owen here by themselves, so I asked Tom Davies to look for her."

"Ah yes, Constable Davies has told us that he knows you."

"Mrs Griffin," the female officer interrupts, "did you argue with Rhiannon before she disappeared last night?"

Diana puts her coffee cup down on the table, careful to avoid spilling it, and answers, "Yes."

"What about?"

"Nothing that seems especially important now. I tried to bring up the subject of her behaviour over recent weeks. Rhiannon can be a difficult girl, you see. She is what you might call…" she pauses, to be sure she finds the right word, "strong-willed, and has a fierce temper. Lately, that temper has flared up against people in an ugly manner. I tried to talk to her about the fact that this is not acceptable. She became defensive and, unsurprisingly, angry. She shouted – something insulting, I forget what – and then stormed out of the house." Diana sips her coffee as she waits for the officer to finish scribbling notes.

"And has this happened before?"

She raises a single eyebrow. "Are you asking if the teenage girl I am raising has ever argued with me before? Of course she has! And we have accepted that it works to allow one another some space after these exchanges. I assumed Rhiannon felt that going to her room was not sufficient this time, but that she would come home later."

It is the other officer's turn to interrupt. "Mrs Griffin, would you mind clarifying your relationship to Rhiannon Morgan? You are her legal guardian, I believe?"

"Yes, and also her aunt. She is my late sister's daughter, and my husband Edwin and I were named Rhiannon's guardians in her will. Frankly, I still haven't got over the shock that Elin thought to make a will, but people do surprise you. And I had been helping her to care for Rhiannon long before that, of course."

"But you've never formally adopted Rhiannon? I see that she has kept her mother's surname. You aren't her parent by law?"

"No."

"Why is that?"

Diana sighs with irritation. "I hope these questions are necessary, and not just for your own curiosity. After Eira was born, my husband wanted us to adopt Rhiannon. He said it was important for us to show her that she was just as valued as our own children, that she had the same status in our family. He started proceedings, but then became ill. He passed away shortly after Owen was born, and since then I have had my hands full raising two small children and a teenager, not to mention sitting on the community council and having an active role in Llandymna village life. I simply have not had time to look at it again. And it would hardly make a difference in the day-to-day running of our lives."

"I'm very sorry, Mrs Griffin. You seem to have experienced a great deal of loss. Do you think that the very same loss could have caused Rhiannon to feel less stable and secure at home, to prompt her to want to run away?"

Diana casts an eye around her pristine front room, from the white china coffee cups to the perfectly co-ordinated furnishings. "I can assure you, I have done everything a person might do to ensure the continued stability of Rhiannon's life. She has stayed at the same school with the same friends, she has always had a good home here and a routine to her days. And when I am not here, taking care of her, I am busy working to improve this village so that it provides better services and facilities for young people like her."

The coffee pot is empty, so Diana excuses herself to refill it in the kitchen.

"Observations, Matthews?" the older officer asks his colleague, keeping his voice low so as not to be heard from the next room.

"Well, she's clearly hiding something, sir. No one looks that together after they lose one of their children. And she got very defensive just now."

"True, but she strikes me as the kind of woman who would be more outraged at the suggestion that she hasn't tidied her house enough than if you accused her of a criminal offence," he replies.

"Should we be contacting social services, sir? It seems like this girl's family situation is complicated."

"Possibly, but look at the date of birth you wrote down there. She turns eighteen in a few weeks. Not a lot of point putting her into care as and when she turns up. By the time the process was sorted, she'd be an adult."

"*If* she turns up, sir. I've read all the guidelines. We're supposed to consider the worst case scenario. That's what it says."

"It does, Matthews, and we have to entertain that possibility."

Matthews is about to put forward her initial hypothesis – that Diana Griffin has locked her niece away, or even murdered her, to preserve her public image – when Diana returns with more coffee and flapjacks.

"Mrs Griffin, does Rhiannon own a computer?"

"Yes, she has a laptop for her schoolwork. It's up in her room."

"We will need to take that away with us. There may be something on there that gives us a clue as to where she has gone. What about social media sites? Would you know her account details for those?"

Diana shakes her head. "Rhiannon refused to join any of those websites, even when all of her class did. She said they were for narcissists to engage in popularity contests. Her words, not mine."

Matthews smirks. "Smart girl."

"And is there anything about Rhiannon that would make her especially vulnerable?"

"Aside from the fact that she's a teenage girl not at home?" Diana retorts.

"Mrs Griffin, people go missing around the country every day. Most of them turn up safe and unharmed before long. It's our job to assess the risk level to Rhiannon. Aside from her young age, is there anything else that puts her in danger? Any mental health issues, disability, anyone known to you who might want to harm her?"

"Goodness no, of course not," Diana snaps. "Rhiannon is a perfectly normal seventeen-year-old."

"Exactly," Matthews mutters, but Diana seems not to hear this.

CHAPTER FOUR

RHIANNON

I walk back to the woods triumphantly, in one arm carrying a parcel that consists of my coat wrapped around a heavy collection of damson plums. It didn't take me long to find the place where they grow in the little lane; the only difficult thing was making sure I was not seen. It is only my second day and I am already gathering my own food. I will be self-sufficient in no time!

True, there are other aspects of this new life I am looking forward to less. I still do not know how I will fix the roof of my house without nails or string to hold it in place, and the bathroom facilities in the forest are not going to be ideal, but I am sure I can beat these things. And today I will enjoy the first meal I have ever properly worked for, unless you count the times I was told I had to finish my homework before tea. I am too happy to even care that I seem to have lost my phone somewhere; I think I had it earlier today, but it is no longer in my pocket. It was out of battery anyway, so was of no use to me.

I have come to the clearing where I stopped yesterday. The sky was grey and brooding then, casting criss-cross shadow patterns over the leaf litter, but today it is transformed. The light falls in patches, turned greenish by the leaves that filter it, and makes this place look like a fairy glade. There's an ethereal feel to the beauty of it all: as if the stillness is merely that of something holding its breath, waiting.

Waiting for what?

Maebh used to tell me stories when I went to her house after school, and my favourites were the stories of the Sparrow Girl. She was brave and beautiful, though I never understood why she was named after something as boring as a plain little sparrow. I would have named her for a falcon or a lioness, but when I told Maebh this she said that was how the story went and she wasn't going to change it just for me. I never could quite tell which of Maebh's stories were ancient legends from our Welsh past or her Irish heritage, and which were stories she just made up. She told them all with the same reverence for the words, the same glint in her eye as she knew she was coming to the really gripping part where you would find yourself leaning forward, eyes wide as you waited to find out what happened next.

I can picture the Sparrow Girl standing here, in this illuminated glade. She is a figure of legend and fairy tale, one to be taken seriously, or she might knock you off your feet with a quick whirl of the staff she carries everywhere. She dresses in the colours of the forest and sings when she feels joyful, and it is the most beautiful sound you have ever heard, or at least it is in my head when I imagine it. I have never met any living person I wanted to emulate as much as I want to be like the Sparrow Girl. But it's hard to walk with grace and dignity into a sixth-form classroom where the only things that seem to matter to people are alcohol and relationships and occasionally exam results.

I liked the fact that the Sparrow Girl sometimes got angry. Not many heroines in books do, it seems. They are gracious and composed, no matter what happens around them, like Nia Evans who never complains about anything. But one of Maebh's stories about the Sparrow Girl told how the local villagers chased her best friend out of his home and drove him away. And in that story, she raged against their cruelty, furious at the injustice. I think of her when I remember what happened at the school fundraiser incident. That's where I got angry like the Sparrow Girl.

I'd been missing Uncle Ed that day, thinking about how he never did get around to building the treehouse we'd been planning for the garden, and how it would probably never happen now because my aunt would hate the idea of Eira or Owen falling out of a tree. And then I got to thinking about how, if someone met me for the first time now, they would need to know about Uncle Ed and my parents in order to understand me. Sometimes it feels as though I'm defined by all the people I've lost, like one of those negative-space pictures, where what's not there is just as important as what is.

We were at Llandymna Primary School, where Eira started last autumn, and Diana had been asked to give a speech at the fundraising event, because she's supposedly important on the community council, even though everyone knows she can't wait to take over as chairwoman as soon as there's an opportunity. It was meant to be about children who need healthcare supplies in Tanzania, but no one seemed to care about that. The parents were all just very proud of what their own children had achieved, and the headteacher was clearly trying to advertise the school as a seat of moral high ground in the village, and the pupils had no idea where Tanzania was or why they were raising money for it. Then Diana started her speech, and to my disbelief she actually started using Uncle Ed's illness and death as a reason for why she related so much to this cause! She had hardly cried in the last couple of years, barely mentioned his name in front of Eira or Owen, and here she was talking as if she actually missed him, and using that to make an impression with other people.

I'd been slowly realizing for a long time just how much hypocrisy there was among the adults of this village, but this was too much. Somebody had to make a stand, to show everyone how far they had strayed from the good intentions they claimed to have. No one else seemed to have even noticed. So I stood up at the back and did just that. It wasn't the dignified, moving speech that the Sparrow Girl would have given. It was a lot messier and more emotional than that, and ended with a lot more broken glass. Still, I said what was right when no one else would. That has to count for something.

At least now I'm free of all that. Here, as I walk back towards my new home, I can leave behind everyone else's double standards and selfish motivations. I have my first collection of foraged fruit, and a bundle of firewood I will add to later. I will fix the broken roof and perfect my house.

I arrive back at the house and spread out my coat with its harvest of plums on the ground. It must be nearly midday – I can't be sure, because my phone is missing and I don't have a watch – and I have been busy, so I reward myself with one of the damsons. Its skin is sharp to taste, but the inside is sweet. I spit away the stone, and then wonder if I should plant it instead, to grow a new fruit tree. I am not sure it would grow though: I think growing trees is quite hard and takes a long time.

The sudden sound of distant barking startles me, and I jump to my feet. I suppose someone is walking their dog in the woods. They will probably keep to the path and not come anywhere near me. Another animal howls, louder and a little nearer. I think, if I listen hard, I can hear voices somewhere too. People don't normally come into Dyrys Wood in large groups. A horrible twist of fear sets in my stomach: could it be a search party?

I don't want to be found here, especially not by strangers in police uniforms. The only police officer I know is Tom Davies, who lives in Llandymna and seems sensible enough, but he was there after my speech at the school fundraiser, so he knows me as a troublemaker. He might even try to arrest me for what I did there.

I cram all my belongings back into the rucksack. There's no time to put on my coat, so I tie it around my waist. The bundle of firewood could give me away. I scatter it haphazardly over the forest floor, and it looks like no more than a few twigs and branches that have fallen to the ground. With my rucksack over my shoulders, I pause to check which direction the noise is coming from, and then I start to run the opposite way. Behind me, the voices and the dogs are growing louder as they head this way.

The forest is my home and I am safe here, or so I tell myself now. Tearing past tall trunks, stumbling on the uneven ground, biting my lip to stop the cry of pain as I bruise my ankle on a stone, I am heading deeper into the protection of the trees. The sheer vastness of Dyrys is something I'm suddenly thankful for, as it must be possible to lose the search party out here. I run headlong, further than I have explored, far beyond any landmarks I will recognize. I have no idea how I will ever find my way back. Right now, I only need to lose the search party, but I can still hear their shouts ringing in my ears. I look back to check if anyone is still following me, and immediately lose my footing and slide down a muddy bank into the stream. The ground is steep and slippery on either side and for a moment I panic at the thought of being trapped down here. I picture the searchers arriving here to find a bedraggled girl sitting at the bottom of the slope, waiting to be caught and brought home. But I refuse to be found! I splash through the shallow waters until at last I see somewhere I can clamber back out on the other side. I begin to run again. Heart pounding, my feet drumming against the ground, I plunge downhill, dodging beech trees and tripping as I blunder onwards.

In one mad moment, I wonder if I ought to climb a tree. I've heard stories of people avoiding capture this way before. They get up into the top branches and then wild beasts snap at their ankles but can't reach them. But I don't think I would be any good at climbing, and now is not the time to find out. I keep running.

The route I take sends me winding further and further into the heart of the forest. The rucksack jolts against my back with each step I take, the weight of it pulling against my shoulders. I can taste the fear of being pursued, but in spite of this I stop for a moment, needing to know just how near my hunters are. The dogs are quieter now, the shouts only just audible. I take a guess at where I am; I have all but lost my sense of direction in the wood, having run so blindly.

I listen out for any sign that they are coming this way. I sit down on a tree stump and try to catch my breath, for the thudding of the pulse inside my head all but drowns out the sounds further off. After a long while, the shouts seem fainter still, and trail off altogether. Still I don't dare venture back, in case I'm seen. I sit, silent, for what must be hours.

At last, as the sun sinks lower, I feel ready to return to the house. But I have no map and no landmarks to navigate by. *OK, never mind what you* don't *know. What* do *you know?* I know that Dyrys stretches to the west of Llandymna, and I've been running deeper into the woods, so home should be roughly east of here. If I can head east long enough, eventually I will spot something I recognize. It's late, so I only need to follow my own lengthening shadow. As long as I make it to the mill house before it gets properly dark, I should be fine.

When I finally make it back, I look around for tracks of any kind, or a sign that someone was here, scouring the ground for prints and the surrounding woodland for the roughly hacked path of a hunting party, but there is nothing. They didn't find the mill. If they had, they might easily have come back another day and found me, but my secret is safe and I can remain hidden here for now.

LLANDYMNA

Tom Davies finds himself once again knocking on the door of Diana's house with an increasing sense of dread. She answers the door with a teething Owen in one arm. Tom always finds it surprising to remember that Diana is a mother: she is a formidable member of the community council, a campaigner who gets things done in Llandymna, and it's easier to picture her with a clipboard and checklist of action points than with her children. Yet somehow, in spite of the loss of her husband, she manages to raise two children of her own as well as her niece, while still attending every important local event, knowing everybody's name, and managing to reinstate the Llandymna summer festival, regardless of having no funding for the project at all.

"You have news?" she asks with an unmistakable note of panic in her voice. Tom nods, and Diana eyes him expectantly.

"It's not what you're hoping for, I'm afraid. We haven't found her. But we have made some good progress."

Her face falls. Composing herself, she invites him inside, and Tom follows her into the spotless kitchen. Diana sets Owen in his high chair so that she can put the kettle on.

"I'm glad it's you this time," she says. "I found those other officers who interviewed me this morning to be very heavy-handed. I think the woman was trying to imply that I had invented Rhiannon's disappearance as some sort of cover-up for my own crimes. Goodness knows what she thought I'd done."

"We have to consider every possibility," Tom replies with the measured response he is used to giving to indignant relatives. "But there were enough witnesses to the incident on the seventeenth at the school, who heard Rhiannon threaten to run away, that we are treating that as the most likely scenario. And in the meantime, I have been appointed Family Liaison Officer, which means that I can bring you updates on the investigation."

"And have you found anything useful?" Diana asks, taking out two white mugs with yellow lilies painted on them.

"We took a team of officers to search the area surrounding the village today, including Dyrys Wood. There were some footprints in one of the fields that will need further examination to determine if they belong to Rhiannon or not. We also found a mobile phone in a lane leading away from the village, which we believe may be hers."

"Can I see it? I can tell you if it belongs to her straightaway."

"I'm afraid not. It's already gone back to the station in Bryndu. Any evidence we find will be sent there."

"But why would her phone be there? Why wouldn't she have it with her?"

"She may have dropped it by accident, or she may have deliberately discarded it if she didn't want us to track it and find her."

Diana sighs as she pours the tea. "I just can't believe she would actually run off like this! I know she talked about it, but she used to threaten a lot of things when she was angry."

"Well, Rhiannon would be classed as medium risk, considering –"

"Considering what, exactly?" Diana asks sharply.

"Considering that she is an orphan, to all intents and purposes. And despite having been taken in by a stable and supportive couple who were already related to her, she has gone on to lose one of her guardians too. That's a lot of upheaval for a young person to go through."

Diana's jaw tightens and her lips purse, yet when she opens her mouth to speak, the words sound perfectly civil.

"I appreciate this must be a difficult situation for you, Thomas, policing in a serious matter where you know everyone involved. But I am glad that you are on the force, else every officer on this... this 'case' would be an outsider from another village. Llandymna is lucky to have you."

"That's... very kind of you," Tom replies a little formally, taken aback by the unexpected compliment.

"And I assume you have the next steps planned?"

"Yes, of course. There will be further searches and interviews tomorrow, as soon as it's light. And I've been asked to recommend to you that we involve the press in the search. A television appeal for information, with a message directly to Rhiannon inviting her to get in contact, could be very effective."

"I see," Diana replies in an inscrutable tone of voice. "Well, I'll think about it. You obviously know what's most likely to work here, much better than I do."

Tom finishes his tea and ensures that Diana has all the necessary contact numbers in case she should need to speak to somebody. As he leaves the house, the door clicks shut quietly behind him and the sound that follows him down the road is presumably Owen crying.

Later that evening, Tom walks down the track out of Llandymna to the Evanses' farm. He is met at the gate by Megan, the border collie, who considers it part of her duty to her owners to knock every visitor off their feet, by launching herself at them with boundless energy.

"Megan, *dere ma*!" a deep voice booms from the house, as Ifan calls her back. "Evening, Tom! Nia tells me you're joining us for tea."

"Hope that's all right with you."

"Course it is. Come on inside," says Ifan. Tom leaves his shoes by the rack of wellingtons and walking boots in the hallway, and follows the delicious smell that wafts from the kitchen. Above the door is a wooden sign painted with an old saying: *Deuparth gwaith yw ei ddechrau* (starting the work is two thirds of it). Tom smiles as he thinks how apt this saying is in the Evanses' home. In the kitchen, Nia is removing a casserole dish from the oven, while billows of steam momentarily fill the room.

"Hello, Tom. You're just in time," she says, placing the pot in the middle of the kitchen table between the three place settings. "How did it go today? Any sign of her?"

Tom shakes his head. "Nothing concrete. Just a few more possible leads."

"You must be tired."

"Exhausted," Tom replies, but on hearing Ifan snort in response, quickly adds, "still, I know you are both used to long days and tough work all the time."

Ifan seems mollified, but Nia still looks sympathetic. "You sit there," she says. "Don't take the nearest chair; it wobbles a bit. I'll have that one."

"It's been a difficult year," says Ifan, sensing an opportunity to make sure Tom understands. "The snows in March were bad news for our lambing season. We can't afford another spell like that next spring. When your livelihood's tied to the land and the weather, success and survival can be fickle things."

"It's not been so bad –" Nia begins.

"These city folk with their desk jobs," Ifan continues, "have no idea what it's like. Bring 'em out here and we'll show them what hard work is really about."

Tom knows that as a local police officer he does not quite fall into the city office worker category Ifan is so suspicious of, but nor is he a farmer, and that in itself is cause for concern. He knows it will be easiest to keep quiet and let Ifan say all he wants to on the subject. Nia appears to have decided on the same strategy. She serves up the casserole while her husband continues.

"And then there's the dropping prices of milk and lamb, which are driving some farmers around the country into debt and even bankruptcy. As if we weren't still recovering from foot-and-mouth, and the number of farmers around here who lost whole flocks to that! More and more people are following what we've done, and converting spare buildings into guest houses to try to make some money out of tourists in the summer."

"Not just the summer," Nia adds. "We've had an out of season booking for this September. That will bring in some extra income for us."

"My point is," Ifan says, more loudly to convey his annoyance at being cut off and contradicted, "times are hard. And you know what I keep noticing, Tom? Even though we work harder than most, there's not the respect there used to be for a farmer's vocation."

This thought turns out to be the springboard into Ifan's indignation at the general lack of respect these days, and he talks as if he were a much older man until he has properly exhausted all his opinions on the matter. Tom tries to cast a knowing smile at Nia, but she seems not to notice as she turns down the oven to warm the pudding for later. She is hatching her own plan in silence. She has questions that need answering, and tomorrow she will seek out the one person who may be able to help.

CHAPTER FIVE

LLANDYMNA

The following day, after the eggs have been collected and the sheep checked on, the porridge made and the washing cycle begun, Nia leaves the farm to visit Maebh. Ifan has taken Megan the collie and gone to move the sheep into the next field, while Simon who helps out on the farm is shifting hay bales. Nia knows she will not be needed for an hour or so. She walks up to the village, carrying a bag of edible gifts in recycled containers: a homemade stew, an apple pie, and a jar of onion chutney. Though the weight of the bag pulls on her shoulder, she does not lean with it; she may be a slight, pale figure to look at, but Nia is stronger than she seems.

She passes the White Lion, where Terry the barman is hosing down the hedges that mark out the space for picnic tables. He greets her rather gruffly: everyone knows Terry is not a morning person. Nia skips over the streams of water running from the pub garden down into the gutter.

The air is clearer here in the village. Nia often finds that she sets out from a farm shrouded in mist to discover that the centre of Llandymna is enjoying sunlight or, at the very least, visibility. Nia has never minded the mists. She likes the feeling of disappearing into the grey, melting out of sight to become nothing more than another unrecognizable shape in the distance.

She walks by the church hall, where the community council meets, where jumble sales reallocate everyone's possessions into different houses, where the boy scouts learn to tie knots and the ladies' sewing group compare their children's school reports. The hanging baskets outside the main entrance are overflowing with a blaze of bright pansies and geraniums. She keeps walking up the road and around the corner to Maebh's house.

Nia holds out the bag of food as an offering as soon as the door is opened, but Maebh glances from the gift to the woman holding it and says slyly: "Dearie me, I think that might be too heavy for me to lift. You are very generous, my dear. Would you mind coming in and putting it down on the table for me?"

She ushers Nia into the house and suggests putting the kettle on, and before Nia can protest that she did not mean to invite herself in for tea, she is holding a cup and being offered cake.

"It's bara brith. I bet you didn't think an Irish woman like me could master your recipes, did you? My mother insisted we learn it when we first moved over here. She said the same about lava bread, mind, and that turned out foul, and we never ate it again. But bara brith is something I can do rather well when I choose to! Mind you, there's been Irish and Welsh intertwined in this village for centuries." She cuts two slices of the fruit loaf, which fills the kitchen with a rich sweet smell.

"There has?" asks Nia. Talking with Maebh is like sifting through a trove of local folklore. Though she is one of the few Llandymna residents who cannot trace their roots in the village back through the centuries, she knows this place better than anyone. Ever since the O'Donnells stepped off the boat from Rosslare and stood with their backs to the steamer's dark iron chimneys in Fishguard harbour, they immersed themselves in the language and culture of their new home. It is said that Bridget O'Donnell, Maebh's mother, was fluent in Welsh by the time they settled in Llandymna, just two years after arriving in the country.

"Of course. It's in the name: Llandymna. Do you know what it means?"

"Well, the first bit – *llan* – is a church or parish. I suppose the rest is the name of some saint. I hadn't really thought about it."

"It's from *Dymphna*. The name of an Irish saint, though they lost a couple of letters along the way, maybe to make it easier to pronounce. There's tales of there once being a shrine to her, long before the church was built. Of course, once they remembered she was foreign, and Catholic, they were sure to name the church after someone else. But the name Llandymna stuck. Will you have butter with your bara brith?"

Now that Nia will have to stay for at least as long as it takes her to finish her cake and tea, Maebh can proceed.

"So then, how are you?"

"Um, I'm well, thank you," comes Nia's reply. They sit facing one another in the small sitting room, with its outmoded floral wallpaper and display shelf of commemorative chinaware.

"I haven't seen you for a while. I expect you've been busy on the farm, haven't you?"

"Yes, busy as ever. We've got all the hay in now, thankfully. It's been a good summer so far."

"And Ifan – how is he?"

"Busy too. He works so very hard. I never feel like I'm keeping up with my share of the work really."

"I'm sure you do all you can, and more besides." She takes a bite of the bara brith, chewing thoughtfully. "I heard that Tom Davies was going to see the two of you yesterday."

Nia lets a smile flicker over her face in amusement at the way an elderly woman who rarely leaves her house can still know everyone's comings and goings. Maebh is not a gossip in the way that some of Llandymna's residents are. She never tells another person's news just for the entertainment of it, or encourages her visitors to think or speak badly of one another; still, you always know that she is aware of everything happening around her, whether she tells you or not.

"He did come round for tea. I made a casserole. He seems to be finding his work very hard at the moment." Nia reaches to put her cup down on the table, but misses. It falls to the floor and spills its contents over the carpet. She jumps up, apologizes profusely and runs to the kitchen for a cloth to mop up the mess. When she sits back down, Maebh does not seem interested in the spilled tea, but stares at Nia instead.

"You seem distracted, my dear."

"I suppose I am, a little. I don't know who to worry for more: Rhiannon, wherever she may be; Diana, waiting for news from the police; Tom, having to deliver the news of whatever the police find. He's still quite junior, isn't he, in the force? I don't think he's had to deal with anything like this before."

Nia watches Maebh's face hopefully, searching for the signs of reassurance. Maebh, however, does not respond this way.

"The one thing I can always be sure of with you, Nia Evans, is that no matter what happens, you'll be thinking of everyone but yourself. You were that way as a girl too, I remember, forever giving away your toys and spotting the one child in the room who was unhappy."

"How could I possibly think of myself at a time like this?" Nia exclaims indignantly. "There are plenty of other people more affected than me by what's happened!"

"And yet you are affected by it. I know that furrowed brow too well. Something else is troubling you, and I shan't let you fret over Tom or Diana until you tell me what it is."

Nia sighs, and searches around in her head for words to explain something she has not yet articulated to herself.

"It's... unsettling, I think. Llandymna has always felt like a small, stable community. It's familiar and predictable, and I like that about this place. Most of us do, I suppose. The summer baking competition is won by the same people every year, the church always has a congregation of about twenty, except for funerals and Christmas, Elsie Jones tells you the same three or four stories about her brother moving to Canada, Diana Griffin is automatically in charge of everything that happens in Llandymna, no matter what it might be, and nobody moves further than fifteen miles away, and even then only if they marry someone from another village. But ever since the day she disappeared, I've been speaking to people and they all look… dazed. Like centuries of safety have been overturned. I'm sorry – that sounds much too dramatic. And selfish, too. I suppose I mean that everyone thought we were safe from anything like that out here."

Maebh nods, knowing she has made Nia very uncomfortable by insisting she speak all this aloud. She pauses, looks around the room, and then asks, "Didn't Rhys Powell try to set up a Llandymna history society once?"

"I think so," Nia says with surprise at the sudden change in subject.

"If I recall, Diana argued against it, saying that pride in Llandymna was to be found in meeting its admirable current residents and seeing our community at work, rather than leafing through dusty old archives in a dark room."

"That does sound like something she might say."

"Then I shall try not to be surprised at how quickly you forget your own history here."

"I'm sorry?" Nia is puzzled.

"You say the people of Llandymna believe they lived a peaceful, respectable existence until two days ago? They said the same thing when Elin Morgan came back over the border after five years living in London, and wherever else she had been. She kicked up a mighty storm, did that one. And she wasn't the first, either."

"She wasn't?"

"Gracious, no. I know you young folk think everyone my age used to be terribly boring and wear aprons or top hats in the days of black and white photography, but we had our troubles and scandals too. That history society might have dredged up all sorts, had it ever been allowed to begin. So if it's their peace and quiet people are worried about, tell them not to fret. Llandymna recovers from its traumas and forgets them faster than you'd think."

"What do you mean? You can't be suggesting we forget about Rhiannon and stop looking for her?"

"No, of course not."

Nia senses an opportunity, draws in a breath, expanding her lungs to give the impression of boldness, and asks the question she has been harbouring.

"Maebh, do you know why Rhiannon left? Assuming she has left by her own choice, of course."

"A nice policeman was over here yesterday afternoon," Maebh replies, "and he asked me the same question. He was older than our Tom. And I told him that I had known Rhiannon her whole life, and her mother before her, but that I did not know exactly why she might have run away just now. I did suggest he look for her in Dyrys, but I think they had already thought of that and sent a search party out."

"But do you suspect something – something not concrete enough to be of any use to the police? I think you knew her better than anyone else, after Elin passed away at least."

"Perhaps. Perhaps there is something in this old head of mine that would make sense of it all, but when you get to my age it is hard to access it all."

"I just wish there was something I could do to help," Nia sighs.

RHIANNON

This morning I picked wildflowers and scattered the petals across the floor of my house. They add colour and a beautiful fragrant scent in place of damp moss and cold stone. I wonder how long it has been since anyone took care of this place. Maybe a century or more, unless another fugitive or woodland-dweller took shelter here after it fell into ruin.

I'm getting better at starting up my cooking fire now; today it only took a few minutes to get the flames to really take hold and now there's hot water for me to wash with. I even picked some dandelion leaves and threw them into the first pan of water as a drink. It tasted bitter, but I felt proud of myself for making it nonetheless.

I begin wondering how to make it as difficult as possible for other people to get to my hideaway, in case a rambler loses the path one day and stumbles across this place. I don't want to have to run like I did yesterday every time I hear a footfall. It would be far more convenient to be able to hide instead – clumps of overgrown bramble and thickets of dense vegetation form natural barriers that even a dog could not crawl through. If I could surround my house with a tangle of holly and fallen branches, no one would be able to reach me. It would look as though no one had been this way in years, and they would search somewhere else. I would only need one or two small gaps to squeeze through when I go searching for food and firewood.

I stand up in front of my house and stamp on the embers to put out the last remnants of the fire. If I burned Dyrys to the ground, then I'd be really stuck for somewhere to hide! I pace forward, jumping over the stream where it is narrow enough, and keep going until the house is obscured from view. Next, I look for where the brambles are already growing nearby. This is where I will start my fence. In autumn, I will be able to pick blackberries from it without crossing the boundary.

I begin to pull one of the branches to stretch out to the right, but cannot get a grip on it without the thorns digging into my palm. I pull down the sleeve of my jacket to cover my hand, and this just about stops the spikes. Next, I drag some fallen branches to extend the tangle further to the side, mounding them up so that they seem to have fallen there naturally. It is hard work, and slow, and as the afternoon passes I find it harder to find suitable wood. I have to search further and further away from my house. But every step is worthwhile, because the thicket grows taller and longer. It will take a long time to complete, but when it's done I'll be safe. I wonder if a caterpillar feels this way when it builds a cocoon around itself.

I pause in my work for some food and a drink, deciding water is preferable to my attempt at dandelion tea. From where I sit, I survey the progress I've made on the fence so far. When it's finished, a large circle of land will be mine, perhaps to farm or hunt in, certainly to hide from others passing this way. I shall have my own territory in which to live.

In this rest during my lunch, I suddenly wish there was someone here to tell me a story. It's how I used to spend my evenings, listening to Maebh tell her tales, or reading a book from the school library once I was older. But as there's no one here, I can tell a story exactly as I want it.

Once, in the days when forests and mountains still moved and animals spoke to one another, the magician Gwydion went to battle with an army of trees behind him. Their branches became wooden arms so strong they had no need of weapons, and these soldiers were tall enough to see for miles around, so no one could ever sneak up on them. On the day of that battle, there was the cry of men on one side and the creak of timber and the rustle of leaves on the other. Gwydion's trusted general, the alder tree, led the march, while lithe willows and weather-beaten rowans followed in the ranks, and the solid oaks, most dependable of his soldiers, took up the rear in the march on King Arawn and his army.

Arawn is king of the Underworld in mythology, and Maebh taught me a saying from an old folktale she learned when she first arrived in Wales: *Hir yw'r dydd a hir yw'r nos, a hir yw aros Arawn.* It means "Long is the day and long is the night, and long is the waiting of Arawn". I remember thinking it was one of the most magical and evocative things I had ever heard: wistfulness and perseverance and longing and hardship all rolled into a few beautiful Welsh words.

Perched in the topmost branches of some of these trees were the forest people – those who had left their mud-and-straw houses to live in the woods. They were dressed in green and carried bows and arrows on their backs. The leaders of the forest people, a

*young man and woman high up in the branches of an alder,
could be recognized by the leafy wreaths that crowned their
heads. The young man was the one they called the Boy Who
Shone in his childhood.*

Maebh told me a story about him once, when there were just a
few of us listening. It seemed to make her much sadder than any
other story she had ever told, but no one else I've ever asked seems
to know it. The legend goes that the young man was so full to
the top with goodness, any stone or plant he touched would be
bathed in sunlight for hours after. Alongside him was the Sparrow
Girl, known for her fierce fighting spirit. Maybe I will rename the
Sparrow Girl one day. That is the good thing about telling stories:
you can change them as you wish.

Eventually I go back to work, though it's not like being at home.
There, I would have shaken off the story in order to go back to
normal life, landing with a jolt in Aunty Di's kitchen or a noisy
classroom. People tell me I daydream too much, that I get distracted
from work too easily, so I have to make myself forget the stories
when I am busy running errands for my aunt. But here, there is no
one to complain, no one to interrupt with a question or command
that will catch me by surprise and make it obvious my mind was
a thousand miles away. So I don't need to snap myself sharply out
of the story. Instead I carry on weaving it, even as I weave together
this tangle of stems and branches. As I venture further out into the
forest to look for more twigs and creepers, I walk with the presence
and dignity of the Sparrow Girl. It adds a certain splendour to the
work of finding wood. I pull out branches as if selecting the material
for arrows, or for the walls of a tree house. Time passes more quickly
this way too, and before I have done only half as much as I expected
to achieve today, the sky is greying with the first hints of evening.

A strange cry catches my attention and I look up. In the boughs
of a tree not far away sits a hawk. Its talons are hooked around a
branch. A mantle of grey feathers is on its shoulders, and its beak

curves to a vicious point beneath two gleaming gold eyes. It is looking straight at me.

I freeze, staring back into those eyes. The cry is repeated. All about me, birds trill alarm calls and take to the air in terror. The same terror strikes me, and I turn and run.

Through the darkening forest I flee, back to the safety of my house. The shriek still rings in my ears. *You're being ridiculous,* I scold myself. *Since when are you scared of birds? Some great adjustment to life outdoors, running away from a hawk!* It took me by surprise – that must be it. That, and the way it didn't fly away when it saw me. It had fear in its eyes, as all wild things do, but it did not retreat.

At least now it is far away. I lie still in the shadows and think of something else. I think of my parents.

I've always thought that my father must have been an adventurous, intrepid sort of man, that somehow I must have rivers and sky in my blood. I picture him climbing mountains, but of course no one can tell me if he was really like that. My mother kept him a secret and never brought him to Llandymna. I imagine she wanted to protect him from the people there. Diana would have disapproved on principle, just because my mother liked him. But sometimes I wish she had dared to leave a clue behind, in case I ever wanted to find him.

My mother's name was Elin, a Welsh name meaning light. I think it suited her: I remember her as lively and bright. She brought fun with her wherever she went, according to Maebh. Her sister Diana shares her name with the Roman goddess of the moon. I learned that in our Year 4 project on myths and legends. And like the moon, so serene and quiet, my aunt is dignified and composed. People look to her as a natural leader, though she's not as constant as they think. She reserves her dark moods for when she's at home, when the last guest has handed back their tea cup with a so-kind-of-you-to-invite-me and when the door is firmly closed. The rest of Llandymna doesn't know how she slams things, or how she cleans like a maniac when she's trying not to think about a painful memory.

This year, on the anniversary of Uncle Ed's death, she completely rearranged most of the furniture in the house. That day, Eira came up to my attic room. She brought a stuffed bear with her, and an owl with button eyes and only one foot. We didn't say anything about why she was there, but I let her play in the attic for the rest of the day, and I put some music on loudly, so we wouldn't hear the thuds and creaks of our home's battlelines being redrawn.

Those are the women who raised me: one bright and hopeful, dancing around the house to old jazz songs and letting me eat ice cream for breakfast because she forgot to buy cereal again; the other sensible and respectable, making plans and packed lunches for the week ahead.

CHAPTER SIX

RHIANNON

No matter where I put my sleeping bag, I cannot avoid those early rays of light bursting in through the open doorway any more than I can escape the deep cold of the hours after midnight. On the fourth day of my new life away from everyone, I wake with the sunrise, curled up tightly and wearing all the clothes I have to try to keep warm. I eat fruit and berries for breakfast, and wash in the cold water of the stream.

I am feeling bolder today, so I put four flat stones in my pocket and search the walls of my house for footholds to scale it. I feel around with fingers and feet for a place to grip the surface, and hoist myself, a little at a time, up to the top. I perch on the edge of the roof, my legs dangling down into the drop below. When I have edged my way nearer to the place where it is broken, I lay the waterproof fabric of my bag over the top of it, and then place a stone on each corner, wedging them into a nook or crevice so they will not slip. They pull the material taut across the hole and hold it in place. That should keep out most of the Welsh weather. Overhead, clouds are rolling grey and ominous. We're due rain soon.

I slide down from the roof, dislodging a couple of stones on the way; it isn't far to the ground after all. Today, I have resolved, I will put out of my mind all the things I wish I had: a pillow, dry socks, soap, hot chocolate, a mug, painkillers, plasters, a hairbrush, and a thousand other things. Instead I will think about what I can do with what is already here. What can I make? What can I manage without?

I remember seeing some discarded drinks cans by the path. At the time I thought the litter only an eyesore, but now I think about what I could make from them. The metal would not burn or melt over a fire. If I flattened out one of the cans, I could use it to fry food.

Then there is the mud that lines the banks of the stream. I know the earth around here is full of clay: every gardener and farmer complains about it when they try to plant something new. *Oh, the soil's no more than clay around here – better for sculpting than planting carrots,* they all say. What if they were right? What if I could make pots and bowls from it? I'd need to build my own kiln, but I'm pretty sure that's just a stone housing for your fire.

A sudden noise distracts me from my plans. I look up sharply and see the hawk, sitting on the ground not twenty feet away. It starts to move forward and I rise to my feet quickly.

"That's close enough!" I say. Even though I know it's the sudden movement rather than my words that startles the bird into retreating slightly, I'm relieved to see I can tell it to go away. Now that I look at it more closely, I can see something is not quite right. It looks a little dishevelled and scruffy for a bird of prey. One of its wings sits lower than the other, the long feathers trailing on the floor, like when the wind blows your scarf over your shoulder and it drags along behind you on the pavement.

"You're hurt, aren't you?" I say. "That's why you don't fly away."

The hawk's eyes dart back and forth, in what looks like agitation.

"Well, I don't know what you want from me. I'm not a vet, and I don't have any food for you. Not unless you like fruit."

It tries to move again, and achieves only a pathetic little shuffle. If its wing is broken, it won't be able to hunt. It will probably starve. Hawks take care of their young, but that's as far as the altruism goes.

"No one's coming to help you," I say, and the words come out sounding sadder and more sympathetic than I had expected. I find that I don't like looking at it, so I decide to go and search for those tin cans by the path instead.

Claire Wong

LLANDYMNA

In a rare quiet moment, Nia sits down at the kitchen table and brings out her knitting. The oven hums away as it takes care of its work for the afternoon, and for the next half an hour at least, it does not need her attention. For a moment she listens to the dogs outside and the distant engine whir of one of the farm vehicles out in the fields. Then she focuses back on the teal wool in her hand and the rows already complete. She is making a shawl, though whether it is for herself or to be given as a gift, she has not yet decided. She still laughs at herself sometimes for taking up knitting, when she remembers her nan teaching her twenty years ago. She had made a rather wonky scarf, too small for a person, so it had ended up being worn by one of her toy animals. Then she set aside knitting for a long time, as being "something for old people". But in the long evenings on the farm, she finds it soothing to give her attention to a single useful task. There is a rhythm to it. The repetition is reassuring rather than monotonous. She could happily stay here for hours, but she only completes three more rows before the doorbell rings.

"Nia! There you are."

Diana stands on the doorstep looking, to Nia's surprise, entirely herself. She is wearing her smart coat, the navy blue one she always uses for council business or important occasions. She wastes no time in inviting herself inside, and for all Nia's searching for a sign of strain on her composed face, she cannot spot it.

"Diana, I'm so sorry about what's happened. It must be so hard for you."

"Thank you, dear; that's very good of you to be thinking of me."

Nia feels strangely like a child being praised by her mother for showing good manners. She shows Diana to the sitting room, because she does not feel she can ask her to sit at the kitchen table.

"I don't suppose there's any news?"

"Not yet, but the police are working tirelessly, of course." Diana casts an impatient glance around the room.

71

"If there's anything that we can do to help…" Nia offers. As the room undergoes her guest's scrutiny, she feels suddenly conscious of cobwebs and clutter that had not bothered her earlier. She finds herself straightening the check blanket that hangs over the back of the sofa.

"As it happens, that's why I'm here. There is a way you can help me."

"Really? What is it?"

"The police have the idea that a filmed message might reach Rhiannon, and that it might be a way to encourage her to come back home."

Nia recalls the times she has seen this on the news. She remembers images of brave but visibly distraught parents speaking to cameras and strangers in the hope their child might be among the audience. She thinks of the painful emotion in those voices, the pleading words, and thinks that she cannot imagine Diana ever doing such a thing. Then she realizes that must be why she is here. Her stomach churns violently.

"You don't mean – "

"Nia, you and I both know that this sort of thing is far better undertaken by someone who is approachable, unintimidating, and sensitive. You've known Rhiannon a long time, and you are far more a friend than an authority figure. Your voice will be much more effective than mine in this instance."

"But I can't. Surely it should be you?" Nia pleads.

"Don't be silly. It's perfectly appropriate for a concerned friend of the family to do this."

Nia wonders briefly what people in the village will think if they hear that Diana did not want to face the press. She then remembers that Diana will certainly have considered this at great length, and knows she must be desperate not to do the interview if she would risk gossip over it. Perhaps the fear of letting down her guard in public is worse than seeming not to be fully involved in the efforts to get Rhiannon back. But Nia decides this is unkind speculation.

"Perhaps there is someone more used to speaking in public?" she appeals.

"You're being modest now, but I wouldn't have asked if I didn't have complete confidence in you."

You didn't ask, Nia thinks. She would be reluctant to refuse Diana a request at the best of times, but now that Rhiannon is missing, she feels bound to agree.

She takes a deep breath, reminding herself that she wanted to do something to help. "When will it be?"

"Tomorrow afternoon. I will help you write a statement to read out, of course. The filming will take place over in Bryndu, so you'll need to be there for three."

"It won't be here in Llandymna?" Her voice wavers.

"No, it's better this way. Easier access for press to have it there, and it avoids having journalists descend on our village. I'll come round tomorrow morning then, to agree what needs to be said." She speaks with the efficiency of one used to delegating to others.

Everything appears settled, so Diana leaves. She walks back to where she parked her car in the lane outside the Evanses' farm rather than risk taking it over the bumpy ground past their gate. On the drive back up to the village she does not pass another vehicle – only a kestrel hovering over a hedgerow on the lookout for mice. Ed would have asked her to stop the car so they could watch it. He was like that, her Edwin, always reminding her to stop and just look at things. She would have reminded him that tea needed to be on the table at six if she was to make it to the meeting at seven-thirty, and that there were a hundred things to do before that. But then Rhiannon would have joined in the appeal: *can't we stay just five minutes?* And Eira too, when she was old enough. It was impossible to refuse them, at times like that.

Milk. She needs to buy milk before she goes home. She parks at the White Lion and goes to the little shop across the road. Inside Llandymna's only shop Angie Rees, Callum's mother, is in her usual spot behind the counter, chatting with another woman as she counts out change in five pence coins.

"… in the end, he said, Matthew Pritchard bought it off him for half the price. Sick as a parrot, he was! So it's an afternoon of gardening for you, is it? There's lovely. You know who's just spent a fortune on their garden? That couple who moved up from Newport. You know – the ones on Lon Du. They ripped everything out and put decking in! I say if you don't want grass in your garden, you might as well stay living in a city. Hello there, Diana," Angie says, seeing that she has another customer.

"Afternoon, Angela," Diana replies, pretending not to notice that both the two women at the counter and the few other people in the shop have stopped to stare at her. She walks to the chilled section on the far side of the shop, but even from here she can make out snippets of the whispered conversation.

"Terrible, I know. They say she's run away from home." Angie lowers her voice so that Diana cannot make out the next part, except for the phrase "more likely than kidnapping".

Diana stays facing the shelves as the whispering continues, and she hears the other shopper say, "Looks very together, don't you think?" Suddenly she feels as if every eye is on her. She is acutely conscious of each movement she makes, of what might be read into it. Does the way she chooses semi-skimmed milk in four-pint bottles convey the right response? One muscle out of sync and she might be seen as too anxious or too carefree, too aloof or too emotional. She knows this game. She excels at it.

She selects her purchases and then straightens up and walks to the till, keeping her face solemn until she is close enough to smile a greeting at the two women who have fallen silent. She gives no indication that she has overheard them.

"Diana, we're all so sorry."

"Oh, that's so good of you, Angie, to be thinking of me." Diana knows it is always best to act surprised that people are giving you their attention, no matter how deserved it might be.

"Any news yet?"

"Nothing concrete. They're still looking."

"Is it true they've already searched the woods?" she asks.

"That's right."

Their wide-eyed eagerness to ask more is something they struggle to conceal. This is the most interesting thing to happen in Llandymna in many years. Diana knows that after she leaves the shop, reports will spread from one house to the next, over garden hedges or in passing outside the pub. Everyone will receive the updates, retold with all the compassion and nuance of a sensationalist tabloid headline.

"I'm sure she'll turn up safe and sound eventually," the other customer says. Diana restrains herself from snorting at the ridiculousness of this woman's certainty. How can she possibly be sure of any such thing?

"Oh, I don't know," Angie says darkly. "I can't see why anyone would up and leave of their own free will, now. Can you? This is a good place, and barely anybody moves away. I'd say you'd have to be forced to leave Llandymna."

"Oh, hush now, Angie. You don't want to worry Diana. Pay no attention to her. There'll be some good news soon, you'll see."

Diana acknowledges the reassurance and quickly leaves the shop. She finds it easier not to think about any kind of news. The idea of hearing something good awakens short-lived hope, while the other possibility looks like an abyss gaping open at her feet. She has done the rounds before, cycling between optimism and despair, in doctor's offices with her husband, and then in hospital waiting rooms alone. She knows how to shut out the highs and lows. Life will go on, whatever happens, for Owen and Eira's sake.

CHAPTER SEVEN

RHIANNON

The fence around my little patch of land is taking shape. The east side of it is indistinguishable from the natural woodland. The cost of this success, though, is that my hands are scratched and scraped all over. I hold them in the cool water of the stream, which soothes the stinging temporarily. It feels fitting to be weaving together this mass of brambles in Dyrys, the wood whose name means *tangled*. I am adding to its thickets and its mystery, building something that perhaps always belonged here.

The temperature has dropped, so when I stop working I put on all the extra layers I have. It isn't much like summer today. I've had to stop hauling the branches around earlier than planned, because I am a little weak and lightheaded. Perhaps my diet of berries and fruit is not giving me the energy I am used to having.

My hand goes to the pendant around my neck, which I've worn every day since I was first given it. I trace each part of it: the key, the rose, and the book. I've always liked to think of them as being relics from a fairy tale. The key would unlock the tower room where the protagonist has been kept trapped all this time, like Rapunzel or the Lady of Shalott. Then she would step out from her prison to begin her adventure. I suppose I've always thought that the key stands for freedom.

I look around my land, from the ruins of the mill cottage to today's crop of food wrapped up in my waterproof coat, waiting to be washed in the water of the stream. I suddenly wish that they could see me now, the people back home. No, not home – just in Llandymna. Maybe that never really was my home. I wish they could see everything I have done, and how I am surviving out here just fine without them. I imagine Di's face moving from admiration to sorrow when she realizes how wrong she was about me; how much she wishes I had not left. But it will be too late by the time she knows this, because it is her loss and the loss of everyone else in that village now, because I am happy here, and I am free!

Another benefit of being here is that I won't have to go to her birthday party. She has been planning it for months, and I've been forced to help with the preparations, even though my eighteenth is actually a few days before. She and I both have September birthdays, but mine is always overshadowed.

I want to think about something else. It seems like, no matter how well I do out here, thinking about Llandymna, about my neighbours and relatives, always makes me feel strange, as if my stomach is being twisted and wrung out like an old tea towel. I turn my mind instead to the projects I thought of yesterday. Perhaps I should try making clay pots to keep my food in. It would be better than using my coat as a tray, especially as I think I will need that soon, judging by the dark clouds brooding overhead.

Something just inside the doorway of the house catches the light and glints at me. I go over to see what it is. A few stones have fallen in from higher up, probably from when I jumped down off the roof. Partly buried beneath them is something that looks metallic. I shift the stones out of the way to see what it is. It is round and heavy, and hangs on a chain. My first thought is that it could be a compass, but on closer inspection it looks more like the casing of a pocket watch. It even has initials engraved on one side of the tarnished metal, the letters R and T inscribed in a floral script. I try to open it, but it seems to be rusted shut. It would take someone stronger than me to break it open now.

The watch is old, but not as old as the ruins it was sitting in. So does that mean someone else has been here, sheltering from the elements like me? There is no other furniture here, so they can't have lived very comfortably. I wonder who owned the pocket watch, and what they were doing hiding out here. I like the idea that there was another runaway here once, and that this watch is a message from my predecessor to me.

I picture a young woman, perhaps fifty years ago, hiding the watch in a nook of the house one evening. Perhaps, like me, she learned to take care of herself in the woods. And then maybe one day, when she was transformed by her experiences into quite an impressive figure, she went back home.

On a clear summer's evening, when the sky was blazing golden in the west, and the villagers had been preoccupied with their petty squabbles and hypocrisies, she returned. Not until she was at the very walls did anyone see her, this mysterious woman who had been gone for many years. As she stepped into their midst, with light yet purposeful strides, all fell silent.

Of course, she couldn't be from Llandymna, or I would have heard of her. Maebh would have remembered the story, even if no one else did.

I hold the watch in my hands and momentarily wish there were someone nearby, so that I could tell them everything I have done over these last few days. I would like to see the impressed look on their face, and I would like to tell the story. *Here*, I would say, *look how much food I've collected, look what I've built.* I've always enjoyed doing things more if I know there will be the opportunity to narrate it to someone afterwards: it seems more important as soon as you have an audience. But there's no one here this time, so I stop chattering in my head to an invisible spectator, and look up to the sky instead. The rain hasn't yet begun, though it can't be far off now, so I plan my next foraging trip. There are berries of every kind, and soon there will be hazelnuts and chestnuts to gather. Mushrooms spring up mysteriously in the shady patches, and I hope that bees will be making honey somewhere not far from here.

As if on autopilot, I go back to my food store and inspect it, once again measuring out the number of days it will last. I seem to do this several times a day now, even though I know the counting will not change the result. This time, as I do it, a new and unpleasant thought strikes me. Why exactly am I doing this? I collect food to give me the energy to go out the next day to collect more food, and then what? Day after day, I horde these supplies and work hard just to sustain my own life. But in this forest, there is no one else who will benefit from my presence. I daydream about the people who will follow me and revere me, so where are they? Who will ever tell my story? All these questions and doubts seem to land so sharply and suddenly that my stomach feels as if it has been kicked. I try to shake off these thoughts.

Quick, think of a story. This always works when I feel low. *Once, in an enchanted forest, where animals could speak and the leaves sang to one another, there lived...* Who? A girl who shouted and argued so that nobody cared when she left? Try again. *Once, in a town far away, there were many people...* But it isn't enough simply to imagine friends for myself, is it? Come on, you can do this. *Once...* It is no good. For once, the earth and stones of this house around me, which I can see and touch, are more real than the stories I have woven together. These stones are not here to form part of my story; they are here in spite of me, and they suddenly seem hard and flat and unyielding.

I can't help but laugh bitterly at the realization. I have spent my whole life wishing myself away. Every time the real world became too much to cope with, I would imagine myself off to another place far from family, teachers, and friends: to a wild place like Dyrys. There's a sign in the local library that says: *Humankind cannot bear very much reality.* I think T. S. Eliot said that. He wrote very long poems, about wars and legends and how mundane ordinary life is. I should have read more of him before I stopped having access to books. But now, at last, I am away from all of those boring real people, just as I dreamed. And it turns out that I can't ever outrun my own thoughts. Maybe they were the problem all along.

I feel disorientated, as if a wave has come charging in and knocked me off course, and as I run back outside, the skies finally break.

Rain droplets land squarely on my face and arms, the water soaking through my clothing in seconds. I know I chose this new way of life, but I think I may have made a horrible mistake. I can't see the point to any of it. I cannot see how to make all the days of my future count for anything now.

Long is the day and long is the night, and long is the waiting of Arawn.

I stand in the downpour as it washes pathways through the clay and dirt that streak my skin. I look up to the sky, but not a single beam of sunlight breaks through the grey canopy. I let out a scream at the rain; at the forest; at myself. It doesn't matter any more if I am silent or not, for there is nothing here.

CHAPTER EIGHT

BRYNDU

Bryndu police station is unwelcoming from the outside: little more than a stack of grey concrete blocks with a blue and white sign over the door. Nia arrives early, but knows she will spend all the waiting time adjusting the collar of her blouse. She is unused to wearing such smart things, but her everyday clothes from the farm did not feel appropriate. She tries to straighten her outfit before approaching the front desk. It still feels uncomfortable, as if there are the wrong number of buttons.

"Can I help you?"

"My name's Nia Evans. I'm here on behalf of the Griffin family. Sorry, I'm not really sure how this works…"

The woman behind the desk looks down her list. "Oh yes, here you are. You're early, so take a seat over there and I'll let them know you've arrived."

Nia sits down on a blue upright chair and takes out the piece of paper printed with the words she and Diana have agreed on. *Don't think about the cameras; don't think about all the other people. This is just a message for Rhiannon. Just think about saying it to her.* She wonders what will happen if she starts crying while they are filming her. *But even if you mean it just for Rhiannon, everyone else will see it when they watch the news tonight. Everyone will see you.* She wishes she could just walk out of the station right now, and not have to do this. But she had wanted to help, after all. And if, somehow, Rhiannon hears the message, then it could make a difference.

She rereads the words on the page. Diana redrafted them several times until she was happy with the result. To Nia, it feels formal and speech-like.

On behalf of the Griffin family, your friends, and the residents of Llandymna, I want to urge you to come home, Rhiannon.

Nia sighs, and puts the speech back into her bag. She cannot imagine Rhiannon responding well to the tone of the message. What teenager would?

"Mrs Evans? I'm Detective Inspector Michelle Collins."

The speaker shakes Nia's hand. Detective Inspector Collins is in her early forties, and looks far more comfortable striding about the station in a grey trouser suit than Nia is in her attempt at smart clothes. She invites Nia to follow her, and the two walk down a windowless corridor.

"Now, I'm sure this will be a difficult experience for you, but just try to relax as much as you can and speak naturally. These appeals can be very effective in reaching the missing person or prompting other witnesses to come forward with information."

"I just want to help however I can."

"Well, we have a number of the press here today. This kind of case always attracts a bit of interest. We'll go in there together once we're all ready. I'll give a statement first regarding the investigation, then I'll hand over to you. We've told them we aren't taking questions, so if a journalist tries to ask you anything, you don't need to respond. In fact, it's better if you don't. Ah, here's someone I think you know."

They have come to the door at the end of the corridor. Tom stands outside it in his constable's uniform.

"Good to see you, Nia," he says.

"I'm a bit surprised to be here." Nia gives an unsteady smile and takes a few deep breaths as she looks at the door before her.

"I know Diana appreciates what you're doing. And more to the point, you're doing something good for Rhiannon's sake, which is what matters."

You're right, she thinks. *This needs to be about Rhiannon more than anything.* She thinks back to the carefully crafted speech sitting in her bag. Suddenly, she makes a decision. *Diana is going to be furious with me.*

The doors close behind them, and cameras start flashing. Detective Inspector Collins gives her statement, which describes the investigation in detached and official language – facts that give no indication of what is happening in the community of Llandymna. Then, before her heart has stopped racing at the sight of all these staring eyes, it is Nia's turn. She blinks at the bright lights, searching the rows of reporters for a face that looks friendly so she can make eye contact with someone. Then she takes a deep breath.

"Rhiannon, I don't know if you will see this, but just in case you do, I'd like to talk to you, as a friend, I hope. I can't imagine what you might be feeling right now, and I won't pretend to. I'm worried for you and I'd like to know that you're safe. If you can, please get in touch somehow. Just let someone know you're all right…"

RHIANNON

The rain stopped hours ago. I didn't sleep at all last night: I wandered around the forest aimlessly. Now I see the mess I've become in just a few days. My clothes are torn and covered in dirt; my skin is marked with mud and clay and the juice of berries, all worked into the lines of my hands and under my nails. The pile of firewood is now strewn over the ground. A sparrow is sitting in a rain-filled footprint and chirping happily, but when I move, it flees to the safety of the dense foliage.

I take up a long narrow branch, which I had picked out as a walking stick in case I ever had to scale a steep slope or pick my way through deep mud. Taking it in both hands, I swing it around with all my strength. The movement seems to use up some of my anger as I wield the staff at an invisible enemy. I spin it over my head.

I thought I would like being alone out here. I thought that

with no adults to disapprove and no classmates to jeer me, I would feel free to be myself. But instead, I find I have no idea where I fit or who I am, and those I left behind haunt all my thoughts. Everything I do is to prove something to one of the voices that told me off for being disruptive, or to impress someone who had written me off. Maybe I didn't really want to be away from everyone. I just wanted to be around people who liked me, who would tell me I was doing OK, who I wouldn't disappoint all the time. But I don't think there's much chance of finding a new group of friends out here in the woods.

The noise in my head grows louder, sapping my remaining strength. I stagger and allow myself to fall backwards ungracefully to the ground, where I lie and stare up at the sky. When I close my eyes, I see friends around me here, sitting in a circle around a campfire. We could share stories and cook food together. I see kindness in the way we interact: a depth of compassion I think must only exist in books. As soon as I open my eyes, I am only lying in the mud among the first of the fallen leaves. But if I try hard, I can block out the cold air and the rainwater seeping from the earth into my clothes. I can shut out the bird noise and the pangs of hunger in my stomach, and go somewhere far away.

I need to run. When I was escaping the police and their dogs, it was all I could think about. My head was clearer. Maybe if I start running through the woods now, it will help again. I don't know where I will go, but there is plenty of space out here.

I pull myself up onto my feet and the unsteadiness of my legs reminds me again that I haven't eaten all day. Nevertheless, I pick a direction at random and start to run. I weave between the trees and leap over obstacles, inventing my route as I go. Some of the places I run through are familiar, others I don't recognize, but that doesn't matter. My head starts to feel a little lighter as I think more about not falling over and less about the mess I've made for myself.

I burst into a clearing and startle a fox into dropping its prey and fleeing in a bolt of red. The surprise of it stops me in my tracks. I go over to the small bundle it has left behind. It is a young rabbit, definitely already dead. I step back instinctively: I have never been a vegetarian, so a dead animal should not bother me, but this is different to packaged meat in the shops. I regret scaring the fox. I know animals have to hunt and eat, but now this will go to waste.

Then I have an idea. I take a breath and then pick up the rabbit, holding it at arm's length as I walk back to the stream. I drop it on the ground and sit down a short distance away. I wait.

It doesn't take long. The hawk must have been nearby already. It manages an uneven flight from a tree down to the floor, landing with a bit of a wobble. It hops up to the rabbit carcass and inspects it. I turn away for the next part. Yet I am too fascinated by it to miss the chance to see how the hawk eats, so I find myself turning back to watch it. It is gruesome, but skilful nonetheless.

While the bird focuses on its meal, I risk edging closer. It allows me to approach. Perhaps the effort of flying down from the tree with a damaged wing has taken its toll; perhaps, as provider of dinner, I am not a threat to it.

"No wonder you got hurt if you're happy for a predator like me to come and sit next to you," I murmur, softly so as not to startle it. "Well, maybe we can be friends now."

The hawk ignores me, but I don't mind. I am happy to watch it, and know that I am not alone here.

PART TWO

ROSE

CHAPTER ONE

Let me tell you a story, my children, of the Boy Who Ran. Long ago, in a faraway place, a young man was accused of the worst thing anyone could think of in those days, and he was driven from his home. That was how his adventures began. He started by running away from his accusers and his village, to a place of safety. And as he ran, he found that he was fleet of foot, and as agile as a young fox. So he crossed great swathes of terrain in this way, the soles of his feet leaving only the lightest imprint on the grass or earth, like the tracks of a hare on the morning hillside. He travelled far throughout the country, never tiring once, and he saw such wonderful sights as high grey mountains and shimmering blue lakes. With him came his best friend and closest ally, the Sparrow Girl. She was called that because she could understand the language of the birds, though in truth she would have been better named after something much fiercer, for she was a brave fighter. She had a sharp temper to match her sharp weapons, but the Boy Who Ran knew that they were friends, and he was glad to have her there with him.

He was always afraid that one day he would have run too far and too fast, and that he would turn around to see the Sparrow Girl no longer there. He also knew, deep down, that one day he would want nothing more than to be able to stop running, to sit still in the shade of an old tree and look at the same spot of earth for more than a moment without leaving it. When that day came, the Boy Who Ran would need a new name.

RHIANNON

Twigs snap, and crisp leaves crunch under footfalls in the forest. Two pairs of sturdy boots disturb the silence of this bright September morning. I freeze, halfway through breaking off a sprig of elderberries, to locate the source of the sound. My foraging trip has brought me too far east, too close to the edge of the wood.

Lleu eyes me with a quizzical stare. It has been a couple of weeks, I think, since I fed him that rabbit. After that meal, he let me get near enough to make a support for his wing. I'd seen it done before, one winter when a wild goose crash-landed into the field behind the church. I didn't have a bandage like the one Uncle Ed used then, but I tore a strip off the end of my sleeve and bound it carefully around the wing, copying the figure-eight wrap he showed me. Now the support is off and Lleu can fly and hunt again. He still comes back to me, probably hoping I might catch something for him to eat. But I like to think he comes for the company too. He's taken to perching on my shoulder or arm at times, and it makes me feel like a falconer to a medieval king's court!

Voices drift this way, indistinct, on a gust of autumn wind. One of them is laughing. It doesn't sound like a police search party. I should be able to get back to my house undetected, if I'm quick.

"Don't look at me like that, Lleu!" I say to the hawk. "I don't know who it is, but the safest thing is to stay out of sight."

Lleu responds with a plaintive cry.

"Of course I'm curious to know who's out there! But what if we get caught? I can't fly away like you."

I stuff my coat pockets with the elderberries I've collected and turn back towards home. A snatch of the strange voices reaches me again. I don't recognize them. And if I'm not mistaken, the accents, though Welsh, aren't local. How odd. Could it hurt to try to get a glimpse of them? People come out here so rarely, and it would be wise for me to know everything that happens in Dyrys.

"OK, fine. But we're staying out of sight. And at the first sign of trouble, we run. Well, I'll run. You can fly to safety."

I creep towards the sound, steering clear of the path and relying on the forest undergrowth to conceal me. A spread of tall bracken seems like a good spot to hide. From here I can watch the path, while Lleu perches in a hazel tree behind me.

A man and woman walk down the main track through Dyrys from the east. They are not from Llandymna – of this much I am sure. They look to be in their thirties, dark skinned and dark haired, and ambling through the woods as if there is no destination before them.

"This is it," the man says, looking up at the trees as if they contain something more wonderful than yellowing leaves. "We're actually here!"

"That's the first thing you've said since we set out that wasn't just to cheer me up," says the woman, putting her hands in her pockets to keep warm. She adds, "I'm glad. You should stop looking after me, you know."

He gives a rueful smile. "Wouldn't dare try!"

"I mean it, Kofi! I'm glad you're here, but you can't keep up this concerned big brother thing any more. It's going to be strange for both of us, being here. Let's agree to that now, and stop pretending this is just another research trip."

The mischievous grin vanishes. They are almost level with my hiding place now, so I duck lower among the bracken and can no longer see their faces. But I wish I could still watch their expressions, if only to work out what's worrying the man who sounds so cheerful.

"All right, I can do that. Besides, these days you only call me Kofi when you're being serious. I just wanted to make sure you were OK, coming here so soon after the funeral."

"It'll be fine," she says.

"Now you sound like me. But it's more convincing coming from you, I think," he teases her. "It's the glasses, probably. They add weight to whatever you say."

93

"And don't you forget it!"

"I won't. Whenever we meet any of the locals while we're here, I'll tell them to direct all questions to my wise sister, and let you do all the talking."

"That'll be a first. Wait… What's that noise?"

Lleu has just let out a screech. Now he sweeps across the path and alights in the branches of an oak tree. Though I dare not lean forward to see their reaction, I hear the two strangers fall silent. I may have enough time to slip away while they are distracted, so I crawl further away from the path. I stand up silently, but then, to my dismay, they both look back over their shoulders to see where the bird came from. And of course they see me at once. I jump back as soon as they turn around, poised to run away.

"Sorry. We didn't mean to scare you," says the man.

A thousand questions run through my mind. Have they heard of the runaway from Llandymna? Will they tell the police they have seen me? "Who are you?" I ask, and it comes out fierce and demanding. I steady myself with a few calming breaths as I try to find out as much as possible about this threat.

"My name's Adam, and this is my sister Grace," he replies. I stare from one to the other, scrutinizing their unfamiliar faces. They don't seem particularly menacing. And by now I'm sure their accents are from somewhere south.

"You're not from round here."

"You're right," says Grace. "We've come here for my work. Do you live nearby?"

"Suppose so," I say, relaxing a little as I realize they have no idea who I am. Perhaps the police search hasn't extended far beyond the villages near here. I call up to the oak tree: "Lleu!"

In response, the bird flies down and lands on my left arm. I put my right hand on his back to keep him from flapping his wings. They stare in surprise.

"He seems well trained," Adam remarks.

Well, if he'd healed Lleu's wing and fed him dead rabbit, maybe the hawk would have learned to answer his call too. It occurs to me that maybe these two are walking so aimlessly because they are lost. "If you're looking for the main road, it's that way," I say, ignoring Adam's comment.

"Thank you," says Grace.

I can't think of anything else to say, so I stay silent, watching them.

"Maybe we should go and find this place where we're staying," says Adam. Grace nods silently. "We'll be in the village a while," he adds towards me. "Maybe we'll see you again there some time."

"Maybe," I say with a shrug, not wanting to give anything away about my home.

"Our car is parked just out on the lane at the edge of the woods. Can we give you a lift anywhere – back home, or wherever you're going?"

"No need," I say. "Come on, Lleu. Time for us to go."

I take my hand off the back of the bird's head and he jumps up into the air and flies off. A second later, I run after him, leaving the strangers behind.

Getting back to my house takes longer than usual, because I keep stopping to look back over my shoulder and make sure no one is following. But I hear and see nothing unusual on the way. Once I am the other side of my fence, I know I am safe again.

It's becoming more homely here. The space in the old mill house is filling up, with a good supply of dry wood and a few aluminium cans that I have repurposed into containers for my belongings. I've piled up some dried leaves under my sleeping bag to try to give a softer surface to sleep on, so that my back does not ache quite so much in the mornings. I've also used leaves and moss to stop up some of the gaps in the stonework, now that it's starting to feel colder.

As I build up a fire and set a pot of water over it, I give Lleu my most unimpressed glare.

"I could have stayed hidden if you hadn't given me away like that!" I accuse him.

I used to imagine what I would do if travellers ever came this way, how I would mysteriously appear from nowhere and offer them assistance before vanishing just as suddenly. But now I'm afraid they might report seeing me to someone in the village, and then a search party will come out here again. I'm also cross that I just stood there, staring at them like an idiot. What must they have thought of me?

The thought of my stupidity grows louder, until it rages in my head. I sit still, take a breath to clear my mind, and close my eyes. I try to think of something else. In my head I am sitting with friends in a clearing in the woods, at dusk. There is firelight and music. We pass the time with riddles and songs, and tell stories as old as the sky. It is my turn and I sing a sorrowful song about an old king giving away all the treasures he had collected during his lifetime. Each item is precious and has its own story for the one who receives it. My voice is as clear as running water, as crisp as a winter wind before the first snow falls.

I can feel my shoulders relaxing and my stomach unknotting. The sense of disgust ebbs away. I know it isn't real. I know that depending on my imagination to cope with everyday life probably isn't ideal. But what else can I do? This is the only way I know how to bear reality sometimes. Maybe if the world were not so cold and flat and stony, I would not need to dream of a place full of beauty and joy.

The water is bubbling now, which means it is safe. Time to throw in the ingredients: apples and elderberries today. The apples would be fine raw, but I quickly learned not to eat uncooked elderberries after vomiting up a handful of them last week. I found some rosehips too. It took me a while to risk eating them, because I was afraid they might be poisonous. The bright red colour isn't much of an encouragement. Still, hunger pushes you to take risks. Even though I've learned to ignore stomach pangs, there are days when my legs shake and I know I have to find food quickly to replenish my strength. Sources of carbohydrate are few in the forest, and I can tell my body is starting to use up the excess cushioning of fat that

I had built up before I ran away. I remember my biology classes; I know what comes next. I need to find new food supplies.

I do like living here, away from everyone. It's easier not having to deal with people, with all their faults and unkindnesses. But I'd forgotten how interesting new people can be, when you have to guess at their stories or try to find them out. I sometimes wonder whether flawed friends aren't better than none at all.

I eat the fruit I have cooked, and then prepare for what I must do now.

"What do you think, Lleu? Will they tell anyone they saw me?" I ask the bird that perches in the branch of a hawthorn next to the house. He watches me with his bright yellow stare. "You're right. It's too much of a risk to stay here for the rest of the day. Someone might come looking."

I need to go further into the woods and hide until it is dark. My fence will keep my belongings out of sight, so I do not have to carry them all, but if they bring sniffer dogs, then even a thicket of ivy might not protect me. I put some essentials into my backpack, check the fence for any damage, then slip through one of the concealed gaps in it and head for the depths of Dyrys.

LLANDYMNA

"Well," says Adam, as they find the grassy lay-by where they parked the car earlier. "D'you reckon that's normal for round here? Strange girls wandering the woods."

"I don't know," says Grace. "I wonder if she's OK. She looked a bit… on edge. And dishevelled, like she'd been out walking for a while."

"What was it she called that bird? Clue?"

"Lleu – it's a name from the Mabinogion. He was a man who got turned into an eagle."

"Maybe that's what they do to unsuspecting visitors around here!"

"It reminds me of something. Something on the news, maybe, that might have been from round here... It's no good. I can't remember what it was. I'll look it up later."

Adam cannot resist a last look back over his shoulder to the woods as they leave them behind. Then it is time to complete the journey: their destination is a short drive from here, and there are too few roads for them to get lost.

*

"There's the gate – this must be it."

They pull into the driveway leading up to the farm. A cluster of buildings sits around three sides of the yard: two old cottages, a barn, and some more recent structures in corrugated iron. Hay bales wrapped in black sheeting are stacked at the far end next to a trailer.

"I think there's just the one holiday cottage to rent on the farm here. It wasn't the easiest place to find accommodation in the end. I told the lady we'd arrive about two. What time is it now?" asks Grace.

"Close enough to two. Time to find out if this place lives up to Dad's stories."

As they stop outside the farmhouse, a woman comes out and waves to them. She crosses the muddy yard in her wellies to meet them as they step out of the car.

"Hello. Welcome to Llandymna. I'm Nia. Would you like me to help you with your bags?"

CHAPTER TWO

LLANDYMNA

"All unpacked?" Adam returns downstairs to find his sister stacking folders and books on the kitchen table.

"Just about. You don't mind if I use the table for work, do you?"

"Of course not. We can eat in the living room. Or get some food from the village. I've got a view up towards it from my room and I think I can see a pub. It might be easier to eat there some evenings."

"Probably. I'll be working all day, and we don't want to subject ourselves to your cooking!"

"Grace Ayawa Trewent, you are cruel sometimes!" Adam mimes taking a stab wound to the heart, and staggers back across the kitchen. Grace laughs. "But if it means that much to you, I won't try to cook. I'll find another way to make myself useful."

There is a knock at the door. Adam goes to answer it, and is met by a stocky farmer who looks immediately shocked.

"Hello, name's Ifan. I'm the owner here. Thought I'd introduce myself. Sorry, my wife didn't mention that you were... foreign. Speak English, do you?"

Adam smiles patiently and explains, not for the first time in his life, that he speaks English fluently on account of having lived in Britain his whole life.

"Oh, right. That's good," Ifan flounders, unsure what to ask or say next.

"Your wife gave us a quick tour of the farm when we arrived – it's

99

impressive what you've done here. Have you been farming all your life?"

"Oh yes, I took this over from my dad when he retired – he has himself a nice house in the village now. Nia's parents were farmers too. It's not a big piece of land compared to some, but we do what we can with it."

"I saw you have a river running by here too – do you get many fish there?"

"Yes, we do. Do you fish, then?"

"When I can. My father took me fishing a lot when I was younger."

Grace smiles as she watches her brother do what he has always had a talent for: winning people over. By the time Ifan leaves, he has arranged to go fishing with his new guest and invited the two of them to come for a drink at the White Lion this evening. Grace continues to set up her work station, where she will write up her research over the coming weeks. She places her tree identification guide next to the Ordnance Survey maps, and props up a few ringbinders against the wall. She hears Adam call a cheery goodbye to Ifan from the door, and then return to the kitchen.

"Now, I know you'll be annoyed with me, but I've gone and got us invited to the pub with our hosts this evening."

"I know. You always forget how loud you are when you're being friendly."

"I thought it would be a good chance to get to know people. And that might be useful for, you know, our secondary research project while we're here."

"Investigating Dad's stories, you mean? Be careful."

"When am I ever not careful?" Adam asks. Grace puts down the books she has been arranging and folds her arms.

"Kofi, I'm not joking here. I don't think he left this place on the best terms. I know we could never tell which parts of his stories were real and which were made up – "

"Apart from the one with the sea monster that swam up the River Usk."

"Apart from that one, yes. But I always got the impression there was something not quite right when he talked about this place. There must have been some reason why he never went back, after all those years. I just don't want you to get in trouble if you go asking lots of questions and don't like the answers you find."

"All right, I'll tread lightly. Don't want to go disturbing the peace."

"Thank you. I'll phone Mum now, to let her know we've arrived safely. I want to check how she's doing, anyway."

She leaves her glasses on the table next to the books and files, and goes to find her phone.

That evening, they walk with Ifan and Nia up the road towards Llandymna. Nia asks if they are comfortable in the house, and apologizes that the controls for the central heating are so complicated to understand; Ifan asks why they chose this particular village for a holiday in September.

"It's really only a holiday for me. Grace is doing research and couldn't do all of it from her desk at the university. She's here for fieldwork. She won't tell you this herself, but she's a genius." Adam seizes the opportunity to praise his sister to their new hosts.

"You're an academic then, Grace?"

"Yes, I'm a researcher at Aberystwyth University," Grace explains in a matter-of-fact tone, not showing the same pride in her achievements that Adam feels.

"I see," says Ifan as tersely as if Grace had claimed to be a unicorn tamer. "And what about you, Adam?"

"I've been working with the Forestry Commission for several years, but I'm planning to start up my own business when we get back."

"A businessman, eh? Very good. What will you be selling?"

"Woodwork. Fencing, decking, garden furniture, whatever I can build."

"Excellent. We always need more skilled tradesmen like you." It is unclear whether by "we" Ifan is speaking on behalf of himself and Nia, the people of Llandymna, or the world as a whole.

"Their surname's Trewent," Nia tells her husband. "Didn't there used to be a Trewent family in Llandymna, or am I confusing that with something else?"

"Not sure," says Ifan. "Can't say I've ever met anyone with the name though."

They come to the White Lion, which is warm inside and smells of beer and gravy. Tom and Callum have already claimed the usual table in the corner and are waiting for them. Ifan introduces them.

"These are our guests from the farm, Adam and Grace. These two lads here are Tom and Callum. Best watch yourself – Tom's a policeman, so no drunk and disorderly behaviour in front of him!"

"Great to meet you!" Adam declares with real warmth.

"So where are you from?" asks Callum.

"Monmouth," answers Adam, "though Grace spends a lot of her time travelling on research trips these days. How about yourself? A local here?"

"But where are you actually *from*?" Callum asks again, not satisfied with the answer. Tom looks uncomfortable. Adam and Grace exchange a smile.

"I'll take this one," says Grace. "Our dad was Welsh, and our mum is originally from Ghana. She came to this country before we were born. But we have always lived in the UK."

Nia tenses, wondering if her husband will take the opportunity to share his views on immigration. Fortunately, he does not seem in the mood for this; perhaps meeting a fellow fisherman has pacified him for today.

"Oh, OK." Callum nods, then turns back to Adam, asking a question that shows he has accepted this stranger: "So what team do you support?"

Talk of rugby leads to football, and in almost no time Callum is telling them about the time he scored a winning goal against the rival team from the next village. The Llandymna locals have all heard this story a dozen times before, and it is a sure sign that Callum is keen to impress the new visitors.

"Nice one, mate!" Adam enthuses at the end of the story, offering the approval that was being sought. "Right, can I get anyone a drink? Ayawa, what will you have?"

"Lemonade, thanks, Kofi. I've got to get an early start on my work tomorrow."

Adam and Ifan go to the bar, talking about fishing and laughing like old friends.

"I've never seen Ifan take to someone so quickly," Nia says to Grace. "Your brother has a way with new people."

"Yes, he's good like that. When he meets someone new, he works on the assumption that he is going to be their friend. It's gotten him in trouble with bosses and authority figures in the past though!"

"I can imagine. And these names that you call each other: are they Ghanaian?"

"Yes. Our parents gave us first names that would be easy for people to understand and pronounce in this country, since we were going to grow up here, but then they gave us each a second name in the Ghanaian way, to remind us that we have two heritages. We go by our first names day to day, but in conversation with each other we like to sometimes use our Ghanaian names. Our mother still uses them too."

"I wish I had a cool African nickname," says Callum, earning a despairing stare from Tom. He has started absent-mindedly scratching the edge of the table with his pocket knife, carving a small trench into the wood.

"And I gather you're a researcher," says Tom. "If I ask you what your field of study is, will we understand it?"

"I'm looking at how we can use environmental and archaeological features to reconstruct historical landscapes. Basically, I'm interested in what the land looked like hundreds of years ago. Sometimes even the plants growing in an area will give you an idea of what it used to be like."

"Sounds interesting," says Tom.

"Why research it? If you want to know what this place was like hundreds of years ago, just ask Maebh!" Callum delivers his joke with a tone of triumph. Tom groans and gives Callum a humouring pat on the back.

"Who's Maebh?" Grace asks.

"Maebh O'Donnell is an elderly woman in Llandymna. She likes to tell people about the importance of remembering our own history," Tom explains.

"Not that she ever really tells us what history she's on about," Callum adds. "As if anything interesting has ever happened in Llandymna!"

"Has she lived here her whole life then?" Grace asks casually.

"Yes, just about. Her parents came over from Ireland. Started out on the coast where there was more work to be had, but ended up here as a farm help. She's like everyone's unofficial grandmother."

Grace nods as she logs this information to share with her brother later. Adam and Ifan return with the drinks.

*

"I knew we should have booked a holiday cottage with its own library."

Adam comes downstairs the next morning to find Grace already awake and surrounded by maps. The kitchen table has proved too small a surface, so she has taken over the floor as well. Adam carefully steps over an Ordnance Survey to get to the kettle.

"Sorry. I was going to move these before you came down."

"No problem. Coffee?"

"Yes please, if you're making it. Look at this…" She sets down one map on top of the others. "This is where we are – see, there's the village and this is the farm. Now, see how huge the forest is. It covers most of the map."

"I guess that means you've got your work cut out for you, right? If you've got to study that much land."

"True. But I've been thinking about that girl we saw yesterday. Where was she going when she ran off? There's nothing in that direction that looks like a settlement or even a farmhouse."

"Maybe she was going for a walk first before heading back home," Adam suggests, though he sounds unconvinced by his own theory. She had not looked like someone going for a walk.

"Maybe." Grace looks puzzled, then shakes her head and goes back to work.

Adam makes up two mugs of instant coffee. The first he places in a small square of free space on the table, and the second he takes outside, leaving Grace to work in peace. The morning air is cool, and a thin layer of mist hangs over the fields. He inhales deeply, then takes a sip of his coffee and walks to the bench at the end of the small garden in front of the cottage. From here he can see to the road in one direction, and over to the farmhouse in the other.

A border collie runs up to the hedge and starts barking at this stranger. Adam puts his coffee down on the bench and goes out into the yard where the dog is currently jumping up and down.

"You're a friendly one!" Adam says as the collie launches itself at him.

"Meg!" a voice calls, and the dog runs back to Nia, who stands under the farmhouse porch. "Sorry. I hope she wasn't bothering you."

"Nah, I like dogs," says Adam, walking over to say good morning at a distance that does not require shouting. "Busy day today?"

"Fairly," says Nia. "There's always lots to do before we go to the farmers' market, which is tomorrow. And I've gone and promised to take some eggs and apples over to Maebh today, on top of everything else Ifan needs me to do. Meg, stop that! Sorry. You don't want to listen to me going on like this, I'm sure."

"Why don't Grace and I deliver those things for you, if it'll help?"

"Oh no, I couldn't let you do that. You're not here to help out on the farm – you're guests."

"But Grace wants to visit the library later, so we'll be going into the village anyway. No point you making the trip too."

Nia hesitates as she realizes she has no other objections to this offer of help.

"Well, if you're sure."

"Course. Just let us know the address and we'll drop everything round on our way."

Nia writes down the address on a scrap piece of paper for Adam and thanks him profusely. Adam goes back into the house, picking up a cup of cold coffee on the way.

"Grace, let me know when you want to take a break from work later."

"Not for a bit. Why?"

"You know that woman you heard about last night? The one you thought might have been here at the same time as Dad. Didn't you say her name was Maebh?"

"Yes, that's right. Maebh O'Donnell, they said. Why? What have you done now?"

Adam grins. "I've just arranged for us to go and see her."

*

Maebh answers the door and invites them in almost before they have explained that they are there on Nia's behalf. She offers them tea and lemon cake, and then tells them to sit down.

"You must be Maebh," says Adam.

"For want of another name or face, I must," she says with a mischievous smile, "and for want of a better introduction, you must be the visitors staying on the Evanses' farm. Grace and Adam, isn't it? I'm sorry, dear boy, you mustn't look surprised. I tend to know everything that happens in this village."

As they introduce themselves, she scrutinizes their faces with her sharp glinting eyes. These two are new, different, and yet somehow familiar. There is something about them that tugs at her memory, though she cannot pin it down. A slight movement or mannerism: the disarming openness of one's smile, or the gentleness of the other's voice. She must have seen them somewhere before. She frowns in puzzlement.

"Well now, why would two strangers want to visit me? It was

kind of you to bring those things, not just for my sake but for Nia's. I know she has a lot on her mind these days, poor thing. Tell me, are you here just to help her, or is there something else I can do for you?"

"Sharp as an arrow!" laughs Adam, realizing the complete transparency of his plan now. "I am afraid you're right. We have actually come to ask you something."

"And I imagine it's not to knit you a Nativity set, unless fame of my skill with wool has spread further than I thought." Maebh cackles, amused by her own sarcasm today. Still she cannot place what it is she thinks she recognizes about these two.

"No, we wondered if you might remember somebody who used to live here. We heard that you've been in Llandymna for many years now."

"Ay, that's true enough. Who is it you think I may remember?"

"We think you might have known our father, Emrys Trewent."

Maebh sits motionless as all the familiar expressions and gestures fall into place in her memory, and instead of two faces, she now sees one.

"Emrys," she says, trying out the name like a forgotten word from a foreign language. "That's not a name anyone has spoken in Llandymna for some time now."

"You knew him though?" asks Adam, suddenly animated and eager. "You must have done! This village was never big enough for everyone not to know each other, or that's how it seemed when he spoke of this place. And I think you would have been similar ages – maybe even have gone to school together."

"You say 'knew' and 'spoke', so am I to assume he is dead?"

"Yes. He died about a month ago."

"I see. Losing someone is hard, and you are both young. I am sorry for it." Maebh is silent, contemplating this. The brother and sister watch her face, but she seems for a moment to have forgotten they are there. The only sound is the ticking of the clock on the mantelpiece. Finally she looks up.

"Well, what is it you want to know about him?"

"The truth of what really happened, and why he left here," Adam replies. Maebh gives an incredulous laugh.

"There's a story I've been trying to tell people around here for, oh, decades, and then you two turn up and the first thing you ask is to hear it! Do you know there are people in this village who did everything in their power to prevent a local history society being set up? And they said it was because we needed the resources and the manhours elsewhere, but the truth is they didn't want people learning too much about their predecessors."

"We understand it might not be what we want to hear," says Grace, though she has visibly tensed at Maebh's warning. Adam leans forward, eager to have his questions answered at last.

"Well then, if you're sure you're ready for it. Someone should know his story, after all, and you of all people have a right to it." Maebh sighs and closes her eyes for a moment. Then, taking her time over each word, as if she has been rehearsing this tale a long time, she begins. "Emrys was born just after the end of the war. He was born too soon, they said. His mother went into early labour and the baby was small and frail. You'll know, of course, about his right arm that never quite grew properly."

"Yes," Adam says, "but it never really seemed to hold him back. He'd take me fishing and still be able to reel in the line faster than I could."

He smiles to remember his childhood, but glances over at Grace to check that she is not too upset by this already. His sister's expression gives little away so far: she has always been better than Adam at concealing her emotions.

"That's good," Maebh nods, pausing to picture the man she remembers, sitting beside a river with his son, "but when he was young, Llandymna was much more a farming community. And Emrys was the only son in a farming family. Even though he grew healthier than the doctors ever expected, he never had the strength for a life of work in the fields. His father made no effort to conceal his disappointment at this." She frowns in deliberation over how much to tell them, then decides to be blunt. "He could not see the point of a son who would not inherit the Trewent farm."

Grace arches an eyebrow and Maebh looks sympathetic. Emrys's father would not have thought much of his granddaughter's academic achievements.

"But there was more to Emrys than that," she continues. "He read, and he drew with his left hand, and he did his best to make friends, though most children at his school avoided him because they had been told by their parents that he was somehow different, or not quite right. None of that bothered him. He was always generous in his opinions of others, and there was such a peaceful quality about him. He seemed to feel the pain of others as deeply as if it were his own. Once, I remember, he found a sparrow that had fallen from its nest before it could fly. He and I found a hiding place where we could watch it at a distance, to be sure the bird's parents came back for it, and he painstakingly scared off every predator that came near.

"But then one day, when he was still a young man, strange things began to happen around the village. Some sheep disappeared from their pen and turned up drowned in the river. Some said it was an accident, but others said the animals had been drowned on purpose. Gardens were torn up overnight, and some said it was just more animals escaping, but others thought it was vandalism. And they looked around Llandymna for where to point the finger, but they didn't look for long. Because when they saw Emrys, hanging back from the group because he wasn't used to being around people, that was that. No one could prove anything, of course, because there wasn't a mite of evidence against him, but everyone believed it was him."

Grace and Adam stare in disbelief. In all their father's stories, he never mentioned this. But Maebh's story is still unfolding, and she ploughs on, though her voice becomes graver as she relives those years.

"Emrys had always been forgiving of others when they showed him unkindness. But these accusations were everywhere now. Folk wouldn't speak to him on the street any more, or serve him in shops. He became low. That wonderful heart of his was turned heavy and dark by the weight of what others were saying and doing. He started avoiding people, so as not to give them the chance to be cruel. It made me sad to see him finally defeated by them, after all this time. But I didn't know then that wouldn't be the worst of it."

She reaches for her cup and takes a sip to clear her throat, but when she sets it back down, there seems to be a slight tremor in her hand.

"You understand that it's easier to fear what you don't know? With Emrys hardly seen any more, I seemed to spend all my time correcting other people's gossip. In the years that followed, there were rumours that he lived wild and never went indoors, or that he ate frogspawn and dragonflies. There were all manner of stories of how he hurt his arm, and none of them painted him as a hero. Parents started to threaten their children that if they did not behave, Emrys would come and get them. Then, one day, a child disappeared in Llandymna. A little girl from a family that's been here for generations. And you can guess what everyone here decided had happened, and who they held responsible."

"No," Grace whispers under her breath, suddenly understanding where the story is headed.

Maebh nods sadly. "People were scared and they were angry, and it was easy to blame the strange man no one had spoken to in years. And in those days, Llandymna was even more isolated than it is today. It felt like its own little kingdom away from the world. So they thought they'd confront him themselves, rather than call the police.

"I've had nightmares about what happened that night. Emrys's mind was too overcome with all he'd already been accused of to properly understand what they were saying. And when he could not answer them, a few men set upon him – beat him almost senseless, they did. So when there was a moment's chance, when Emrys was back on his feet, I distracted them just long enough for him to get away. And he ran off into the night. They tried chasing him, and had it been daylight they most likely would have caught him. But it was dark, and Emrys had been an outcast long enough to know all the hideouts and secret paths away from here. He must have kept running until they were too weary to chase him further. He escaped. But I never saw him again.

"And the next morning, do you know what happened? They found that little girl, safe and sound. She'd been playing on one of the farms and had fallen asleep in a barn. She walked herself home the next day, but it was too late by then.

"Rather than admit they'd made a terrible mistake, the people of Llandymna made a silent agreement that day never to speak of what happened. They were ashamed, but not in a way that was going to do any good. So no one names Emrys here. Most young folk will never have heard of him. All I can do is tell stories of heroes who have his kindness and goodness, and hope they will learn to value that in others. The older ones tell themselves it was all fair, all deserved. They retell the story in their heads until they find a version they can live with."

Maebh waits now for Adam and Grace to have time to make sense of it all. As her words sink in for them, she becomes lost in her own thoughts. She remembers the shouting. She remembers running past houses, looking for Emrys, trying to find him before the others did. She remembers watching him disappear into the darkness, and how the next day she went out looking for him, calling his name from the path through the woods. Now she sees his face traced as a likeness upon these two. She wonders: are they like their father?

"Before today, I never knew what became of him after he left this place. I didn't know if he even survived his first winter away from here. But now at least I know he went on to live. Though you seem young to be his children. You must be about thirty, I would guess."

Grace picks up the story from Maebh, repaying her story with the information she wants. "He married late in life, or at least late for what was normal in those days. He was forty when Adam was born. He went to the coast, found work, and met our mother there. He lived a life far more ordinary than what you have described."

"And was he happy?"

"Yes, I believe so. Our mother's faith always seemed to give him strength. He told us stories of this place, but never spoke of what happened. He never seemed bitter or angry. Though we knew something wasn't right, we would never have guessed at the truth."

"And he died just a few weeks ago. How?"

"His lungs. He'd been having trouble breathing for some time. It was peaceful in the end."

Maebh thinks of all the possible outcomes and imaginings she has ever dreamed up of what may have become of Emrys – all the stories she has told children of the Boy Who Shone in the hope she could somehow make these happy endings real for him. Now she knows the truth, and reality carries with it both relief and disappointment.

CHAPTER THREE

LLANDYMNA

Adam and Grace walk through the centre of the village on their way back to the farm.

"Funny to think he would have walked down here fifty years ago," says Adam. "That would've been his post office there, and that corner shop."

Grace is silent.

"I know. Not the history we were hoping for, is it?" he continues. "But at least it's filled in the gaps. We know now why he didn't talk much about it."

His sister continues to focus on the road ahead. Her jaw is set, all the muscles tightened resolutely.

"Ayawa, it'll be OK –"

"OK?" Grace finally answers. "Kofi, for once it's not OK! It was supposed to be a lovely meaningful thing, to go back to where Dad grew up. To bring back stories of his childhood for Mum to enjoy. But now we know… what these people did to him… I can't even think about it." She chokes back tears, and her brother hugs her. "How could they do that?"

"I know, I know. It's not right."

A man walking a dog crosses the street away from them, clearly taken aback by this display of emotion.

"Look," says Grace, catching her breath, "if you don't want to stay here now, that's fine. I know you offered to keep me company while I'm doing research here, but now that we've found what we came here to ask, I'll understand if you want to go back. I need to be here for a week or two, but you don't."

"And leave you here to face it all on your own? No chance. I'll stay until you've finished your work."

They continue walking and pass the church hall, which is the site of a flurry of activity. Large crates of food are being carried into the building while trestle tables are hauled through the doorway. Two men are on step ladders attaching orange and green bunting to the outside of the building, while a woman with a clipboard stands on the steps and directs them.

"Higher on your side, Rhys, or it'll look uneven," she calls. Rhys obediently raises his end of the bunting until the effect is perfect symmetry.

"A bit early for Halloween, isn't it?" Adam remarks to Grace as he takes in the bright decorations, spotting the chance for a much-needed distraction.

The tactic works, and Grace cannot resist sharing a deep-buried piece of trivia from a book she read perhaps a decade ago, in favour of dwelling any longer on the day's revelations. "Maybe it's a wedding with a bold colour scheme. Roman brides used to wear orange veils."

Adam laughs. "There's no end to the strange things you know, is there?"

The woman with the clipboard has spotted them and is walking over at a brisk pace. She greets them each with a firm handshake.

"Hello there, I'm Diana Griffin. You must be Ifan and Nia's guests I've been hearing about. Welcome to the village. I hope you're enjoying your time here."

"It's a beautiful place," Adam says, so as to seem to be answering her.

"It is, isn't it?" Diana nods, apparently not spotting the slight evasion. "And you've come at the right time for our harvest festival. We have it every year in September. There's a big meal to celebrate later on today. You can see we're busy setting up for it here. You should come, if you have time. Everyone is welcome."

114

"That's very kind," Grace says guardedly.

"Thanks very much," Adam adds. "Sorry we can't stay, but my sister needs to get on with her work, so we need to get back."

"We're going to that, aren't we?" Grace says resignedly as they turn the corner and head back towards the farm.

"What? No, not if you don't want to."

Grace gives a look that says she is not taken in by her brother's nonchalance. "I know you, and I know that even after everything we've learned today, you can't resist the idea of being around people – and food, for that matter."

"Well, I was thinking it sounded like a good opportunity to meet locals," Adam admits, "but you don't need to be there if you don't want to."

"Don't be silly – someone's got to keep an eye on you. Though at this rate, I'm never going to get my work done."

RHIANNON

An invasion of gold is fast banishing the green of the forest. The trees blaze all about me in their new colours, but in spite of this brightness the sky is growing duller every day. The days when it rains non-stop are the worst. Then I can do little but shelter, cold and miserable, waiting for the downpour to be over. Today, a chill in the air clings to my skin with keen fingers as I set out into the dew-glistening forest.

I know my way around well now, though I trip still from time to time when I forget to watch the ground as much as the path ahead. As I walk out, I notice that many of the flowers have died down into the earth, and I can only hope that they will be here next spring, along with so much else that will try to outlast winter.

Yesterday I ventured deeper into the woods than I ever have done before. I was scared of being caught after I saw those two strangers here. I expected them to rush back and send a search party to find me. But they must not have said anything, because no police patrol came into Dyrys all day. I would know, even if I didn't see them. Police officers wear heavy shoes that leave deep prints. Being in a new part of the woods gave me access to new blackberry bushes I had not come across before, so I ate well at least. But I am starting to worry about what I will do when this year's crop of fruit has died back. So far I have only ever collected enough for that day and the next, but I need to start thinking about a proper store, of things that will not rot or attract insects.

The school term will be underway by now. The rest of my year will be back in the classroom being told they aren't nearly stressed enough yet about their A-levels. I wonder if they miss me, or envy me, not having to think about things like exams. I sometimes miss my books though. We were going to be doing *Hamlet* this year.

In the distance, I hear the faint peal of bells from St Luke's. They ring on Sunday mornings, and it's the only way I have any sense of the days of the week any more. I can gauge the time of day pretty well by the shadows on the ground, but it's far harder to keep track of the calendar. All the same, I could swear I heard those bells more recently this time around. And I know it is not morning. The sun has started creeping around to the west. Something is different today.

Then I remember. Every year they have a harvest festival in the village, and they ring the church bells for a good half-hour in the afternoon to signal it. That must be happening today. It's strange to think that I know what everyone there will be doing. Diana will be bossing people around and loving every moment of it. Eira will be smiling at everyone and twirling in her new dress so that they all think she's adorable and sneak treats off the food table for her. The Evanses will be there, even though Ifan will complain about having to leave the farm for so long. Sometimes even Maebh comes, but she depends on other people remembering to help her make the journey over to the church hall.

If everyone is going to be at the meal this evening, then that means the rest of the village will be empty. It would be the perfect time to sneak over there and stock up on some supplies I cannot get in the woods. My heart races as I realize I am planning a mission that will depend on stealth, but could mean I don't starve or freeze to death in the coming weeks!

LLANDYMNA

That night, the church hall is full. Diana has overseen its transformation, and the effect is striking. Long tables run down the centre of the room, decorated in rustic colours. The food is served from buffet tables at the side, set around a centrepiece of a loaf shaped like a wheatsheaf.

Reverend Davies stands up to welcome everyone in his rich, booming voice. He says a prayer of thanks for the harvest this year, and for all that the people of Llandymna have, and then invites everyone to help themselves to the feast that has been prepared. The children, being small enough to run under the tables as a shortcut, make it to the food table first, followed by their parents, who are quick to moderate their portions with warnings of: "Make sure to leave something for the grown-ups to eat," and: "That's horseradish sauce, not yoghurt – you don't want so much of that on your plate."

"Don't be polite," Ifan tells Adam. "You'll never get anything to eat that way. You've got to push your way forward!"

Adam greets Ifan warmly. "How's your day been, mate?"

"Hard work, I can tell you! I always say you don't know real work till you've spent a day on a farm. You're not an intellectual like your sister, are you?"

"Me? No, I was never clever enough for university. I inherited good looks rather than brains from my parents!"

Ifan laughs heartily as he manoeuvres his way to the food and starts filling up his plate.

"Your sister must be quite the clever one to have done all that studying. But I always say there's no school that can teach you common sense, and that's more important than any exam."

"You're right there, but Grace has plenty of good sense too. She keeps me out of trouble most of the time."

"Women tend to do that, don't they?" Ifan says in his most knowing tone.

"That stew's not vegetarian, is it?" asks a voice behind them. They turn to see Callum peering over their shoulders at the options.

"Looks like lamb," says Adam.

"That's all right then," Callum says. "Last year I got a huge helping of what I thought was a proper meat pie, only when I sat down and started eating it, it turned out to be filled with potato and stuff."

He takes the ladle and starts pouring lamb stew onto his plate until it looks likely to overflow.

"You got enough there?" asks Ifan.

"Why would I leave space? What am I going to fill it with? Salad?" He reaches past Adam to grab a chicken drumstick from a platter, and balances it in the middle of his dish. "I'm starving," he explains.

"Why? Exhausting day of watching football, was it?" Ifan asks.

"Yeah, three matches on this afternoon. Did you see any of them?"

"No, I was busy working."

They weave their way back to some seats around the central table.

"So how long has this been a tradition, then?" asks Adam, wondering if his father might have sat in this hall at a previous harvest.

"Years," says Callum, setting his overloaded plate down carefully to ensure he does not lose even a morsel of it.

"Hundreds of years," adds Ifan. "As long as there's been a church and a farming community here, I reckon."

Adam looks around the room and tries to picture it: the same occasion, but fifty years ago. Would the young Emrys have been here, or would he already have been too ostracized by the village to show his face? He glances around for Grace, regretting making her feel she needed to be here tonight. But she is chatting with Nia and Tom, and looks happy enough. For his own part, Adam is finding the interactions of this little community fascinating. He has always enjoyed seeing what drives people, and in this village of only a few hundred the relationships seem magnified and intensified.

"Ifan, I hoped I would see you!" Diana's voice cuts across their conversation as she marches towards them. "I've been meaning to talk to you. The community council would value your input on something."

"Oh yes?" says Ifan, sitting a little taller. "What can I help you with?"

Diana lowers her voice enough to denote that this is not public information, though not enough to prevent those sitting nearby from overhearing. "We're looking at an application for a sports facility in the village. It would mean doing up the old scout hut, and would border onto your land. Can you come to our next meeting on the seventh? We need more local people involved in making the decision on this."

"A sports facility?" repeats Callum eagerly. "Like, a proper football pitch or something? Can I be involved? I don't mind volunteering if it means we get some decent space for games round here."

Diana eyes Callum. There is a pause before she says, "Thank you, Callum, but at this early stage we're just discussing it among the adults. Maybe later on you can be involved."

"Well, I'll be there," Ifan says. "Happy to help the council if it needs my input."

Speechless, Callum scowls into his food and starts stabbing pieces of lamb with his fork. Diana, powering through a to-do list in her head, has already moved on and does not notice. She spots Adam and smiles.

"Hello. I'm so glad you decided to accept my invitation to come here today. It's Adam, isn't it? And this must be your sister Grace coming over to join us." Diana takes the empty seat opposite Adam as Grace, Nia and Tom all come to sit with the group. "It's so good to see some new faces in Llandymna!"

"Thanks!"

"We don't get many visitors here, though I'm sure that's not in any way the fault of your hosts." Diana casts a glance down the table at Nia that suggests she very much suspects it is her fault. "So we're delighted you've decided to come and stay here – is it a week you're here?"

"Two weeks," says Adam.

"Excellent. And am I right in thinking your sister will be working here, and that you are looking for ways to occupy your time?"

"You're very well informed."

Diana looks flattered. "I do my best to know what's happening – this is my home, after all. Well, I gather you have some experience in woodwork. If you need a project to keep you busy, I may have just the thing. Tom here is putting up a fence for me next week, to keep the chickens from escaping or getting under my feet in the garden. I'm sure he'd be happy to have some help. By the way, Tom, I want to speak to you later about another matter."

Everyone at the table turns serious, as if they all know what this other topic is. Only Adam and Grace are left in the dark, but they judge from the troubled faces around them that it is best not to pry.

"I'm sure he doesn't need me," Adam answers, fairly sure that Tom's need for help has been decided for him by Diana. "But by then I'll be in search of something to do, else I'll get in Grace's way while she's working. Tom, if you don't mind having the company, I'd be glad to lend an extra pair of hands."

Grace chuckles as she watches this exchange. For all that she is less outgoing than her brother, she shares his keen eye when it comes to people, and it amuses her to see him restoring the pride of strangers as fast as it can be knocked down. She knows her brother is better and more natural at this than he ever realizes, and it will not have occurred to him yet how much these people like him already.

"They've both been very helpful to me too," Nia adds, only just audible over the background din of conversation. "They helped me get through all my errands today."

"Isn't it wonderful to have such generous people around to help us when we fail to manage our own time well?" Diana remarks with an arch smile. Nia looks disheartened and apologetic. She glances across to her husband, whose expression has not altered. He seems to have missed the insult in Diana's words. The rest of the table have not, however, and there is an awkward pause.

"I think someone's trying to get your attention," Grace says to Diana, nodding over to the child standing behind her chair.

"Yes, Eira, what is it?"

"Owen won't eat his carrots," Eira says sadly. "He keeps throwing them on the floor."

Diana excuses herself and goes to attend to her children.

Everyone at the table sits looking around at one another, wondering what to say to their new friends about what has just passed.

"Now you've met Diana," Tom states.

"She's on the Llandymna community council," Ifan explains. "Basically the best person round here at getting things done. She organized all this too." He motions at the room around them. Callum sniffs loudly and announces he is going up for seconds.

"Second helpings sounds like a good idea," says Adam. "Those pasties were good. Can I get anyone anything while I'm there?"

"Can you see if there's any more of the pork pie left?" asks Ifan. "I'll have another slice of that if there is."

Adam follows Callum up to the food table.

"You all right there?" he asks.

"Yeah, fine," Callum mutters, but is convincing no one.

"That's good," says Adam, and then waits.

"I can't believe she said I'm not one of the adults!" he says after a gap of only a few seconds. "I'm *twenty*. I finished school ages ago. I don't get it. Why does she think I'm still a child?"

"Why does it bother you what she thinks?"

"It doesn't. 'Cept that round here Diana's opinion of you makes a difference. She decides things, you see. So if you want to be involved in something in the village, and she doesn't think you're good enough, she can talk to people and make them see things her way. I reckon it's the only reason everyone runs around trying to keep her happy. I reckon if you asked people what they really think, they'd say they can't stand her."

Callum's voice has grown louder during this speech, so Adam steers him towards the doors before he is overheard. They sit down on the steps outside the hall, with their plates balanced on their knees.

"Ugh, I got the wrong flavour crisps!" Callum's latest misfortune seems to add to his sense of outrage. "Yeah, everyone wants Diana to like them. You saw how Nia tried to get back in her good books there, right?"

"Has Nia upset Diana?"

"It was the interview. She went off-script. Diana hasn't forgiven her for it. Says she made her look stupid on camera."

"What interview?"

"Oh yeah, you won't know about that. I forgot. It was a police thing – an appeal to try to find Rhiannon. She's Diana's niece. She went missing in August. Nia was meant to read something Diana had prepared, but she gave her own appeal instead. It was kind of nice really, what she said. The sort of thing that'd make you feel it was safe to get in touch. But it wasn't what Diana wanted."

Adam stops eating and slowly straightens up. "This niece of hers – did they find her?"

"No. No one knows where she is, or if she's even still alive. That's probably why Diana's getting worse lately. I bet she feels guilty about what happened and is taking it out on the rest of us."

"And is she about your age?" Adam asks, trying to keep his tone free of all signs of urgency.

"Who? Rhiannon? Couple of years younger. She's still in school. Why?"

Adam stands up. "Listen, don't worry what Diana thinks about you. If you want people to see you as an adult, don't try proving it to anyone, just go and be an adult. People will notice soon enough." With that he leaves Callum sitting on the steps and goes inside to find Grace.

"What is it?" Grace asks when she sees her brother's face.

"Callum just told me that Diana has a relative who went missing a month or so ago. A niece who's the same age as the girl we saw in the woods."

Grace's eyes widen.

"We need to go and tell her," Adam says, and is about to go looking for Diana, when Grace catches his arm.

"Wait. We can't do that."

"Why not?"

"We don't know enough about what's happened here. If that girl is the missing niece, then maybe she ran away to escape something. Maybe there's something, or someone, here that she's afraid of. If we tell her family and neighbours, we could be putting her in danger. We need to go to the police first."

They spot Tom standing by himself at the edge of the room. Reaching him means weaving between the tables and bypassing a large group gathered around Ifan, who is holding their attention with a loud and highly exaggerated anecdote.

"Hi Tom, can we talk to you in your police capacity for a minute?"

Tom sighs. "I'm not really on duty at the moment. I mean, it *was* a police matter – the thing that Diana asked to speak to me about – but that was a special case really. Is it urgent?"

"We're not sure. We might have information about a missing person."

Tom's whole expression changes and he ushers them outside at once. Callum has disappeared from the steps, but they still walk a way down the road to be sure they won't be overheard.

"Have you seen Rhiannon?" he asks.

"We think so," Grace replies. "We saw a girl in the woods yesterday, about the same age as this Rhiannon, and looking, not exactly dishevelled, but not like someone just out for a morning stroll either. We didn't know whether to make anything of it, until Adam heard just now that you've got a search on for a missing person."

"Can you describe her for me?"

Grace thinks. "Long, light brown hair, and her face was slightly tanned. Shorter than me, so maybe about five foot four? She was wearing jeans and a thick waterproof coat – the kind hikers go for."

"It could be her," says Tom, taking a notebook out of his pocket and hastily scribbling something in it, "but we've searched those woods multiple times already."

"I was about to go and ask Diana where we could find the girl's parents, until Grace sensibly stopped me and said we should come to you first," Adam adds.

Tom nods. "That was wise. And you would have had no luck finding her parents. Her mother died some years ago, and she never told anyone the identity of Rhiannon's father, but it's generally accepted that he wasn't from round here. Diana's her legal guardian, but she's been through a lot already. We don't want to get her hopes up until we have some evidence that it was her niece you saw. Right, here's what we'll do. I'll report to the station in Bryndu that we've got a possible lead. Tomorrow morning I'll come over to the cottage with a picture for you to identify whether you saw Rhiannon or not. If it's her, I'll need you to show me exactly where you saw her. I'll be round at nine tomorrow, if that's not too early for you."

CHAPTER FOUR

RHIANNON

They walked in slow single file, the women cloaked in a blue as dark as the twilight sky. As they trod a path through the woods that only they knew, they resembled a funeral procession, as well they might. They were the last survivors of the coastal villages that were drowned by the sea all in one night, as if the waves rolled forward to take a great bite out of the land, and never receded. Their old homes now lay underwater somewhere, with pathways carved out on the sea floor, gold trinkets sitting uselessly on small wooden tables surrounded by seaweed. These women with their torches were the only ones who escaped that night. They walked the land looking for a new place to settle, but they were too restless ever to stop, and so the procession continued.

The afternoon is a waiting game, and I spend an hour or so of it immersed in the story of *Cantre'r Gwaelod*. This is, of course, one I first heard from Maebh, though I later found it written down in a book of Welsh legends in the library. It says that Wales used to be a bigger land, but that a huge chunk of the west coast was covered over by the sea. I added plenty to it, since there seemed to be vital details missing. I wanted elegance and beauty in the story, and to dive into the loss that would be entailed in that kind of catastrophe.

When evening falls, I get ready. I leave behind my coat, even though the sky is overcast. It rustles too much when I move, and might give me away. I empty everything out of my bag, to make room for what I need to bring back. Then I carry out one last check of my fence before slipping out. I make sure the lighter is in my pocket – I will need some light on the way back. If the clouds do not clear to give some moonlight, it will be pitch black in the forest later.

When I get to the edge of the woods, I sit looking down towards the village for a while. It's hard to be sure of the time, but I can see lights in windows shutting off as people leave their houses to go to the festival. When most of the village is dark, except for the street lamps on Church Road, I venture down the hill towards the river.

Maebh once told me that fear was invented to keep us safe and out of danger, but that sometimes it gets too comfortable. She said it likes to set up home and start rearranging the furniture where it doesn't belong. I think of that now, as my heart pounds with every step I take towards Llandymna. This is my mind telling me that I won't be safe if I go into the village, but this is also one of those times to overrule that fear and remind myself of what I need to do. I avoid the roads, just in case anyone is driving out tonight, and walk through the fields instead, following the line of the hedgerow down the valley.

Once over the river, I skirt around the edge of the village, steering clear of the busy spots like the pub, until I am near the road where I used to live. There is a little path that runs along the foot of the gardens, and I use this to get to Diana's house. I know she will have been out for most of the day, but her neighbours might be at home. I find the space in the hedge where I used to build houses for pixies out of twigs and moss, and crawl through.

The flowerpots by the back door are arranged exactly as they've always been. I lift up the geranium, and there is the spare key. This is going to be easy. I unlock the door that leads into the kitchen and step inside. I don't dare turn on any lights, in case one of the neighbours is still home to see and mention it to Diana. She mustn't know I was ever here. In the dark, I reach down to undo my laces and leave my boots on the doormat. I used to hate having to do this when Diana insisted on it to keep her floors clean, but now it's a matter of secrecy.

Even though the house is empty, I still tiptoe up the stairs, avoiding the steps that I know will creak under my weight. At the top of the second flight is the attic room that was mine. I open the door.

It feels like stepping back in time to see all the parts of my old life laid out here. Everything is as I left it, except for where Diana has tidied up some clothes I left on the floor. And my laptop is missing. Maybe the police took it: I know they do that sort of thing on detective shows. I feel angry at the thought of them having access to all the songs and photographs I have saved on there, but at least nothing will lead them to me. That is one of the advantages of not having planned my disappearance: I had no opportunity to leave a trail of clues as to my intentions.

The bed looks so comfortable that for a moment I consider just lying down on it. But I know that if I do, it will be too easy to decide to stay here, to come back home. Aunty Di could get back from her evening out to find me back here, and we could just return to normal life, the way it was. But I don't want that life back, and I don't think it would really be that easy to pick up where we left off. Instead, I go to the wardrobe and chest of drawers, and pull out a few things: a jumper, a pair of trousers, and some fresh socks and underwear. I also grab the blanket from my bed and stuff it into my bag. Next I open up the drawers where I kept my toiletries and pick out some essentials. I have missed feeling clean!

On the windowsill is an array of ornaments – beautiful things I had collected from the craft stalls at farmers' markets and school trips – model ships and boxes with Celtic designs on them. I am surprised to remember how many useless things I used to own, but at the end of the sill is a small silver lantern with a candle inside it. That would be worth having, if I can fit it in my bag. I push the clothes further down to squeeze everything in. It is harder to leave this room than I expected, but I close the door behind me and go back downstairs to the kitchen.

There is so much food here. It takes most of my self-control not to consume everything in the fridge and cupboards. But I need to make sure no one notices I was here. And Diana will spend far more time in this room than the attic. So I can only take things that will not be missed. Reluctantly, I leave the fresh loaf in the bread bin and the cake in its tin, and instead fill a freezer bag with rice from the huge jar, and another with porridge oats, then take a couple of tins of soup from the back of the cupboard – tomato flavour, Diana's least favourite, so she will not notice they are gone. I then remember the picnic things under the stairs, so I go and pull out a plastic mug and plate that will not be required now until next summer.

I'd like to take a thousand other things: a wooden spoon, a pillow, a hammer and some nails, the bar of cooking chocolate I used to sneak squares from before tea time, the whole chicken sitting in the fridge waiting to be roasted, and some shoes that aren't covered in mud. But that would draw too much attention. Before I leave, I run to the hall and pick up one last item: a book from the shelves by the door. It belonged to Uncle Ed and is called *A Guide to Foraging in Britain*. Now my bag is heavy on my back as I lock the door behind me and slip the key back under the flowerpot.

To be extra safe, I leave the village a different way, taking the road that goes past Ifan and Nia's farm. They will be away this evening, celebrating the harvest. But some of their crops will still be on the trees or in the ground, not gathered in. The harvest festival is a tradition these days, not tied to the actual bringing in of the corn. Surely they wouldn't miss some of their vegetables? I suppose it is stealing really, to help myself to their food, but if I only take a little bit, that can't be so bad. I know they struggle to sell the misshapen ones anyway, so perhaps if I take those, then I am not depriving them of any income.

I climb over the gate, because I don't want to risk letting the dogs escape. Megan immediately comes yapping towards me, but I quieten her quickly when she recognizes a familiar person.

"Shh girl, it's just me."

She thinks I am going to play with her, and follows me across the yard. I let myself into the vegetable garden at the back. It is hard to see what is what here, but I can make out some tall leafy bean plants with fat pods hanging off them. I decide to take from the end furthest from the farmhouse. I don't know why. Maybe it feels as if they will be less likely to miss the food further away. I leave the greenhouse alone, because I know that whatever is in there will have taken more work to grow, even though I am aware of the hypocrisy of drawing ethical lines across my theft. I take some beans and two cabbages from the end of their rows.

"Sorry, Nia," I whisper as I climb over the fence with my plunder. I never liked Ifan enough to feel I need to apologize to him now.

Once over the bridge, I scramble back up the hill. Under the cover of the trees, it's as dark as I expected, so I take the lighter from my pocket and the lantern from my bag. The candle gives a flickering light that casts just far enough to see where I am putting my feet and keep me from walking into a tree trunk, but it also throws shadows that dance eerily around me, so I walk as fast as possible back to my house. When I get there, I set the lantern down in the doorway and unpack my new treasures. I use the candle to start my cooking fire and then wrap myself up in the blanket as I sit and prepare a feast from what I have gathered today. Tonight, I won't go to sleep hungry.

*

I wake with the birds again. I heat up some water to wash with, and unwrap the bar of lavender soap I took from my old bedroom. I even wash my hair, scrubbing it until I can feel that the grease is gone, then rinsing it out over the stream. I change into the fresh clothes, then set about washing my old ones. I hang them over a holly bush to dry out.

The exhilaration of making it into and out of the village unseen has not dissipated yet, and the feeling of being fed and clean adds to the effect. I take Uncle Ed's book and go for a walk, to find a good reading spot. The ground is still too dewy to sit down though, so I decide to be a bit more adventurous. I find a tree with some low branches, and clamber up onto one of them. This must be the view that Lleu gets as he flies through the woods, scanning the leaf-strewn ground for his prey. I sit with my back against the trunk and my legs dangling in the air, and I open the book. I know at once it is going to be a lifesaver. On every page are photographs of native plants, annotated with information on where to find them and how to eat them. A few carry warning symbols if part of them is poisonous. There are so many things in here I would never have recognized. I will have things to eat other than berries and apples for a change!

I come to a page that features a picture of plantain, and realize that I recognize it. There is a clump of it growing right next to my house! The page tells me how the leaves are edible but fairly disgusting to taste, and that they are traditionally used as an anti-inflammatory or for healing cuts to the skin. There is even a section on mushrooms, but I am not sure I am brave enough to risk those. I know it's easy to pick the wrong thing and poison yourself by accident.

I am so enjoying this feeling of sitting with a book on a sunny autumn morning that I forget to be alert for sounds around me, until the approaching voices are coming from just around the bend in the path. There is no time to run, so I clamber up to the higher branches, above the leaf cover. Moments later, three people appear on the path. I pull my knees up under my chin and try to keep as still as possible. Through a gap in the leaves, I can just about see them. One is wearing a police officer's uniform. It's Tom Davies, and with him are those two strangers I met in the woods a couple of days ago.

"It was around here somewhere, I think," says the man, "but to be honest, it was the first time we'd been here, so it's hard to say."

"A little further that way," says the woman. I think her name was Grace. I remember thinking it was a beautiful name. They take a few steps forward and stop right under the tree where I am sitting. I hold in my breath.

"Thank you," says Tom. "And can you remember anything else from the meeting? Anything distinctive? Any recollection of which way she went when you parted ways?"

"I don't know which way she went," says the man, "but she had this pet… woodpecker… thing."

I stifle a laugh.

"It was a sparrowhawk," Grace corrects him, "and she didn't say much."

"She gave us directions back to the road though."

"Wait," says Tom, "you're telling me she has a tame hawk now?"

"Yes," says Grace. "She'd given it a name, too. Something from Welsh legend."

"Just when I think I can't be surprised any more," Tom mutters, and starts scribbling in his little notebook. "I was afraid she'd be here. Do you know how hard it is to find someone in a place like Dyrys? Even our thermal imaging equipment doesn't work if there's a leaf canopy in the way! We'll have to make some more searches on foot. One more question. Can you tell me why you were in the woods that day?"

He is still writing, so I think he misses the glance the brother and sister exchange, but I see it from my vantage point.

"This is where I will be conducting much of my research," says Grace. "I was keen to see the area where I'll be working."

That does not seem like the sort of information that warrants the look between them. I wonder if they are lying to Tom and, if so, why. What are they up to?

"OK, thank you very much," says Tom, as he starts to lead the way back down the path out of the woods. "You've identified that it's Rhiannon and been able to confirm the clothes we believed she was wearing when she disappeared, so I think that's all I need from you now. Except to ask – and this isn't so much for the investigation as for her friends and family – how did she seem to you?"

Tom's question jolts me with surprise. He sounds as if he is actually concerned for me. I know this was what I wanted, in leaving, but I find that I don't feel the triumph I had expected. They are walking away, so I cannot make out the answer even though I lean forward on my perch and strain to hear it.

I have always liked Tom. I know some people think he's boring and quiet, and he never spoke to me much because he's a few years older, but he also never tried to show off.

I wish those two had not told Tom they saw me. But I suppose I'm not so surprised. Now he will have to call his colleagues out and spend more hours searching the woods. And they will just waste their time and get tired, because I already know how to stay hidden.

I wonder who this brother and sister are, though. Maybe I will make up a story about them this afternoon, to while away the hours. Will they be heroes or villains? I haven't yet decided. But they are more interesting than any of the people of Llandymna, I am sure.

I go to my house, where I change the bandage I have had to put on my arm. It is just a strip of cloth torn from the sleeve of one of my tops, to stop the bleeding where Lleu's claws have scratched my skin. I like the grandeur of having a bird of prey perch on my arm, as if I am a falconer, and it is nice to have some company in the woods, but there is definitely a cost to it. Also, I suspect he will soon realize that I have no intention of fetching him food again, and will leave completely. And how could I, of all people, blame him for that?

CHAPTER FIVE

LLANDYMNA

Maebh sits in the front room of her house, dreaming. No one has been to visit her today, and in the quiet of a morning spent between a few small rooms, her mind has reached back into old memories. She is thinking of Emrys: that boy who would spend hours watching the wind. Some days on the walk home from school she would spot him, hiding in one of the farm fields to be free of the taunts of the other children. And there had been times when Maebh was one of them, and then Emrys would hide from her too. She hates those particular memories. His face, his eyes so determined not to show any fear, his rare smile: these images have faded with time, but remain in her thoughts. It had taken her so long to see the injustice of how he was treated, and only then had she seen that there was something wonderful about the boy who looked so weak on the outside, as if all the strength he was owed had been exchanged for kindness and gentleness.

Before the accusations, before he became withdrawn and despondent, there had been a quiet, calm light that shone out of him. Maebh was always surprised when others could not see it. She thinks she has seen something like it in his children. Grace has the gentleness, the calm that can be mistaken for indifference. Adam, on the other hand, has the open, unthreatening demeanour. Talking with them yesterday, she felt almost as much at ease as she did all those years ago. Maebh stops herself abruptly. What right has she to decide what they are like? She clears away the attempts to pin down their characters. The clock on the mantelpiece ticks away, and Maebh finds the sound irks her more than usual.

RHIANNON

The police have been back here again. I knew they would come, after those two strangers brought Tom into the woods. They formed a line, like an infantry squadron readying for battle, and then beat their way through the undergrowth around the place Tom was shown. It scared away every bird and squirrel in the area, so how they thought they would catch me like that, I don't know.

All the same, it felt strange to see. It reminded me of news reports where the police search for a body rather than a missing person. I found myself wondering if they've ever considered that I might be dead. I am almost glad those two visitors saw me, so at least there will not be some kind of murder investigation. I wonder who they would suspect in that case. Would Diana be accused of breaking under the strain of bereavement and taking it out on her troubled ward?

I watched the searchers from a safe distance until Lleu started circling, and then I became afraid he would give me away, so I withdrew inside my camouflage fence. I didn't dare light a fire until they had gone, so I am eating late now. I have some rice boiling away slowly on the fire. Then it will be time to work again.

After eating, I take my bag and my knife and go out. I have been watching the hazel trees for a few days now, as the nuts grow pale and fat in their green wrappings. Today I intend to find out if they are ripe or not. I go to the trees and sit down among them, and wait. I listen for the right sound. Sparrows chirp amicably to one another, a blackbird trills, and a jay shouts as it flies low through the woods in a flash of pink feathers. Then I hear the chatter I am listening for, and look up to see branches bend and spring back under the weight of a grey squirrel darting from branch to branch. It leaps into one of the nearby trees, and I watch as it takes a hazelnut, inspects it, and then bounds down the trunk to the ground, where it begins to bury its treasure among the leaf litter.

"You'll never find it again," I tell the squirrel, who ignores me, "but thanks for checking them for me."

Now I know the hazelnuts are ripe enough to eat. The squirrel would not bother trying to store something it couldn't dig up for a much-needed meal on a cold winter's day.

I fill up my bag with as many hazelnuts as I can reach from the lower branches. Then I take a long stick from the ground and use it to shake the higher branches. The crop starts to rain down around me, and I gather them all off the ground. The squirrel retreats to a higher point in the tree, nervous of the competition for food. I test a few of them, and they are good. What's more, they will last better than the fruit I have been gathering. I can store these for days when there is nothing on the trees or hedgerows to feed me.

Something cracks, not far away. I drop to the ground. Have the police come back? I peer up over the slope where I lie, and see a lone figure through the trees. It is not a police officer. Of course, it couldn't have been. They always come here in groups, and they never venture this deep into the woods. It is that woman from before – Grace. She is dressed in sensible clothes, with her hair tied up in an olive green scarf, and she carries a clipboard in the crook of one arm. She seems to be writing something on it.

She hasn't spotted me yet, and there's enough distance between us for me to slip away unseen. I begin to edge backwards, staying low to the ground. I reach behind me for my bag, which I dropped when I heard the noise. My fingers close around it and I turn my head to look for my best path to escape. As I do, there is an all-too-familiar cry overhead as a grey shape swoops down towards me.

"Lleu!" I hiss at the bird, though I know he cannot understand. "Why did you have to show up right now?"

Lleu sits in the branch of the hazel tree, and the squirrel jumps for the branches of another and then runs along the forest canopy to safety.

The woman has, unsurprisingly, looked over this way after hearing Lleu. I crouch low, hoping she will decide to ignore the sound, but she starts to walk towards me. I can stay lying here or I can run for it, but either way she will see me. I decide I would rather have the head start, so I spring to my feet and turn to run.

"Wait!"

She has seen me. I don't know why, but I hesitate. She stops walking any nearer, and we stand there, facing one another.

"It's OK. I'm not here to harm you," she says.

You'd better not be, I think.

"We met the other day, when my brother was here. Do you remember?"

Does she think I am stupid? I nod.

"I'm Grace. You're Rhiannon, aren't you?"

How strange, to be called by my own name again. I nod a second time. "I'm not coming back, if that's what you're thinking," I tell her.

"That's not why I'm here," she says. "Actually, I only came here for my research. And I won't force you to come back to the village. How could I? Besides, maybe you had a good reason for running away. But will you answer me one question?"

I say nothing, and she seems to take this as agreement.

"Are you all right? I mean, are you safe?"

"I'm fine."

"Because if you need help, there are plenty of people out there who can support you without making you go home."

"This is my home!" I say, surprising myself with the ferocity of it.

"Is there anything I can get you? Anything you need?" She looks hopeful.

"I look after myself now."

"All right. How about a message to your friends? They're worried about you, you know."

I think about this for a moment.

"What's the date today?" I ask.

"September the twelfth. A Monday," she says, visibly puzzled.

I know what my message will be. "Tell them I'm fine and that I'm not coming back, and they won't find me, no matter how hard they look. Not that I think they'll look much more after Thursday."

"Why Thursday?" she asks, but I decide I will need to run now. She keeps asking questions, and I fear she will try to make me go back with her, whatever she might say. I run in the opposite direction to my house so that she will have no way of knowing where I live. I glance back over my shoulder a few times on the way, but she hasn't followed me.

CHAPTER SIX

LLANDYMNA

On Monday afternoon, Tom arrives at Diana's house to construct the fence, as agreed. He sighs inwardly as he approaches the house. This fence is one of Diana's projects, he knows, but so is he. She never does anything without a reason, and asking him for help will be part of her grand plan to improve Llandymna. Perhaps she views him as insufficiently practical compared to the other men of Llandymna, and thinks that some good DIY time will fix that. Perhaps she wants to keep an eye on one of the team charged with finding her niece. Perhaps she already suspects that Tom knows more than he is admitting. He has agreed with his superiors that it is better not to tell her about the sighting of Rhiannon just yet. He suspects it would lead to further interference in the case.

There is no answer when he rings the doorbell, so he lets himself into the garden through the side gate. Everything is set up in preparation for him. The materials are all laid out on the lawn, and the hens have been shut away in their house until their territory has been re-marked.

"All right there?" Adam is already here and pouring tea from a flask into two sturdy mugs before Tom can suggest that they should probably do some work before taking a break.

"Is Diana out?" asks Tom, surprised that he has not already been ambushed by the homeowner, who should surely have handed him instructions of some kind by now.

"Yes, she's taken the kids out for a walk."

"She's what?"

"Well, we were chatting," says Adam, apparently unaware of the rarity of this event, "and she was telling me how busy she always is. So I asked if she got to spend as much time with her children as she wanted, and it turned out the answer was no. So I told her I'd take care of things here until you arrived – woodwork is my trade, after all – and that she should take Eira and Owen to go jump in some piles of leaves."

Tom is stunned into silence. This stranger has somehow managed the impossible: to make Diana do something she had not intended to do. And apparently he has achieved it all without angering her too.

"So," Adam continues, "it looks like we've got everything we need. Shall we make a start?"

The fence Diana has chosen is like something out of an American suburb: evenly spaced white posts with pointed tops. Its components lie on the neat lawn, which is bordered by rows of Michaelmas daisies.

"You met her children, then?" Tom says, as they position the first panel.

"Great kids," Adam smiles, "and clearly a very proud mother."

"She's got their whole lives planned out, you know. Eira's apparently destined for Oxbridge. Never mind that no one round here goes that far away to study. And Owen's going to be a great leader one day."

"He's got the determination for it. He decided to throw a bowl of peas at me rather than eat them. Pass me that mallet."

It surprises Tom to hear Adam speak with real patience about Diana and her children. He suddenly feels ashamed of his sceptical exasperation where she is concerned. He decides to stop complaining and focus on the work in front of him.

"What about their father?" Adam asks, after they have put up the first two panels in silence. "She didn't mention him."

"Edwin died within a week of Owen being born. We knew he was ill, but most of us didn't know how serious is was."

"That must have been tough for them all," says Adam, pausing his hammering and straightening up to give proper space to this information.

"It was, and I suppose all the worse because her sister Elin died before her time, too. Not many people talk about her these days, least of all Diana. It was years ago now – must be something like a decade, I reckon – but Elin was always good with us younger ones: this is back when Callum, Nia and I were all still at school. She liked helping us get into mischief, teaching us tricks to play on our parents, that sort of thing. You wouldn't think she was the older sister, out of her and Diana."

They talk as they work, about Llandymna and what little of its history Tom has picked up from Maebh, from the selling of farms to the feuds between local families. When at last they reach the end of the task, Adam passes the hammer over to Tom to put the final nail in place. Then they stand back to view their work.

"Not bad," he says.

"Thanks for your help," says Tom.

"Not at all. I know you could've easily done it on your own. I think Diana was being kind, giving me a way to get out of the house, but thank you for being so gracious about it. Grace is out in the woods today, doing her surveys of plants. I'd have gone all day without talking to anyone and be going mad by now. Anyway… time for a drink? We've earned it."

They put away the tools and walk through the village to the White Lion. When they arrive, the Evanses' car is parked outside. Ifan is holding an animated conversation with the barman in front to the pub, while Nia stands some distance away.

"Afternoon, Nia!" Tom calls. "Been at the farmers' market today?"

"Yes," she smiles. "We're just stopping off to pick up a few things from the shop."

Tom and Adam glance from Nia, standing beside the parked car, to Ifan and Terry. Ifan is waving his arms expressively to make some point to the barman, who is used to talking to people who are the worse for drink, and seems to be humouring him. Whatever shopping the Evanses needed to do in the village has clearly been sidelined.

"Maybe I should see if he's ready to go," Nia says, and hurries over to the two men, tentatively joining herself to the already imbalanced conversation.

"Might be a while before we get a drink at this rate," Tom remarks to Adam, as the barman shows no sign of being able to extricate himself and return to his pub. Just then, Diana and her two children appear around the corner. Eira is skipping and jumping wherever she sees a pile of fallen leaves.

"You've finished, then?" says Diana in a tone half impressed, half threatening. Adam wonders what would happen if they had not.

"All done," he says.

At once the warning drops from Diana's voice. "Well, I'm looking forward to seeing your good work!" she says. "The garden will be much neater now that the hens can't escape and destroy my lawn. But what are you doing out here?"

"We had planned a quick drink to celebrate finishing the job, but the barman seems distracted right now," says Tom. "Poor Nia's been waiting here a while, I think."

Diana sniffs sharply at the mention of "poor Nia", reminding them that she has not forgiven Nia for the unsanctioned appeal she gave on camera. Tom looks pained by this reaction, and opens his mouth to say something, but Diana strides off to speak with Ifan before he can find the words.

Callum emerges from the doorway of the White Lion. Adam and Tom, mindful of the last exchange between him and Diana at the harvest festival, quickly walk over in an effort to intercept him.

"Thought I recognized those voices. What's going on out here?" he asks.

"Nothing that a cup of coffee or two won't fix," says Tom, nodding over towards Ifan.

"Ifan's had too much to drink at the farmers' market again, then?" Callum observes, unsurprised. Before Tom can stop him, he heads over to Diana, unable to mask the eagerness in his voice. "I was hoping to run into you today, Diana. I've been thinking about this sports thing you've got planned for the village. I've got some great ideas –"

"Oh Callum, I think you must have misunderstood me," Diana cuts in smoothly, changing her tack from the last discussion of this. "Really, there's no actual plans at the moment. If there were, I'd be sure to involve you."

"Oh, right," Callum says, his voice devoid of emotion, as though the wind has been knocked out of him. He looks from Diana to Tom and Adam, as if appealing for some translation of this platitude. Tom, who is more used to Diana's tactics, is almost certain the plans are being discussed and that Diana wants no interference from Callum, but decides it would do no good to explain this.

"Let it go, mate," Adam murmurs so only Callum and Tom hear. "She doesn't mean any of it. You know she's dealing with a lot at the moment."

"He's right," Tom agrees. It strikes him, for the first time, that Callum is not so unlike Rhiannon. Perhaps Diana struggles being around a strong-willed young adult with lots of ideas and opinions.

"Some things," Ifan declares, oblivious of their attempts to calm Callum, and lent conviction by the amount of beer in his bloodstream, "need experience and common sense. There's no substitute for that. When you're older, you'll understand that, Callum."

"Well said, Ifan," Diana nods approvingly, and gives a smile that looks a little smug, though she cannot help wrinkling her nose at the smell of alcohol on his breath.

Callum flushes a deep shade of red. With clenched fists, he stares at the ground, unable to even look at Diana as he next speaks.

"You care so much what everyone else thinks, don't you? But you're unable to see how much people can't stand you! I bet I'm not the only one who sees right through you. You're self-centred and controlling, and people are laughing at you behind your back for it."

He looks up now, exhilarated at having spoken his mind at last. He flashes a glare first at Diana, then at Ifan, whom he regards as her accomplice in all this, then stomps back into the pub, avoiding meeting Tom's disappointed expression.

For a second, no one seems to know how to respond. Diana seems unrattled by the tirade, gives a knowing look that says *This is exactly what I expected of him*, then remembers that her children have overheard the whole exchange, and rushes to distract them by asking what they would like for their tea tonight. Nia is wide-eyed with shock. Terry's face is a picture of confusion. He prides himself on knowing all the generational feuds in Llandymna, many of which go back centuries, so no one quite remembers how they began, and he knows of no disputes between the Rees and Griffin families. Ifan takes a little longer to process it all, and then starts seething with rage.

"Hey, come back here!" he roars. His hands curl into fists and he starts to follow Callum.

"No, I don't think you want to do that right now, Ifan," says Tom. "Let's get you home instead."

It takes both Adam and Tom to restrain him. They steer him on unsteady feet into the passenger seat of the car. He shouts angrily, but does not put up a struggle.

"Thinking he can insult me like that, in front of – in front of *everyone*! The boy's barely out of school and already lost all his manners. When have I ever picked a fight with him?"

Realization dawns on the faces of everyone around the car.

"He thinks it was directed at *him*!" says Tom. He looks over to Diana, hoping she will march over to resolve the misunderstanding, but she is deep in negotiations with Eira about dessert. "Will you be all right getting him home, Nia? Would you like one of us to come back with you?"

"No, that's fine," Nia murmurs as she gets into the driver's seat and quickly closes the door behind her.

As they drive away, Adam says to Tom, "Grace and I can check on them later and see if they need anything."

"Thank you," says Tom.

They watch the car disappear, while behind them Eira can be heard talking to her mother as they walk home.

"Why was that man being rude? Grown-ups aren't supposed to do that."

*

Adam returns to the cottage, where Grace is surrounded by books and handwritten notes. He steps over the pile of ringbinders on the floor and turns on the oven.

"How was your day? I've bought some things to make tea."

Grace puts down her book. "Thanks. It was… interesting."

Adam laughs. "That sounds mysterious, and a lot like my day. Do you want to go first?"

"Well, I went out to do the first survey, got lots of good data too, but then I decided to go deeper into the woods, and while I was there I saw the missing girl again."

"Have you told Tom? Or anyone else in the police?"

"Yes, I phoned him not long ago, on the number he gave us. He said you'd just left the village and were on your way back. I told him I'd seen her, and I passed on a message she had given me."

"What was it?"

"She said, 'Tell them I'm fine, and that I'm not coming back, and they won't find me, no matter how hard they look.' And then she said something about how they wouldn't look for her much after Thursday."

"Why Thursday?"

"I asked Tom about that. He said that's Rhiannon's eighteenth birthday. After that, she stops being a missing young person and

145

legally becomes an adult. He says the investigation will become lower priority and resources may be moved elsewhere."

"Seriously? They'll stop caring about bringing her home because of a date in the calendar?"

"The thing is, I think she really doesn't want to go back. She seemed scared that I would try to drag her kicking and screaming into the village. Not that I'd have stood a chance of doing that if I'd tried. She's fast when she wants to get away from you. But I still feel we should do something."

"And the police still don't want to tell Diana and raise her hopes of getting her niece back?"

"I guess not."

"Well, she's obviously living somewhere in the woods and doesn't want to be found. I wonder how she's surviving out there."

"I've been wondering that too. She doesn't look as if she's starving to death, but what on earth is she eating? Where does she sleep?"

"I'm kind of impressed," Adam muses.

"What about your day? What happened that was so interesting?"

Adam tells her how Callum's temper got the better of him after another snub from Diana, and how Ifan seemed ready to take a swing at him, thinking he was the one being insulted.

"Hopefully he'll sleep off the drink and forget about it, or else Nia will tell him what was really happening. Otherwise I think the lad might be in trouble."

"Ifan doesn't strike me as the best listener. Do you think Nia explaining it to him will make a difference?"

"I don't know. This village seems to get more and more complicated every day we're here."

Grace sighs. "I know what you mean. This place is like knotweed, all tangled up, with roots you can't see the ends of."

"Tom was telling me more about Diana – she's been through a lot. Lost her husband *and* her sister, both really young. And for some reason, she doesn't talk about her sister any more. Don't know why, though."

He sounds tired, suddenly. He has made friends here, finding things to like in people despite their strange foibles, because he has told himself that the cruel treatment of his father is something confined to the past, not these people's responsibility. Suddenly the injustice done to Emrys seems more immediate.

"It's starting to get to you, isn't it?" says Grace, watching her brother as he walks over to the window to look out at the farmyard and the heavy grey sky that hangs over it.

"A bit," he agrees. He can see Simon, who has looked after the farm while Ifan and Nia were away at the market today, whistling to himself as he sets off home after another day's work.

"You're wondering if you're angry with your new friends," she says, beginning to tidy her notes away.

"You don't sound very worried about it!"

"I'm not. You like people too much to let yourself get bitter towards them. And if you won't grow bitter, I don't need to worry about you. You'll still be you."

Adam laughs. "You are very wise, you know."

"It's true, I am," Grace says with a straight face. The weight in the air lifts, and Adam seems to relax.

"Thanks, Ayawa."

"Let's make a start on tea. I saw you brought rice back with you from the shop, and you know you always undercook it."

"Only because I'm too hungry to wait!"

Grace takes charge of the cooking of the rice, while Adam chops up the other ingredients. They eat their meal on the sofas, since Grace's work still covers the kitchen table.

As they are finishing washing up, they hear, over the clatter of plates in the sink, the dogs in the yard start to bark. Then there is a noise like shouting outside, and the slam of a car door before an engine starts up. About a minute passes before there is a knock at the door. Nia stands on the step, looking paler than ever.

"I'm so sorry about this, but could I possibly borrow your car?"

"Is everything all right?" Adam asks. Nia is wide-eyed and clearly shaken.

"Ifan's just gone back up to the village. I told him he wasn't fit to drive yet, but he wouldn't have any of it. He's looking for Callum."

"Presumably not to shake hands and make up?"

"I don't know what he'll do. I have to stop him!" She looks frantic.

"Can we warn Callum and tell him to stay out of the way?" asks Grace, taking a step forward and speaking calmly as she offers up a practical solution. "I mean, if Ifan can't find him at the pub, he'll have to come home, right? And by tomorrow things might have quietened down."

"I don't have a number for him, or I'd call him. I think Ifan had his number saved, but he's taken his phone with him."

"He was with Tom!" Adam remembers. "I left them both at the pub after you'd gone. We've got his number here somewhere."

He finds the card that Tom gave them in case they had more information for the police lying on the hall table.

"Thank you," says Nia. "I'm so glad you're both here."

*

Tom and Callum have been in the White Lion for several hours. They have exhausted the line of conversation that began with Tom asking, "What were you thinking?" Callum has not been keen to dwell on that. He already regrets losing his temper with Diana, and fears what she may do in retaliation. If she seemed not to take him seriously before, he dreads to think what his standing in the village will become now. Tom's phone rings, and Callum finishes his drink in silence while his friend is distracted.

"Right," says Tom, putting down his phone, "we need to leave."

"What? No, I don't want to go home yet," Callum protests.

"Well, that's tough, because your moment of stupidity earlier is coming back to bite you. Ifan is on his way over here right now."

"Ifan? What's he coming here for? And why's that a problem?"

Tom shakes his head. "You don't know, do you?"

"Know what?"

"You lashed out at Diana. But from where Ifan was standing, it sounded like you were having a go at him. And that stuff you said about not being respected by anyone… well, you can imagine how deep that would cut him. After you left, he wanted to confront you over it, but we got him into the car and sent him home with Nia. She's tried telling him that you weren't insulting him, but he's got it into his head that you were, so he's looking for you. And you know this will be the first place he checks."

Callum's stomach jolts at the idea of facing Ifan tonight, but he quickly conceals this. "So? I'm not scared of him."

Tom rolls his eyes. "From the sound of things, he's in a right state. And if he beats you to a pulp outside the pub, you know who'll have to write up the notes on it tomorrow morning and document exactly how many of your teeth are scattered over the street? Me. And I'd like a quiet day at work instead. So we're leaving."

Callum is sufficiently surprised at how unsympathetic his friend sounds to agree to this. Tom marches Callum out of the White Lion and points him in the direction of home. They have only taken a few steps, however, when they see a car parked on the opposite side of the road. Tom catches sight of Ifan behind the wheel, and seeing the look on his face, says to Callum, "You should get out of here, quickly!"

"No way. I'm not running."

Ifan gets out of the car and storms towards them.

"What's the matter, Ifan?" Callum asks, trying to sound nonchalant.

"Nobody insults me like that and gets away with it!"

"Ifan, the drink's confused your brain. You've got the wrong end of the stick, mate."

"*Ca dy geg,*" Ifan snaps, and he calls Callum a few names that, though Callum does not understand the exact meaning of the Welsh, clearly are not compliments. "So no one respects me, do they?"

Tom steps forward. "Ifan, don't forget I'm a police officer, even if I am off duty. And if there's any violent behaviour here, I will arrest you and take you to the station, where you can sleep in a cell until you calm down."

Ifan stops in front of Tom. "That's true. You will, won't you?"

Without warning, he swings his right arm and lands a blow that knocks Tom to the ground.

"Now then," he says, looking back at Callum, who has not moved. The younger man stares, open-mouthed, at his friend lying on the floor, then turns back to Ifan.

He lunges forward, but Callum is expecting this and jumps out of the way. Callum is not as strong as Ifan, and knows this, but he has the advantage of having drunk less today. He waits for Ifan to rush at him again, and this time he dodges and manages to trip him up at the same time. Ifan hits the ground, but seems not to feel the impact.

"Get up, old man," says Callum, standing over him. Ifan pulls himself off the floor and faces his opponent again.

A second car pulls up behind them. Nia, Grace, and Adam jump out and run towards the fight. Ifan ignores them and this time he manages to land a punch on Callum's jaw that sends him staggering backwards.

"Stop!" a woman's voice cries through the fog of Callum's throbbing pain and Ifan's slurred rage. Ifan hits out again and this time Callum falls down. As he looms over his rival, there is real fear in Callum's eyes.

"You think that hurt? I'm just warming up," he manages to spit out. Callum scrabbles frantically, but Ifan stamps down on his ankle to stop him getting away. He howls in pain. Looking up at Ifan, Callum suddenly begins to feel afraid of how much damage Ifan might be willing to cause. As Adam reaches them and tries to break up the fight, Callum decides it is time to bring this to a halt. He reaches down to his pocket and pulls out his penknife, which he holds out, pointing the blade at Ifan.

"Stay back!" he says. Adam stops trying to pull Ifan away and gives Callum his full attention now instead.

"Be very careful with that," he warns.

"I know what I'm doing. Back away, both of you, or I will use this!" If he can just sound threatening enough, Ifan will surely withdraw. And then tomorrow, in the clear light of day, Callum can go round to the farm and set the record straight with him. Then he'll only have Diana to face, and her tactics are very different.

Ifan stands over him, swaying slightly. A crowd seems to have gathered around them. The noise has drawn drinkers out of the White Lion onto the street. Tom is back on his feet and walking towards them, holding the side of his head. Ifan cannot quite remember how he got here. He knows he has been fighting with Callum, and that now the boy is beaten, for everyone to see. One more punch should do it. Then he will be satisfied and go home. He swings his arm again to land the last blow. There is a flash of metal and a scream.

Callum lies on the ground holding the knife that is now stained dark red. His relief at not being knocked senseless, or anything worse, swiftly turns to panic as above him Ifan claps a hand to his chest and looks surprised. He staggers back, and the onlookers who have held back until now rush in. A clamour of first aid and phone calls for an ambulance takes over, while Ifan maintains his state of shock.

"He stabbed me," is all he can manager to utter as he slumps to the ground. Everyone remembers this. They look around, but Callum is already gone.

Tom knows he needs to take charge of the situation, but his head is pounding. He calls the station to request a car be sent over with two officers, but he knows the roads between Bryndu and Llandymna are bad, and it will be some time before they arrive.

"What can I do?" asks Adam, appearing in front of him with perfect timing.

"The ambulance is on its way, and Ifan's in no position to give a statement just now. Your sister's looking after him – she told me she's trained in first aid. Next priority is to look for Callum. Can you help me?"

"Course. Let me just tell Grace and Nia where I'm going."

He walks back over to where Nia kneels on the ground next to her husband, while Grace has used her jumper to put pressure on the wound and soak up the blood.

"How long till the paramedics get here?" she asks, her hands pressed against the place where the knife went in.

"Not long. How bad is it?"

"I'm not sure. I don't think the knife hit any major organs, but there's a lot of blood. That's right, Nia, keep him talking. He needs to stay conscious."

"Will you be all right if I go and help Tom? He needs to find Callum."

"Go. There's not much you can do here. I'll look after these two," says Grace. Adam looks at Nia's stricken face and realizes Grace is right to be worried for her as well as her husband.

"Call me if you need to," he says, and then leaves his sister with the wounded man, the distraught wife, and the crowd of fussing spectators. He goes back to Tom. "Right, where do we start?"

"We'll go to Callum's house first, see if he's gone there."

"Will you press charges against Ifan too? I'm assuming that black eye isn't from walking into a lamppost."

"We'll see," says Tom. "Right now I can't believe I'm having to hunt down my best friend."

They cover the streets from the White Lion to Callum's home. The roads are strangely quiet and peaceful, and each lit-up window represents someone going about their evening unaware of what has just happened in their village.

*

Callum catches his breath once he finds a shadowy corner behind the old scout hut. From here he can look out from Llandymna

152

over the dark fields, to see a blue light hurtling around the hill and towards the village. Is it an ambulance or a police car? Now that he has stopped running, which was agonizing because of the damage Ifan has done to his foot, he can feel the cold sensation of blood on his hands; it has trickled off the knife and is cooling now in the evening air. What if he has killed Ifan? He'll go to prison for the rest of his life, and that's assuming no one else gets to him first, given that people clearly like to dispense their own justice around here.

He limps forward.

"There you are," says a voice. Adam rounds the corner behind the scout hut. Callum freezes.

"Is Tom with you?"

"No, we split up after we looked for you at your house. Tom spoke to your mum, but she hadn't seen you. I thought you might have come here."

"So you're all looking for me. Tom's going to arrest me, isn't he?" Callum says, eyeing up his escape routes even as he talks with Adam.

"I don't know."

"I didn't mean to do it. But Ifan was acting like he was going to kill me."

"I know you didn't want this to happen. Come back, explain that, and it'll get sorted out."

"Not if Ifan dies, it won't. Then it won't matter what I say."

"Well, what are you planning to do?"

"I'll wait. I'll hide until I know how bad it is – whether Ifan dies, or he lives and yells for my arrest. When I know what I'm facing, then I'll talk to the police."

Callum decides he will not be able to get past Adam and will need to get away in the opposite direction, if he can just find a way to make sure he isn't followed.

Adam looks grave. "And how exactly are you going to hide from the police?"

"You think I can't? Or do you just want to try and stop me?"

153

Callum raises the knife towards Adam. There is still blood on the blade.

"Careful. I think you've done enough damage with that for one day."

Callum brandishes the knife in what he hopes is a convincing manner.

"I don't want to hurt anyone else. But if you try to follow me, I will stop you, I promise. I'm going now. Tell them I'll come back when I can."

Adam's eyes are so full of sadness, Callum almost feels sorry for him. But he sticks to his half-formed plan and hobbles backwards, still holding out the knife, until the shadows have enveloped him completely. Nobody else sees him disappear.

Adam returns to the road outside the White Lion. Ifan and Nia have already been taken in an ambulance to the nearest hospital. A police car is parked outside the pub and two officers are taking statements from witnesses. He finds his sister sitting alone on the low wall by the pub.

"You OK?" he asks as he sits down beside her. Grace stares ahead.

"I'm going to need a new jumper," she says, mustering humour but not the light-hearted tone that should go with it. Tom joins them on the wall.

"Well, it's official. I'm not allowed to be involved in the case. Apparently it's too personal for me, what with Callum being my friend." He looks up at the sky and sighs with relief.

"It must be hard, doing your kind of job in a place where you know everyone."

"It can be," says Tom, "but only on days like today. It's not normally like this. We're a quiet village. Nothing much happens."

"If you're not involved in this, as a police officer I mean, can I ask you a question?" asks Adam.

"Go on," says Tom, intrigued.

"Hypothetically, if you were still on the case, and if – hypothetically – I had seen Callum this evening, but had no information about where he now was, only that I'd spoken to him and that he'd threatened me with that knife, and if I told you all this in a statement, what would you do?"

Tom inhales deeply. "Well, I'd be in a difficult position. Hypothetically, that information might mean we'd have to class Callum as a 'dangerous' fugitive, since he'd threatened another person. And that might change things significantly. And even though I'm certain Callum isn't a danger to anyone else, because I've known him all his life, as a police officer I'd still have to recommend a manhunt for him. Officers might be instructed to make use of firearms against him."

"And if, continuing this scenario, Callum assured you he would come back and hand himself in as soon as he heard that Ifan was all right, would you believe him?"

"I would. He's an idiot, sure, but he's honest. But I wouldn't be allowed to trust him, of course. That's not how it works."

"Right, thanks," says Adam as an officer approaches to take his statement.

"I'm sorry about my brother," says Grace, as Adam and the officer walk over to the police car together. "He thinks he's being clever, but he's put you in a difficult situation now."

"Not at all," says Tom. "We were just talking hypothetically. We can hopefully avoid anyone else getting hurt tonight. But I would remind you and your brother that I will have to report anything you tell me about Callum's whereabouts, just in case you do end up knowing anything."

*

Callum stops to catch his breath. He has no idea what to do next. He has nowhere to go now. There will be no buses or trains away from any of the nearest towns or villages until morning, by which time people will no doubt be on the lookout for him. Besides, if he did find transport, where could he go? He has an aunt in Neath who might take him in – until she found out what he had done.

Then he would probably be thrown out of the house. It is not so much that he is afraid of the police, or even prison. It would be fair, he supposes, if a bit steep a punishment in his opinion. It is the thought of facing his friends and family that drives him away from the village.

Maybe tomorrow there will be good news. Maybe Ifan will wake up and decide to put it all behind him. Then everyone can go home. He just needs somewhere to shelter for the night. A barn would be ideal. The Evanses' farm is nearest on this side of the village, and they have probably left Llandymna in an ambulance by now. But even if they stay there overnight, in the morning someone might find him. It feels too much like adding insult to injury, to hospitalize Ifan and then hide on his land.

There was always the woods. Callum has never liked Dyrys much. He prefers to be at home, near a television and a fridge filled with beers, than out in the countryside. But it would provide him with some cover from the cold, and a place to hide until morning.

As he starts to hobble his way up the hill that leads to the woods, Callum reflects that he would never have expected the day to end like this. He makes slow progress, because he cannot bear to put much weight on his left foot, but eventually he reaches the edge of the forest.

"Well, here goes," he mutters to himself, taking a deep breath as he steps into Dyrys.

CHAPTER SEVEN

DYRYS

Callum wakes up to find himself slumped under an oak tree, cold and in pain. Confused and disorientated, he tries to stand but cannot, and immediately remembers what happened to his foot last night. With that, all the other memories come racing back.

He needs to find out what has happened to Ifan. He cannot go back to the village yet, in case the reports are bad. He takes his phone out of his pocket – the battery icon shows ten per cent left. He cannot call Tom. Though probably his best friend, he is also a policeman, and likely taking sides against him right now. He scrolls through his contact list, looking for someone to call. Not his mam – she will be too emotional right now to be any help. He doesn't need someone to cry down the phone to him; he needs information. Then he spots the number for the Evanses' guest cottage. He helped with some of the renovation work on the building last summer. There was lots of coming and going, and he ended up with the landline number saved so that Ifan could call him while he was out buying hardware for the house. Maybe Adam or Grace will help him. It seems like his best chance, so he presses the button to call them.

"Hello?" Adam's voice answers.

"It's Callum. Any news about Ifan? Is he alive?"

If Adam is surprised to hear Callum, his voice does not give it away. "They aren't back yet from the hospital. Grace is going to see Nia later this morning. We will know then. Would you like me to call you back when I have an answer?"

"No, that's no good; my phone battery won't last much longer."

The line crackles, and Callum tries hobbling around to find a place where the reception is better. If he leans against a tree trunk, he does not have to support his weight on the foot that is in pain.

"Well, you could call them yourself now."

"What? Call Nia? After what I did! Are you joking?"

"Not at all. I'm very serious about helping you come back home. Are you somewhere nearby? Can I come and meet you when I have news?"

Callum pauses. It could be a trick, to get him to give up his location. Maybe Adam will call the police immediately after this conversation.

"There's a path that leads west of the village, into Dyrys Wood. Do you know it?"

"Yes, I do."

"The first crossroads after that path enters the woods. I'll meet you there, at midday. But don't bring any police with you. I'll be watching to make sure you don't."

"Understood. Midday then. I hope I'll be bringing you good news."

Callum hangs up. Now he will make his way to the crossroads and hide somewhere nearby to watch the path until Adam arrives. He limps forward. His foot might need medical attention, but he has no idea if that will be possible. He takes a few steps and then steadies himself against another tree trunk.

It crosses his mind that he may not yet be safe, and maybe because this thought makes him more alert, he thinks he can hear someone, or something, approaching. He tenses up and looks from side to side, well aware he can hardly run away if the police have already found him.

A few dry leaves crunch underfoot, and his eyes dart about frantically as he tries to pinpoint the source of the sound. For the third time in less than twenty-four hours, his hand goes to the pocket knife he has been carrying, his only defence now. Then he sees what the noise was.

A girl stands almost knee-deep in brambles. In one hand she holds a long stick, like a wizard's staff, and in the other is a bundle of something that looks heavy. Her face is more gaunt than when he last saw her, which makes her look older. She eyes him with an expression of wariness and disappointment.

"Oh," she says, "it's you."

For a moment Rhiannon observes him leaning against the tree, then turns to leave.

"Were you expecting somebody else?" he snaps crossly. His surprise at seeing Rhiannon fast turns to annoyance that his predicament is of so little interest to her.

"What do you care?" she retorts. He does not find an answer to this, so she adds, "What are you doing here anyway?"

"Avoiding being arrested or beaten to within an inch of my life."

At this, her knuckles tighten as she checks her grip on the staff she is carrying. Callum sees the effect his words have had, but Rhiannon's reply does not betray it.

"Then you've come to the wrong place. There've been more police in these woods in the last month than in all the time we've lived round here."

"Wasting time and effort looking for you," he accuses, as it occurs to him that Rhiannon's decision to run away might have worked against him, if it means that the police already know the surrounding countryside better than he does.

"I didn't ask them to. Anyway, what did you do?"

"What d'you mean?"

"Well, if you're on the run from the law and afraid for your life, you must have done something."

"Thanks for having so much faith in me. Didn't it occur to you it could have been a case of mistaken identity, or a false accusation?"

"Well, was it?"

"No."

"There you go then. So what did you do?"

He grimaces, not wanting to acknowledge last night's events. "I got into a fight."

RHIANNON

Now that the initial shock of finding Callum out here has worn off, I relax a little. Everyone knows Callum gets loud and antagonistic after his team loses a match. That must be what has happened.

"Who with?"

"Ifan. Remember him?"

Of course I remember him. Does he think I would forget everyone in the time I've been gone?

"I can't imagine *he's* hiding from the police though," I say.

"No, he's in hospital, fighting for his life."

"What?" I gasp, instinctively taking a step backwards, away from Callum. This doesn't sound like a post-match quarrel any more.

"Yeah," he says, and I can tell he wants to sound nonchalant, but it isn't working. "Guess I don't know my own strength."

I think about this. If Callum really is unable to go back to the village, then he can't tell anyone he saw me, and I am safe. Then again, if the police are after him, they'll be patrolling the countryside around here even more, just when I thought they were going to call off the search. My food-gathering trips will be more risky. Even lighting a fire might become impossible.

"Well, you can't stay here," I say.

"What? I didn't think you were so attached to Ifan. Didn't you call him a hypocrite to his face, along with several other people, at that event at the school?"

Of course he'd have to bring that up. I scowl involuntarily at the memory of it.

"I'm not the one who tried to kill him though, and then ran away."

160

Callum raises his eyebrows and pulls a horrible mocking face. "That second bit was me following your great example."

He is making fun of me. This is exactly why I am happier out here. I don't have to put up with stupid people like Callum, who think they are funny but have no idea what they are talking about. I want to walk away and leave him here, but it occurs to me that he might have more information about others from Llandymna, so I linger a little longer.

"Got anything to eat?" he asks suddenly.

"Nothing that I would want to give you."

"I see life away from home has done nothing for your manners. Don't you care about a hungry fugitive, all alone? It could be your good deed for the year, if you like."

My expression tells him that I do not care in the slightest about his welfare.

"Well, how about a trade, then?" he carries on. "I'll tell you everything you've missed. You're a girl, you like gossip. Give me some food, and I'll tell you all about Aunty Di, all your friends, Maebh, Nia, and two strangers who turned up recently."

I had intended to refuse this bargain, until he mentioned the two strangers, who must be Adam and Grace. Something about them interests me.

"Wait here," I say, and head back to my house.

"Don't worry," he calls after me. "I won't be going anywhere."

On the walk back, I realize that he has never thought very highly of me, and now is my chance to prove to Callum that I can look after myself. I fill a clay bowl with a stew I made from some of the vegetables I took from the farm. I take this back to the oak where I found him, but walk along a different path this time, to show him how well I know my way around.

I give him the food and he takes it without thanking me.

"Not very good, is it?" he says, after tasting the stew. Now I wish I had not wasted the best of my supplies on him. He eats it all anyway, and I sit down, a good distance away. I can see no reason why I have to trust him, or pretend to be friendly.

"The news, then?" I remind him as he finishes the last mouthful.

"Oh yeah. Let's see. There was a lot of fuss about your disappearance at first. Your aunt convinced Nia to go on TV and ask you to come home, which was clearly a waste of time unless you have a satellite dish attached to a tree somewhere round here. The best thing about that was seeing Nia of all people stand up to Diana and say what she thought was right, not what your aunt told her to say. You should have seen Diana's face after that! Tom's been kept busy, having an actual interesting case to deal with for a change, instead of investigating whose dog is knocking over bins, or telling the Bryndu kids that drugs are bad."

"What about Maebh?"

"What about her? She's Maebh. She hardly ever leaves her house. People visit her, and she talks nonsense to them."

"She doesn't talk nonsense!"

"Oh yeah, I forgot. You two speak the same language, don't you? All that stuff about stories and imagining and everything being very noble, right?"

"What about the two strangers?" I quickly change the subject.

"Their names are Adam and Grace. They're brother and sister. I thought maybe they were a couple when they first arrived, but they're not. They look foreign, but they aren't actually, but their mam was from somewhere in Africa – can't remember where. They're pretty cool, really. Be a shame when they leave."

"What are they like?"

"Like? Dunno, really. He's good at building things, she's more the clever type. Studies something to do with trees, I think."

"But what kind of people are they?"

"What kind of question is that? You look too deep, Rhiannon. That's why you hate everyone."

"I don't hate everyone!" I snap back.

"So when you scream at people and break things, it's meant to be a friendly gesture?" he asks, looking pleased with himself. He wasn't even at the fundraiser at Llandymna School. He must have heard about it from his mother, Angie Rees, who runs the local shop and is the worst gossip in the village. I bet she made it sound far worse than it was.

"A lot can change in a month."

"Like your character? Yes, it's like you're a different person. All warmth and welcome now, aren't you?"

I had forgotten how sarcastic he could be. All this scorn is more than I can stand, so I turn my back on him and march away. He doesn't call anything after me, but I feel as though I could drive a knife straight through him just to get rid of that horrible jeering smile.

Lleu meets me on my way back, and flies ahead of me, knowing which way I will go. I start to wonder if I was too rude to Callum, given that he is only the third person I have spoken to since leaving home. Maybe I shouldn't have let him goad me like that. But he deserved it. No wonder I left Llandymna, if it's full of people like that.

LLANDYMNA

It is almost noon the day after the fight before anyone thinks to tell Maebh what has happened to Ifan and Callum. After she puts down the phone and takes in the news, she sits in her armchair with her head in her hands for several minutes.

"Not another," she whispers sadly. Then she gets up slowly and goes to the hallway to look for her shoes. She takes her walking stick and her coat from their place by the front door, and leaves the house with the determination and purpose of a woman on a mission. She knows it will take her a long time to reach her destination, but she has nowhere else to be today, and the weather is good for walking.

"Now then," she says to herself, "let's see what we can do about all this mess."

On her way through the village, she passes Diana and waves cheerily to her. *I'll get to you later,* she thinks as they smile at one another and remark on the clear skies.

It takes her nearly an hour, with several breaks to sit down and rest wherever there is an available bench, but at last she knocks on the door of the farmhouse.

"Maebh!" Nia is understandably startled.

"I thought I'd visit the patient and see if I could be any help to you."

"Maebh, did you walk all this way?"

"Yes. I felt like some fresh air. Don't look so worried, dearie. I'm not going to collapse and give you another invalid to nurse."

Nia invites Maebh inside, and immediately apologizes that she has so little to offer her guest by way of food and drink. "I'm in such a muddle today, with looking after Ifan and trying to keep everything going on the farm."

"How is he? I'm surprised to hear you've come back from the hospital so soon."

"It's almost miraculous, Maebh. They said somehow the blade didn't touch any vital organs. There was a doctor there last night who was able to stitch him up straight away. They kept him in overnight for observation, but this morning they said we could come home. Apparently they're going to send out a nurse to change the bandages until it's all healed up. If you'd been there last night – when it all happened – you wouldn't believe it was possible he wasn't more seriously hurt."

Maebh smiles to see Nia's relief. "That's wonderful news. Now, you go and see to whatever you need to. Don't stop on my account. I'll make us all a cup of tea for when you get back."

Nia thanks Maebh for understanding, puts on her wellies and heads out to the fields. Maebh pours three cups of tea and puts one on the kitchen table for Nia to find. The other two she places on a tray and carries out. At the foot of the stairs she looks up, like a mountaineer viewing Snowdon, and begins her slow ascent.

Ifan is lying in bed, propped up on pillows. He seems drowsy, which Maebh suspects will be courtesy of some powerful prescription painkillers. He turns his head towards the door as she enters with the tray of tea.

164

"Maebh," he slurs, "worrayoudoinghere?"

Maebh sets the tray down on the bedside table and sits herself in the chair by the window.

"Here you go, my lad. Some of the finest medicine you'll ever drink. They've stitched you up and sent you home, then."

Ifan gives an affirmative grunt and reaches over for the mug. He winces as he moves.

"Slowly now, don't spill it. In a lot of pain, are you? Well, I hope you're not trying to blame anyone but yourself."

"Wascallum," Ifan insists, earnest if not articulate.

Maebh looks out through the window to the fields where the Evanses' sheep graze.

"In my day, we took responsibility for our actions. But I've noticed something about your generation. You're all desperate for it not to be your fault. And it's not because you're especially afraid of the consequences of your one action. You're afraid of what that action might say about you to other people. You're afraid that if you're wrong about one thing, it will build up with all the other things you've got wrong, to make you look weak, or bad, or unkind, or whatever you don't want to be. Most likely weak, in your case.

"And I bet no one has dared tell you the truth about what really happened yesterday? Mmm. Yes, that's right. I know something you don't, and I wasn't even there! It was never about you, Ifan. Callum's words were meant for Diana. The boy wanted to be treated the way you are, to be listened to instead of patronized. But in the end he found it easier to be angry at Diana than to wait for her to approve of him. You see? None of that ever took you into account. And don't think I don't know who landed the first blow in that fight."

Maebh has no idea how much of this will stick in Ifan's drug-muddled brain. She hopes enough of it will sink in to make some kind of difference. Ifan's expression is too vacant to indicate any epiphany. Maebh sips her tea.

"One more thing," she says, more sternly this time. "I will not have any more of this village's young people run away and never come back. Do you understand me? As soon as you're up and about, you'd better drop all charges against the boy. We both know the fight was your idea and your doing, and you'll only get the police involved to save your pride over the fact that you lost it. Well, you'll have me to answer to. And I may have the reputation of a kind grandmother figure in this village, but believe me I am tired of playing along."

She gives him her fiercest stare and then leaves the room. As she returns to the kitchen, Nia also reappears. "All well?" Maebh asks.

Nia nods, and spots the cup of tea on the table. "Thank you! That's just what I needed today. But you mustn't walk all the way back, Maebh. I'll see if Simon can drive you home."

Maebh insists on washing up the mugs before she leaves. Nia goes to the kitchen window, her eye caught by some movement outside.

"Oh, there goes Grace up to the woods again for her research. And her brother's with her this time. He must be helping her today."

Maebh joins Nia at the window and sees the siblings walk out to the gate. Adam has a rucksack on his back that looks heavy.

"Hmm," is all she says.

DYRYS

Callum chooses a large tree near the crossroads and sits behind it. This way, he will be able to hear Adam approaching without being seen. Time seems to pass slowly while he waits. He would normally check his phone, but he has switched it off, remembering that in films the authorities can use a suspect's phone to track their location. There is nothing much to do. For a while he idly flicks the pocket knife open and closed, but that makes it hard not to think about last night.

He misses his headphones. He listens to music whenever there is somewhere to go, and it means he can avoid moments like this, of being left alone with only his thoughts for company.

As if on cue, the forest suddenly rings with song; not just the birds overhead, but human as well. Loud and cheerful, if not completely tuneful, Adam's voice goes before him and announces his arrival as he marches down the path.

Nid wy'n gofun bywyd moethus,
Aur y byd na'i berlau mân:
Gofyn wyf am galon hapus,
Calon onest, calon lân!

Callum knows the tune, of course. They used to sing it in school all the time. He tries to peer round as subtly as possible to check that Adam is alone. His sister is with him.

"Hello!" Adam calls. Callum is annoyed that he has been seen already. His careful movements were more obvious than he had hoped.

"You didn't come alone!" he shouts back from behind the tree.

"That wasn't what we agreed," Adam reasons, "but I haven't brought any police with me."

Callum decides this will have to do and steps out from his hiding place, onto the path. He could do with a walking stick like the one Rhiannon had if his foot is going to keep hurting like this.

"Hungry?" Adam asks, stopping at the crossroads and setting down a bag on the ground. "We've brought you something to eat."

Callum hobbles forward as Adam opens his rucksack and takes out some sandwiches and a flask of hot coffee.

"You need to see a medic about your foot," Grace observes as Callum leans his weight against the nearest tree trunk. He ignores her as he unwraps the sandwiches and devours them. Given the circumstances, he hardly cares that cheese and pickle is not his favourite filling.

"Mind if I join the party?" a voice behind them asks. Rhiannon steps out onto the path.

"Hello again," says Adam. The girl seems less on edge this time, and she actually manages a small smile today. She stops a few paces away from them.

"Oh great, she's back," groans Callum. "Seriously, when can I come home? It's like having the grouchiest neighbour ever, being out here."

"Whenever you like," says Adam. "Ifan is out of hospital and expected to make a full recovery eventually."

"And he's said he won't press charges against me?"

"Not yet," says Grace. "We called in this morning just after they came home, and Ifan was too groggy from the pain relief to say anything very coherent."

"Well then, I can't go back yet."

Adam and Grace look disappointed.

"I thought you said you were only running away to make sure you weren't wrongly arrested for murder. There's no chance of that now. The only accusations you'll face will be ones that are fair."

"Not necessarily. Someone might say I meant to kill Ifan and failed in the attempt. Ifan might say I started the fight."

"But there's a witness who will say that's not true: Tom Davies, a police officer, who was there the whole time!"

"They'll say he's biased against Ifan for punching him and that's caused him to give false evidence."

Grace sighs with exasperation. Adam shakes his head.

"Paranoid, isn't he?" says Rhiannon, who has stayed a safe distance from the rest of the group and only now given any indication that she has been paying attention to the conversation.

"What exactly are you doing here?" Callum snaps crossly. "Hoping I'll throw up so you can get your breakfast back?"

"Actually," she says with a smile, turning from Callum to the others present, "I was wondering what the noise was – it frightened Lleu."

"'Twas I, the woodland bard," says Adam with an elaborate bow, apparently unashamed to learn that his rendition of *Calon Lân* has been heard so widely across the woods.

"Who's Lleu?" asks Callum, looking around for a fifth person.

"A hawk," she answers.

"As in, a bird? You really have got desperate for company if you're naming animals. I guess befriending people was never really your strongest skill though. What's this tree called?"

Rhiannon makes a noise of disgust and turns away from Callum.

Adam continues, "Callum, I don't think you've thought this through. If you stay away until Ifan is fully conscious, what are you going to do? Where will you live? What will you eat?"

"I dunno. But if she can manage it, it can't be so hard," he shrugs, pointing to Rhiannon. "Where do you live then?"

"As if I'd tell you!" she snorts.

Callum turns back to the other two. "You try asking her. She doesn't seem to hate you."

RHIANNON

They turn towards me. I don't know why, but I am starting to trust Adam and Grace. They have had the chance to make me go back to Llandymna, and not used it. Callum is right: I don't hate them. I am intrigued by them, which is what compelled me to interrupt their meeting at the crossroads. Maybe it's like the song Adam was singing. There's a line in it that means "only a pure heart can sing", which I know isn't strictly true, but how could anyone scheming to hurt others march through the woods belting out traditional songs like that? Not that I will tell them where my house is, if they ask me. That's too big a secret to share.

"I don't think that's the best plan," says Grace, to my relief.

"All right, Callum," says Adam. "Tom said he believed that when you said you'd come back, you meant it. So if you want to stay out here a while longer, we won't stop you. We'll even bring you food. We can come to the woods each day for Grace's research and bring some supplies up."

"Can you get me a tent too? And a gas stove? And a solar powered battery charger for my phone?"

I can't restrain a laugh at the things he thinks are essentials.

"I don't know," Adam frowns. "I think those would be harder to conceal in a bag. And might attract attention. But I can show you how to build a shelter using just materials you'll find in the woods."

I suddenly wish Adam had been around and dispensing knowledge when I first left home. I think he would have got on well with Uncle Ed.

"Can it be somewhere not too far from here? I'm not feeling up to a long hike."

"Sure," I say, "if you want to make it really easy for a rambler or dog walker to stumble across you."

"She's right," says Adam. "If you're committing to this plan of hiding for a day or two, you need to go deeper into the woods."

"Oh, fine then," Callum says, dragging himself upright again.

"Like to help?" Adam asks me. If I say no, I can leave before Callum is rude to me again, and before Grace can suggest I need to go home. But then I won't be able to make sure they stay away from my part of the woods. I will feel safer if I know exactly where Callum is and therefore how to avoid him. I agree to go with them.

The path is only wide enough for us to walk two by two, so Grace and I walk side by side ahead of the others. I become conscious that her clothes, though practical for outdoor weather, look far cleaner than mine.

"Listen, Rhiannon, I'm glad you're here. I wanted to talk to you again," she says. "I passed on your message to Tom Davies. He told me what you meant about them stopping looking for you. I know it's your birthday the day after tomorrow."

The point of that message was to get people to leave me alone, so I could enjoy solitude in these woods. That plan does not seem to be going very well.

"So I guess you're planning to stay out here long term then, right? You don't share Callum's eagerness to get back to family, or central heating and a roof over your head for that matter?"

I'm tempted to tell her that I do have a roof over my head, albeit one that I have had to patch up myself, but I don't want to risk giving her information about where I live.

"I realize that's your choice, but I just want to be sure you're safe out here. If you were hurt and needed help, would you know where to go?"

"I'll just have to make sure I'm not clumsy enough to get myself hurt."

"But is there someone you could go to, someone you trust? I'm sure you don't need the help, but please humour me. You know what adults are like: we tend to worry a lot."

It's strange. She speaks to me as if I am an adult too.

"Maebh. I suppose I'd get a message to her somehow."

Grace nods. "Good choice."

"You know her?"

"We met her on our second day here. She told us a lot about the history of this place."

Maebh says our history is a part of us; that we build the present out of it without even realizing. But while I know she weaves stories of her childhood into the tales she tells us, I can never fully tell fact from fiction. When I asked her about this once, she said I had missed the point.

"She gave me this for my fourteenth birthday," I say, pulling the pendant on its chain out from under my jumper.

"That's a pretty gift."

"My aunt never liked it. She said it was childish, having little charms instead of proper jewellery."

"But you could tell a story with them," says Grace. "Think how many adventures could start with a key, a rose and a book!"

I stop a moment on the path, looking to the left and right. "I think we should go this way," I say, pointing right. "There's some flatter ground near the stream. He'll need to be near water." I don't mention it also takes us further away from my home.

"Just as well someone knows where we're going," says Adam. It may not quite be a compliment, but it is a welcome change from all Callum's jokes and jabs at me. I smile to myself when no one else is looking. We take my route, downhill towards the stream.

"This is far enough," Callum declares aloud, rather than admit that the walk has tired him. Here the trees are a little further apart, and there is bare ground between vegetation.

Adam paces up and down, testing the ground and scanning the area for materials.

"Right then," he says, "here's what we're going to do. Since we don't have any tools, we're going to copy a very old style of building."

"Wattle and daub?" asks Grace.

"The very same!" her brother nods.

"What's that?" Callum asks.

"It's how Celts used to build their houses," Adam explains. "It's weatherproof, and you can make it just using things you'll find in the woods. But it'll be a big task and hard work. So we need to get started now. First off, we need lots of long, bendy branches. Gather any you can find, and bring them back here. Go!"

We get to work collecting all the fallen branches we can find, bringing them back to the spot where Callum's shelter will be. Meanwhile, Adam takes some sturdier branches and uses Callum's penknife to sharpen the ends into stakes. Then he drives them into the ground so that they mark out an oblong shape.

"It's not very big in there, is it?" Callum comments.

"Maybe we'll come back tomorrow and build you an ensuite, if you're nice to us!" Adam says. Next he shows us how to weave the longer branches between the stakes to build up the walls.

I find a good branch that seems supple enough to be woven into the wall, and try to dislodge it from the tangled undergrowth of the forest. It feels stuck. I pull all the more determinedly, but to no effect.

"Here," says Adam, appearing beside me. At first I fear he is going to brush me aside, declaring I am too weak for the task and that he will take over. I could not bear the humiliation of that, or

172

the way Callum would crow with triumph at my failings. To my relief, he says, "Let me help you."

Adam takes hold of the branch alongside me and we try to pull it free with our combined strength. It shifts a little, but not much. Adam follows the length of the branch to where it is caught up in a mess of other branches and brambles, all bound together with matted ivy tendrils. He asks me if I have anything we could use to slice through this, and I throw Uncle Ed's knife to him. He cuts through some of these stems close to the ground.

"Let's see if that has made a difference," he says, as we try again. This time the branch breaks free almost instantly. It comes loose so surprisingly quickly that I let go and jump back to make sure I keep my balance. Adam does not, and falls to the floor.

He doesn't seem embarrassed. In fact, he is laughing. The sound rings out between the trees. I'm glad it was he who fell and not me. I don't mean that maliciously – he seems kind – but I couldn't have borne that indignity so lightly.

"Nothing broken," he says, getting to his feet and brushing dead leaves off his clothes, "except this." He passes the branch to me and I take it to where the house will be, and weave it in between the stakes. The wall is growing higher all the time.

The roof is awkward, but we take two tall stakes with forks at the top and drive them in at opposite ends of the hut. Then we balance another branch as the roof beam in the forks.

"OK," says Adam, "time to cheat a bit. We'll use one bit of help from the outside world to fix this roof."

He takes a roll of twine from the rucksack and explains his plan to bind more branches to the roof beam and then to the top of the wall. By now we are searching further and further away for building materials.

"You said it was going to be weatherproof, right?" says Callum. "I reckon there are a lot of gaps in there at the moment."

"That's step two!" Adam announces. "And for this part it's good that we're near the stream, because we're going to need mud."

He stoops down and picks up a handful from a puddle that has not yet dried up from the rain three nights ago. Callum jumps as Adam hurls it past him so that it lands over the woven wall.

"There's your insulation," he says. I copy him, scooping up mud and throwing it so that it sticks to the side of the house. Grace and Callum join in.

"Just picture the face of someone you don't like," Adam says with a wink and a mischievous smile.

"You'll be spoilt for choice," Callum says to me. I don't bother replying to this, but I doubt he will be able to guess whose face I am thinking of. I pour all my energy into the task, and it does seem to help. I feel less anxious or angry, and the hut starts to look sturdier.

"That's a good day's work," says Adam eventually. "Well done, everyone."

As he starts talking Callum through how to build a fire, Grace takes out a bottle of water and pours a little over her hands to wash them, then offers it around to the rest of us.

"I'm starving," says Callum. "Did you bring any more sandwiches?"

"No," says Grace. "We were expecting you to have gone back home by now. And speaking of which, we need to head off soon. It's getting dark. If we raise any suspicion among your neighbours, you could end up in even more trouble."

"At least one of us should be able to come back tomorrow with more supplies," says Adam. "We'll get you some blankets as well as food."

"Fine."

I wish they wouldn't bring food for Callum. So far everything has been quite easy for him, and I think that's why he is being so rude and ungrateful. I'm almost surprised he doesn't put in a specific request for bacon rolls or something else ridiculous like that. Maybe if he were to go twenty-four hours without food or help, he would behave less like he is entitled to everything they give him. But Adam and Grace don't seem even slightly bothered by how he takes what they are doing for granted.

"Do you have the map with you?" Adam asks his sister. Grace takes it out, and as they frown at it I realize they have no idea how to get back to the main path from here.

"I'll show you the way," I offer.

"Thank you. That would be a big help."

"Now remember what I said on the walk over here," Adam says to Callum. "Stay warm and drink plenty. Your body will cope with being a bit hungry, but not with dehydration."

Grace puts the top back on her bottle of water, which is now only half full, and hands it to Callum. We say goodbye to him, and he acts cool about the situation, but clearly he does not look forward to being left alone in the woods. I lead the way, striding back the way we came; behind me, I can hear Adam and Grace following. After a while, I slow down to let them catch up. Now that we are walking level with one another, some kind of conversation is probably necessary. I want to ask why they have come here. I know Grace keeps talking about her research, but I don't see why she had to carry it out in Dyrys, or why her brother needed to come too. But maybe it is rude to ask. I don't know: I was never much good at this sort of thing. The silence is waiting for someone to speak, and I haven't had to bother with this nonsense of civility for ages. Maybe I should express sympathy for Callum, but I doubt I could feign that right now. Eventually it's Adam who speaks.

"Can we trust you not to kill him if he stays out here for a couple of days?"

I laugh at his directness and his mock-seriousness. He isn't a particularly tactful man.

"It'll be hard, but if you really think his life worth sparing, then I suppose so," I respond with a pretend sigh. I think this is the first joke I have exchanged with anyone in a very long time. The novelty of it makes me bolder, and I blurt out the question I have been turning over. "Why did you really come here? Aside from your research, I mean. There's something else, isn't there?"

Adam and Grace exchange glances. I wonder whether that is

175

something siblings can do: communicate without saying anything. Perhaps if Eira and Owen were closer to my age, I would know the answer.

"That's very sharp of you," Grace answers. "We came here to learn more about our father."

"Was he from here?"

"Yes, but he left a long time ago, before you were born."

"He left?" I repeat. I wonder what they mean by that. Did he pack his bags and move to a city one day, or did he run away like me? Now I hope these two do come back tomorrow, because I have more questions I want to ask them.

"It's left here, after that fallen tree," I tell them.

"Left? Good thing you're here to guide us. I could have sworn it was a right," says Adam.

"If you went that way you'd probably end up falling down where the land drops away steeply at Owl's Ledge," I say. Technically, I made up the name Owl's Ledge after I heard a tawny owl near there once, but they don't know that.

"There's nothing we like better than a broken leg to make the afternoon more interesting," he says, and then adds more sincerely, "But thank you for the warning."

I want to laugh at Adam for being so strange and light-hearted about everything, but his eyes look kind, so I can't bring myself to make fun of him. It would feel unjust.

"And here's the path," I announce as we reach it. "Head that way and you'll be out of Dyrys before too long."

"What will you do now?" Grace asks.

"I'll go back and finish my work before it gets dark. I'll see if I need to make any repairs to my house or the fence, and then make some soup."

"What kind of soup?"

"Nettle. It's better than it sounds – it tastes like spinach."

"Impressive stuff. Well, thank you for all your help today. I hope we'll see you again soon."

The politeness makes me uncomfortable, and I don't know what to say, so I just nod and point them in the right direction. They follow the path out of the woods, and I go back to my house.

DYRYS

"So," says Grace, as they reach the edge of Dyrys, "another day that turned out nothing like we expected. I thought this would be a good location for research because it would be quiet and distraction-free!"

"I'm sorry," says Adam. "I've dragged you into helping Callum, and I know we're going against the law in doing that."

"You can't stop yourself, can you?"

Adam sighs. "Anything else seems cruel. He's young, and more scared than he'll admit. And so is Rhiannon, for that matter."

"Fear can make people do terrible things, though. Be careful. You don't know these people. I know you think you do, but we've only been here a few days."

They walk down the hill and cross over the river. Up ahead, the windows are lit up in Ifan and Nia's house.

"What would you advise?" Adam asks.

"I want to tell you to go to the police again. To show them where to find those two so they can arrest Callum and take Rhiannon into foster care for the last two days she's legally a child. It might not do them or anyone else any good, but we'd have done the lawful thing and could leave here with that to reassure ourselves. But I know I can't tell you to do that. I'm not even convinced it would be the right thing. So I'll stick with this: talk to somebody local. In fact, talk to Maebh. She's seen a lot in this village, and she's a good judge of people. She'll know what to do."

In the silence that follows, there hangs a loud but unspoken idea that Maebh will want to avoid repeating what became of Emrys, and that she might know how best to help another runaway.

RHIANNON

I almost hadn't noticed that Lleu was missing earlier. When I return home, he is perched in a tree above my fence, his gold eyes glimmering in the fading light.

"Where were you?" I demand. He gives a cry that is not especially repentant, yet when I reconsider it, I don't mind that much.

I slip through a gap in the boundary and enter my land. By the doorway to my house, I build up the fire and, as the evening chill sets in, I wrap the blanket around my shoulders like a cloak. Today has been a good day.

CHAPTER EIGHT

LLANDYMNA

"I thought I might be seeing you again," Maebh says the following morning, opening the door before Adam has even finished knocking. "Come in. You're just in time to hear the end of Gwern's adventures."

He steps inside. In the living room, three children sit cross-legged on the carpet, eagerly waiting for Maebh to continue the story he has just interrupted. He recognizes one of them as Diana's daughter Eira, and the two boys look older. Adam takes a seat near the door, and Maebh picks up where she left off.

"... And at long last, Gwern came back to the foot of that mountain, and he looked up to his old home, now half destroyed by the fearsome giant. Smoke was still rising from the roof, where the giant had made a campfire out of the thatch and roasted a whole sheep from Gwern's flock for his dinner. But this time Gwern's spirit was not shaken, and he showed no fear. For he looked around him at the friends and allies he had gathered on his many adventures since he first fled from the giant's attack on his home, and he took heart from seeing them beside him.

"To his left stood all of Dyfed's men, ready to repay the debt of gratitude they now owed to Gwern by standing guard and keeping watch on the giant. To his right was Scáthach, the fearsome Irish warrior woman who used to teach fighting until, as you all remember, Gwern broke the magic spell that prevented the chieftains of all the local tribes from agreeing to be at peace with one another.

"'Shall we attack?' asked Scáthach, whose thoughts still went first to warfare. She drew her sword and was ready to start running up the hill. But Gwern stopped her battle charge with a motion of his hand, and told her there was no need for that yet.

"'It is enough, first of all,' he said, 'to see my old home after all this time. Tomorrow we will reclaim it from that giant, but tonight let us rest and regain our strength after the long journey.'

"And so everyone set down their burdens at the foot of the mountain, and lit fires to cook themselves a good hearty meal. They feasted and rested, and Gwern told them stories of what his home had once been like. The fires burned so bright that they caught the attention of the giant, who had been busy whittling arrow heads from the bones of cattle. He had heard rumours of Gwern's adventures, and now that he saw the man not far away, he was afraid. He knew that Gwern was joined this time by Scáthach and Dyfed, and a whole host of men. He had heard it claimed that Gwern had defeated all the chieftains of all the tribes and that this was why they had stopped fighting one another.

"'This Gwern must have become a terrifying warrior since I drove him out of his house,' growled the giant. 'See, he arrives here and doesn't even worry about catching me by surprise. He just camps out in plain sight of me. He must be very strong now, to be so brave.' The giant looked down again to the fires, and saw that Gwern's men did not completely surround the mountain, but were only stationed on one side of it. He saw a chance to outwit Gwern and avoid being defeated by this famous warrior.

"And so, on the next morning, when Gwern climbed the steep slope up to his old home, he found no trace of the giant, except for some very big footprints leading down the other side of the mountain, as if someone very large had run away very quickly in the middle of the night. So Gwern regained his land, and his house and livestock, without shedding a single drop of blood. Dyfed's men put their shoulders to heavy timber and helped him repair his damaged home. And fierce Scáthach saw for the first time what peaceful living looked like, and she thought it a fine thing indeed."

The children let out a sigh, as if they have been collectively holding in breath ever since Maebh first mentioned the giant. Eira smiles with satisfaction at the happy ending.

"Now, let me see the time. I think your parents will be coming to take you home for your dinner soon."

"Is there time to build a castle in the garden first?" asks one of the boys.

"Not this time, Luke. But why don't you draw me your best picture of a castle instead?"

This suggestion seems to satisfy the boy, and the children are kept occupied until their parents arrive minutes later to collect them.

"Do you often look after your neighbours' children?" Adam asks when everyone else has left.

"Some of them come here for a few hours to play in the mornings, or after school. I like having the house full."

Adam realizes it must be very quiet for Maebh on days when no one comes to see her. He moves to the chair nearest her so that they can talk more easily.

"And you're clearly a master storyteller."

"Ha! Some parents don't like me filling their children's heads with fairy tales. People think that stories are a way of escaping reality, but I always say they are a way of making sense of it. In stories, we find space to imagine how we might make our world better, whether it be a more exciting, more hopeful, or more beautiful place. Our stories are a part of us. You can tell a lot about someone from the kind of stories they tell."

"You tell stories that seem fun and fantastical but have lessons hidden in them."

"Very good." Maebh eyes Adam and adds, almost wistfully, "You do look like him."

"It must be as strange for you as it is for us, to learn about the parts of his life we didn't know about before."

Maebh makes a "hmm" noise, but gives no reply to this. This tells Adam enough, and he changes the subject.

"I've come to ask your advice."

"Well, of course you have, young man. Why else would you be here?" Maebh says impatiently.

"You already know about Callum and Ifan's fight, and how Callum has run away rather than face the police on a heightened charge."

"Yes," Maebh says, and she narrows her eyes so that she looks almost birdlike, "and I also know that he is hiding in Dyrys Wood and that you are helping him."

Adam laughs in surprise. "How —"

"I saw you going up to the woods yesterday. I was at the farmhouse with Nia at the time. If you mean to keep on breaking the law, you need to be more careful than that."

"Clearly. Does Nia suspect anything? Grace is going to see her today."

"No, she thinks you were helping Grace with her work."

"Good."

"But let me ask you a question now, Adam. Why exactly are you helping Callum?"

"Why?" Adam sounds surprised again. "Why not?"

Maebh does not accept this as an answer, and leans forward to press the point further. "Are you helping him for his own sake, or is it because of what I told you about your father? I wonder if you will give up and leave as soon as you realize you cannot fix the past. He is not Emrys."

"Nor am I," Adam replies.

She pauses, not used to having her own words turned on her. "I know that."

"And yet you do see him in me," he continues, his voice gentle and his face level with hers, "and I know you also wish you could change the past. We have the same cause now."

Maebh's face looks so sad as she stares back at Adam that he

182

thinks for a moment she may crumble under it all. Then she collects herself and chuckles quietly.

"I think you would make an excellent storyteller too," she says. "So, tell me, what advice do you want about Callum?"

"How would you convince him to come back home?"

"Ah, now there's the question. How indeed, when running away seems like the only option. He is a headstrong boy, and desperate for people to think well of him. That is what has got him into this situation, after all. I think you must either appeal to that side of him, or wait to see if he mellows with time. In the meantime, I have spoken with Ifan. I hope he may decide not to try to blame Callum for his current state. That may take away some of Callum's fear of coming home."

Adam thinks he sees a glimmer of how many worries have been placed at the feet of this woman.

"I saw Rhiannon yesterday," he says.

"You found her?" She looks up at him abruptly.

"She found us, really. I don't know where she's living. But she came and joined us in setting up a shelter for Callum."

"And who have you told about this?"

"Only the police, via Tom, and now you."

Maebh narrows her eyes as she thinks this through. "You've kept it from Diana. I can see why, but that is a hard choice to make."

"I know. I often wonder if we should tell her too. But we've left it to Tom to decide that."

"How is she? Rhiannon, I mean."

"She's surviving very well, I think. She's making her own food, and has some kind of house she's living in."

"She'll have learned all that from Diana's husband, Edwin, I suppose."

"Our dad used to talk about you," says Adam suddenly, and immediately wonders if he should have built up to this more gently.

"Did he?"

"Not by name, but when we were children he told us stories about the quick-witted Sparrow Girl, who ran so fast she seemed to fly, and was the only true friend he knew in this place. She had adventures with the Boy Who Ran, who we finally realized was Dad himself."

Adam thinks it best not to add how Emrys would then always laugh and say that he pitied the man who had the misfortune of such a wife, and how every time he said this he would fail to meet his children's eyes.

"Yes," says Maebh, "that sounds like the stories we used to make up when we were young. But I am sorry that he saw himself only as someone who ran away. He was much more than that."

*

While Adam visits Maebh, Grace goes to the corner shop to find something to take when she visits Nia later today. When she arrives, two middle-aged women are standing outside, talking together like conspirators.

"… always been happy to talk about the news around here, but as soon as it's her son involved, it's not the same," she overhears one of them say.

"I know! And I heard he's on the run from the police now, and no one knows where to find him."

They see Grace watching them, and switch to speaking Welsh. "*Mae'r euog yn ffoi heb neb yn ei erlid!*"

"*Wrth gwrs!*" the other woman nods vigorously.

"Excuse me," says Grace. "Is the shop open today?"

"Yes," says one of the women.

"*Diolch yn fawr.* I thought you might be standing out here because it was closed. *Hwyl!*"

She walks past them into the shop, leaving the two gossiping onlookers to wonder whether or not that is all the Welsh she knows.

Angela Rees looks fraught as she serves customers and tries to avoid talking about yesterday's events. It seems that everyone has assumed she will be the usual source of information about Llandymna's dramas.

"You must be so worried for your boy Callum," the man at the till is saying as Grace enters the shop. "It's very hard for someone as young as him to go to prison."

"I heard Ifan needed major surgery last night," adds the woman queueing behind him, "and that he nearly died. Joan Perry says she thinks they should both be locked up for fighting in the street like that."

Grace selects a packet of biscuits and joins the queue. Angela sends her customers on their way as quickly as possible today, disappointing them with her silence. She does not make eye contact with Grace as she scans the packet and takes a handful of coins from her.

"I'm sorry about your son," says Grace. "I'm sure he didn't intend for any of this to happen."

"Thank you," Angela replies, but she makes no exception for Grace, and hands over her change without another word.

*

"Sorry they're from the shop, but I've never been much good at baking," Grace says as she enters the farmhouse and gives the biscuits to Nia. "I just wanted to come and ask how you are all doing."

"Thank you, that's a lovely thought," Nia smiles. "We're all right today, too. Come in. I'll put the kettle on."

She welcomes Grace inside warmly, but paces to the kitchen with an urgency that suggests she has grown used to rushing around. Her shoulders are hunched as she walks, as if she has been carrying something heavy.

"How is Ifan recovering?"

"Getting better. I wanted to thank you again for your help the other night. The doctors said it could have been much worse if you hadn't been there and known what to do to stop the bleeding. He's not needing quite so much pain relief this afternoon. He's asleep just now I'm afraid, but he'll be glad to know you asked after him."

Grace wonders if this is really true. She and Ifan have hardly exchanged more than a few words since she arrived in the village. Nia continues to rush around the kitchen, turning on the washing machine, putting away a stack of plates, opening a window.

"How can I help?" asks Grace.

Nia looks puzzled by the question. "I – I'm not sure. I think it's all things I need to do."

Her face looks thinner, her eyes greyer, and Grace suspects it is not simply busyness that has brought about this change.

"You don't have to do everything, surely?"

"It's only right, really."

"You don't blame yourself for what happened?" Grace realizes what is driving Nia to work herself so hard. Nia's shoulders drop and she leans on the back of a kitchen chair. Grace stands on the opposite side of the table. Nia looks down as she speaks next.

"I could have stopped it all if I'd only managed to explain what Callum had meant. I knew it wasn't intended for Ifan, but I didn't try hard enough to tell him that when we got back home. And I'm sure part of why Diana's been so sharp lately, with Callum and others, is because I upset her when I gave that interview. There was no need for a fight, but I didn't prevent it like I should have done. I've always been too quiet, but then the one time I speak out, this happens."

Grace sighs to hear what this woman really thinks of herself.

"You know you asked me about our Ghanaian names when we first came here?" she says after a pause.

"Yes," Nia replies, her uncertain tone showing she does not follow the connection here.

"Well, my middle name, Ayawa, is traditionally given to girls born on a Thursday. And Kofi means that Adam was born on a Friday. But there are different traits associated with children born on different days. A bit like the old rhyme 'Monday's child is fair of face'. You know the one? A child born on a Thursday is expected to be observant, a good listener, and quietly analytical. A child born on a Friday is traditionally a natural leader with a good heart."

Nia laughs. "That seems to describe the two of you very well!"

"And our names are a reminder that people are different, with different strengths. I don't believe I am the person I am because of when I was born, but I do know that while my brother is an expert at making friends and bringing out the best in people, I am good at reading situations and taking in information. And those differences between us make us suited to the different work we have chosen. Adam would hate academia, but I could never do what he does either.

"Do you see my point? Our characters are different, but that doesn't make one better than the other. I don't think you should beat yourself up for being someone who is quicker to listen than to speak. And you definitely shouldn't blame yourself if other people don't listen to you properly, which I suspect may be what has happened here."

Nia smiles, for she sees Grace means to be kind, but it is hard to process any thought that goes against all that she has accepted for years to be true.

"If I speak and nobody hears," she replies, "do I blame the whole world's ears, or my one voice?"

RHIANNON

Last night I watched a hedgehog shuffle past my house, its black nose sniffing for the chance of a meal, its spines as sharp as the knife I reached for when I first heard the movement outside. But it wasn't the danger I had imagined. Then, rather than stay awake all night with my heart pounding and my ears alert, for a change I managed to drift back to sleep before I had told myself more than a few lines of a favourite comforting story.

This morning I noticed a gap in the wall, and spent a long time repairing it. I would rather destroy my land than let Callum find it. I'm glad his foot is injured, as it makes it less likely he will wander far enough in this direction to stumble upon the fence, and even if he does, he will surely mistake it for a thicket, as was always my intention. But once I'd used up all the nearby brambles and fallen twigs to rebuild the boundary, I had to travel further to find firewood. So here I am, trampling over the browning undergrowth, with branches bundled under my right arm. Perhaps it is not entirely coincidental when two figures come walking through the wood and catch sight of me. I'm not far from the main path.

"Hello!" Adam calls out to me. "Is Callum still alive?"

"If he isn't, it's no fault of mine," I answer, deciding that if he won't be serious, then neither will I. It's not that his expression gives much away. In fact, if I were to describe only his face now he might sound almost solemn. It's more the way he swings his arms when he walks, and always looks as if he is preparing a joke he wants to tell. Grace walks alongside him, far more collected than her brother, but not in a proud way like Diana, and she looks amused by my retort.

"Shall we go and see if a tree has fallen on him?" asks Adam. I am about to readily agree when I remember why I'm here in the first place. I explain that I have to take the firewood home first, but say that I will meet them afterwards.

I head back to my house, checking over my shoulder a couple of times that I am not being followed. I do like Adam and Grace, but I'm not completely certain yet whether I can trust them. Most of the adults I have met up to now have had their own secret agendas and have feigned friendliness to get what they want, like the way Diana canvasses for support in the village to gain influence. Actually, the young people I've met have been just as bad – it was simply more of a surprise to discover that grown-ups can be petty and hypocritical too.

I put the firewood in a pile just inside my house, where it will stay dry if it rains later today, then grab a handful of hazelnuts to eat on the way back. If we are going to be working hard again, I don't want to be too weak to pull my weight. I find that I'm walking too briskly to eat though, almost breaking into a run. I don't want to miss out on anything interesting.

When I eventually arrive at the shelter we built yesterday, Callum looks tired and miserable from his ordeal of sleeping in the woods. He is wrapped up in a blanket now, watching Adam build a campfire. I feel a pang of jealousy: there was no one to help me when I struggled my way through the first few days in Dyrys.

"What's she doing here?" Callum demands when he sees me.

"We invited her," answers Grace. "You might be able to help us answer a question, Rhiannon. Which is the best way to the stream from here?"

"They're trying to poison me by making me drink muddy water," Callum adds.

"It won't kill you; just boil it first," I say, amazed at how little he knows or is prepared for life in Dyrys. "If you want to avoid the steep drop over Owl's Ledge, where the waterfall is, you need to go that way." I point northward, through a part of the forest that is overgrown with brambles, but the ground is at least flat.

"Great," says Callum. "I guess I'll get lost or eaten by bears every time I want to wash."

"Yeah, you want to watch out for those Great Welsh Bears, mate," says Adam, laughing. "They're infamous around here. Maybe we'd better clear a path for you. Rhiannon, could you show Grace the way to the water, while Callum and I go through the supplies we've brought and check we've got everything he needs?"

"Sure," I say.

"We'll need a couple of sticks for beating down the brambles," says Grace. "Here, this one could do."

I quickly find a long branch that can be used for the task, and we set off towards the stream, flattening nettles as we go.

"Don't you feel guilty, killing all those plants?" I ask.

"A little, but you'd be surprised how quickly they grow back. Come springtime we'll be flooded with green again. What's this in my face? Oh, woodbine. Tread softly, or you'll wake the dormice."

A song thrush is pecking at berries overhead and does not notice us. I pause to watch it for a moment, before hurrying on to catch

189

up with Grace. As she forges on, pulling aside any obstacles that might keep Callum from his water supply, I kick the broken stems out of the way so that the floor of the path will be earthy and even, all the while directing Grace towards the stream. Every now and then she points out something of interest: a patch of woundwort, which was used by healers long ago to treat all sorts of ailments; hemlock growing closer towards the stream, which makes a poison; a blackthorn thicket rich with sturdy branches and deadly sap. I take all of this in; it could save my life one day.

"So all this is part of your research?" I say, wondering what kind of academic knows the folklore of herbs.

"More or less. I study what the landscape used to look like, so I've had to learn to spot the kind of plants that have been native to our countryside for hundreds or thousands of years. These oak trees, for example, may well remember the days of the civil war. And out in the hedgerows of the farms near here, I've found hart's tongue fern and a whole host of other plants that tell me these woods probably once stretched much further than they do now."

"You mean all of Llandymna was once covered in trees?"

"Quite possibly."

I like that thought. I imagine trees filling up the streets of the village, their branches pushing through the concrete and entwining themselves in the buildings, until nature has reclaimed it all.

"You must know a lot about plants too, if you're foraging for your own food," Grace says.

I shrug. "I've picked bits up from my uncle's books. He used to take me and my cousin Eira for walks, before he died."

"I'm sorry," she says. "You must miss him."

I try my best to sound mature and rational as I say, "Can't do much about it, really."

I start to beat the undergrowth around my ankles with renewed energy. This is the sort of work to make your arms ache after a while, but I have spent days hauling firewood around and shaking the branches of trees until they release their crops. If ever I were to be prepared to clear this path, it's now. Sometimes the stems have grown too thick to be broken easily, and then I crouch down and cut through them with my knife. When I get stung on the wrist by a nettle, it only heightens my determination to get rid of them. When I pause I feel calmer and refreshed.

"When all this is done," says Grace, "we'll go back and have something to eat with the others. We've brought a flask to make hot drinks too."

For a moment I am inclined to think her shallow, that she should have something so mundane on her mind when I am sorting through the intricacies of my thoughts, agonizing over deep emotions that require the distraction of hard work to make them bearable. But then something about that simplicity makes me laugh quietly. I find that lunch is a better thought than many of the ones running round my head recently, and I agree with her that this sort of work does make you hungry. I look forward to reaching the stream.

DYRYS

Callum seems glad when the other two return and Adam suggests that they stop for food. His foot is improving from what appears to have been a bruised bone rather than any breakages. Yet he still cannot walk properly. Adam unpacks the food they have brought, while Rhiannon arranges some twigs on the ground.

"What are you doing?"

"It's an arrow, in case you forget where the path is," she says with a mischievous smile.

They set out the food as a picnic between them. Adam and Grace have brought bread and ham, oranges, a cake and some crisps. They also have plastic cups and a flask of tea. Callum helps himself at once, but Rhiannon hangs back and stares at the spread before her. Tentatively, she takes some bread and chews it slowly, as if tasting something new and unfamiliar.

There is a buzzing sound, and Adam takes out his mobile phone and looks at it with surprise. "Interesting," he says, and walks a few paces out of earshot to answer it.

"I miss having a working phone," Callum sighs, counting up the hours since he last had access to technology and the civilized world. Grace passes around drinks, while Rhiannon watches Adam pace up and down the clearing as he talks.

"That was Tom," says Adam, returning to the group. "He had news for you, Callum."

"I thought he was off the case," Grace says.

"He was. But there's not going to be a case any more. Apparently there were witnesses who had seen Ifan begin the fight, and he was facing charges of assault. Someone seems to have advised him that even though he came out the worse for the fight, it would look bad to a jury that he incited it. And so he's decided to drop all charges."

"Convenient," Callum remarks with a tone of scepticism. "So as soon as he thinks he might be in trouble, he stops wanting justice?"

"*Now* you claim to care about justice?" Rhiannon sounds incredulous. "You weren't so much a fan of it when you thought the consequences would apply to you!"

"That wouldn't have been justice. That would have been a one-sided version of events leading to only me being punished."

"I think you're missing the point here," Grace interrupts. "You no longer have any obstacle to going home."

Callum thinks about this a while. "Maybe. So I'm no longer a wanted man. That's good. What about everyone else though – everyone who isn't the police – what are they saying? They're on my side, right?"

The silence that follows this question gives him the answer he does not want.

"Come on, it's not as if I don't have any friends back there!"

"You're right," says Adam at last. "There's been some gossip in the village, because people get excited when life gets dramatic, but it's nothing you can't handle when you go back. Quietly, a lot of people are on your side –"

"They're *quietly* on my side?" exclaims Callum, suddenly angry. "What good is that? I don't need their pity. I need people to speak up for me. Do you know the power of a bit of gossip in a village like ours? Even if the police aren't interested in me any more, if everyone else decides to say I'm to blame, it may as well be true. You don't get it – you aren't from our kind of community."

"Perhaps not," says Adam, "but I do get how these things work. And I know, as I think you do too, that you need to face Ifan, and talk to him, if you want to get on with your life. And I know that once you've done that, it won't matter what your neighbours say about you."

Callum seems to ignore this advice and switches to another strategy. "What about getting someone important to speak up for me? Could you get Diana to say something? Everyone listens to her."

"For one thing, that would be a way of you avoiding the issue," says Adam. "And for another, it sounds like it might be too late for that. Tom said that the decision to drop the charges and end the investigation was announced at a public meeting in the church hall earlier today, and then Diana made a statement denouncing violence and drunkenness in the community. Just because Ifan misunderstood who your outburst was aimed at, I don't think we can assume she did. She's not taking Ifan's side in this, but she's not taking yours either."

Callum nearly explodes with rage at this. "After everything! I ran errands for her. I didn't complain when she sent me on search party after search party for *her*." He nods over at Rhiannon. "I might have lashed out on one occasion, but Diana ridiculed me in front of everyone plenty of times. I wouldn't even be here if it weren't for her. Was she ashamed to be linked with me – was that it? Did it harm her reputation? Or is she just petty enough to hold a grudge over being called a couple of names? That two-faced –"

"I know it seems unfair," says Adam, "but you had the chance to do things the lawful way and go straight to the police after the fight, and you chose to come out here and wait for people to calm down. Your absence is just giving them space to fill in the gaps with their imagination. Come back and show your face, and it will all die down."

"I can't believe she's still making things worse for me," Callum grumbles. "Isn't it enough that she runs the village already? Now she needs to control the lives of people who've left Llandymna too."

"She's a strong character," Adam reasons, "but it's not as if she doesn't think of other people. You can see how much she cares about her children, and she made a real effort to help us make friends when we first arrived; I think she just doesn't realize that other people don't all think the same way as her."

"This is my aunt you're talking about," says Rhiannon, with a slight tone of warning to her voice. They fall silent momentarily.

"I'm sorry. We were forgetting that," says Grace. She catches her brother's eye, and both are thinking the same thing. They have been uncomfortable with the decision not to tell Diana that her niece has been seen, alive and well.

Callum completely misinterprets the glance between the siblings at this remark, and he breaks the silence by taking on a nastily cheerful tone: "Interesting, isn't it, that she hasn't come out here looking for you? I mean, we all know you're here, and so do the police – they've searched the woods a few times for you, haven't they? And yet Diana's just sitting at home, looking after her own children and hardly caring whether you come back or not."

"Callum, there's no need for that." Adam and Grace try to silence him, but he ignores them. He has lost his friends, his home and his life in one blow and now he despises this stuck-up little girl pretending to be independent from all the world.

"I bet you thought you were making a big statement, running away from home, didn't you? I bet you thought we'd all be devastated and not give up until you were found and brought back. And you know what? No one even talks about you any more. It's like you've just been forgotten. Even by Maebh." He cannot deny his glee as she repeats this name in shock.

"Maebh?"

"Yes, I thought that was very strange. I mean, she was like a grandmother to you, and yet it seems she didn't really care what happened to you once you were gone."

"Callum, that's enough," says Adam. Callum looks taken aback by Adam's tone. He falls silent, but too late. The girl in front of him is ashen. She stands, open-mouthed, taking in all these things. Then she gives a thin, empty smile to everyone, and with near-perfect composure turns from them and walks away.

Adam shakes his head in utter disbelief. "Why did you have to say that?" he demands.

Callum shrugs. "The truth hurts, doesn't it?"

"I don't know how much of that you made up, and how much is true, but either way she didn't need to hear it all now."

"Took her down a few pegs though. You can't deny she needed that."

"You're very quick to decide what other people need."

"I've known her my whole life. She's always thought she was too good for Llandymna and the rest of us."

"You know how angry you were at Diana for only seeing the immature teenager she thinks you still are? That's exactly what you're doing right now to Rhiannon."

Callum gives a snort and pulls a face at Adam to show he thinks he is overreacting. Grace joins in on a different note.

"Look, if you aren't going home today, do you really expect us to stay here and keep bringing you food every day? We'll be going back to our own lives sooner or later, but Rhiannon is the one staying. She's your best chance of surviving out here."

"I don't need her help."

To Callum's annoyance and surprise, Grace laughs at him. "And you accuse her of pride!"

"What do you want from me?" he asks angrily, aware that in earning the disapproval of these two he has crossed the only people likely to help him survive or return home on his own terms.

"Apologize to her," says Adam.

Callum searches his face hopefully for some sign that this is a joke, but he is disappointed.

RHIANNON

I think I kept running until I fell into the stream, but I don't remember very clearly. I know my hair was blowing in front of my face, and that is why I didn't see the bank in time. By the time I realized I had lost my footing and was sliding downward, it was too late to stop, so I accepted that I was already falling and waited for my arms and legs to collide with the muddy ground and freezing water. I know I sat there for some time before I could make myself get up. The water ran around my ankles and knees, soaking through my clothes. When I eventually clambered up, the wet material clung to my legs and made walking slower.

Now I stand in the clearing, an open space in the forest that feels so dense and suffocating today. I turn around slowly. The trees encircling me seem further away than before. I take a few deep breaths to calm myself, and try to think clearly. Though Callum only said a few words, there is so much meaning for me to make sense of now, to compound in my mind and understand how my view of the world and my birthplace has changed, and will be different forever. I hold the wooden stick I used to beat down brambles earlier: it is now a staff in my hands.

I start at the beginning of this new information. *Diana has forgotten me.* I swing the staff to the right and then in a loop over my head. The weight of it in my hands is something real to hold on to while my mind races in these mad directions.

Maebh no longer thinks of me. I can hear the rush of air as the wood sweeps past. It is swifter than the silent wingbeat of any hawk. I might be holding the staff too tightly now: my palms will probably be red raw and marked later.

They are all glad that I left. I am spinning around, faster and faster, and the wild speed lends something to the way I feel, a kind of mad rage perhaps. The trees are a brown blur, with some green clinging on into autumn, but mostly now the world is copper and crimson. As I spin, the bright burning colours merge so that it is as if I am surrounded by a circle of fire. I see at once when this space is invaded. I know a shape that should not be there stands before the trees. I stop abruptly, my eyes blazing in anger at this trespass. Callum doesn't take the glare as a hint to leave.

"Go away," I say simply and coldly. Still he doesn't move. Is he really so wooden-skulled? Has he come to taunt me some more?

"I've been told to speak to you," he says uncomfortably. He looks down at his feet.

"Well, I don't want to listen."

His sullenness turns quickly to a pointed jibe. "Still running away, then?"

"No," I snap. "I'm warning you, go away."

He feigns fear and looks at me condescendingly. Why won't he go? Fed up with not being taken seriously in my demand that he leave, angry at the mocking smirk on his stupid face, I bring the staff around and hit him heavily on the shoulder. He jumps back and clutches the top of his arm.

"You hit me!" he exclaims indignantly.

"And yet it seems I really don't care," I reply coolly, coming to my senses a little more now. Callum, on the other hand, looks shocked and furious. He takes out a knife, presumably the one he used on Ifan.

"Seriously?" I say, trying to look unimpressed rather than afraid. "Is that your answer to everything? You've taken out your temper on me and now, rather than back down, you're going to stab me. Is that it?"

As I say it I realize that if Callum really did want to attack me right now, there is no one to stop him but me. If I shouted loudly enough, perhaps Adam and Grace would come running this way, but would they get here in time to stop him killing me? Not that I believe that is really what he plans to do, but it's frightening to think how easy it would be if he did.

"Nah," says Callum, throwing down the knife. "I don't fight girls."

I am relieved and insulted all at once. As fear gives way to indignation, I find myself sweeping the staff around a second time, and knocking him sharply in the stomach. Why did I do that? A moment ago I was worried he was going to kill me; now I am trying to goad him into a fight. I think I want him to stop seeing me as the old Rhiannon, the angry teenager with a grudge against everyone.

"What was that for?" he cries, and tries to grab the staff from me. He fails, as I jump back out of the way, so he reaches for another fallen branch about the same size, which he holds up defensively, to block any further hits I might try.

We face each other, and I size up whether I could win in a fight now. He will be stronger than me, without a doubt, but I am probably faster and more agile. Could that be enough?

"Did you mean it all?" Since we are here and currently not fighting one another, I may as well ask the burning question.

"What if I did?" He gives a retort rather than an actual answer. "Bothers you, does it, knowing your plan to make everyone miss you failed?"

"You don't know anything about my plans."

"I know by the state of you that they aren't working out so well," he says. So now he's resorting to insulting the way I look. I should not be surprised.

"When you've lasted more than a month on your own, then you can talk to me," I say, "but I reckon you'll have used up your last breath whining about how you miss takeaway pizza long before then."

198

He looks put out by this, and I use the distraction to try to knock his staff out of his hands. But he spots it just in time, tightens his hold and blocks it. As I guessed, he is stronger than me, and I leap to one side before I can be pushed back.

Now he has had the same idea of disarming me, and he aims for my arms. I block and jump out of the way again.

"Why don't you get that pet bird of yours to rip my eyes out?" he jeers.

"I think he's happier just watching from that tree behind you."

Callum doesn't fight the impulse to look around quickly enough. While his head is turned, I whirl the staff around and knock his feet out from under him. He hits the ground with a heavy thud.

"Look," I say, standing over him, with the end of the staff jabbing at his throat, "you may have strength on your side, but I will always be quicker, and I know these woods better. If you ever try anything against me, even something like stealing food from me, I will have a hundred ways of getting you back. Do you understand?"

"I understand," he says, holding his hands up. "Truce?"

I nod. "Truce."

I take a step back and he scrambles to his feet. We have reached an impasse. No one is hurt, or likely to be.

"Is it true, then?" I ask.

"What?"

"Are they glad I left?"

Now that he is obliged to live and let live, he thinks more carefully about how to answer, and reluctantly mumbles, "Not as much as I said."

"And Maebh?"

"I don't know, to be honest. I haven't seen her in a long time. But she was the one who suggested you might come here when we were first searching for you."

"So you were part of the search party?"

He begrudgingly allows me this truth rather than deny it. I suspect this is as close as Callum can ever get to apologizing to someone. I want to laugh – not out of scorn, but at the sight of his face: he looks as if he would have preferred to lose a real fight than be put through this. It occurs to me that he can't possibly have volunteered to back down. So someone else must have told him to apologize. Either Adam or Grace stood up for me. For me!

"I was probably a bit harsh in saying you were guaranteed to die out here, too," I say, looking away as I make this admission.

"Not overly though," says Callum. "I'm not really cut out for this kind of thing. If there was anywhere else I could hide out, I would. But at least with you I know you aren't going back into Llandymna any time soon to tell them where I am."

"Believe me, it would take a lot more than the thought of getting you in trouble to make me want to ever go back there. And it's not so bad, looking after yourself out here. It's a good time of year for finding food. You'll survive."

"Of course I will," he snaps, determined suddenly that he will not have my sympathy. "I can look after myself."

"Then you'd better get back and make sure that roof is secure. Those clouds are coming in fast, and that means we'll have rain before it gets dark."

He is glad to be given an excuse to leave after the awkwardness of being civil to me, and hurries away in approximately the right direction.

It looks as though we have agreed not to be enemies, for the sake of convenience if nothing else. I doubt we will ever be friends, but it's something at least. I have no friends here, unless Lleu can be counted, and I seem to see him less and less all the time. He has flown down from his perch to sit on my shoulder, and is trying to rip my hair out with his beak right now. But Adam and Grace must have taken my side instead of Callum's! Even as I think of this, a smile grows on my face. Lleu flies away, flustered, when I start walking too fast for him to keep his balance.

They took my side, they took my side; they agree with me; they think I am not in the wrong. They told Callum to do something about it!

I pass the boundary and see that it is broken again, despite all my work this morning. I should be annoyed, but I don't care. I walk straight past it and head for my house. In the doorway is the pile of firewood where I left it earlier. I had almost forgotten that today is my last day of being seventeen: of being counted as a child. From tomorrow I am anyone's equal.

CHAPTER NINE

RHIANNON

I have been awake for what feels like hours. It's cold even wrapped up inside the sleeping bag, and my back aches. Every time I turn to try to get comfortable, there seems to be a stone or knot of hard ground digging into my shoulder blades. I curl up with the blanket drawn around me and through the doorway watch the sky slowly lighten beyond the tops of the trees. As it turns first grey and then gold with the slow sunrise, I find myself humming "Happy birthday to me".

I am eighteen, but this is not the start to my adult life I ever imagined. It prompts me to think further ahead than I have done for a while. I've been so focused on what I will need to survive the coming winter, I've barely considered what I will do after that, with all the years that will follow. I find that I can't imagine them at all. *Long is the day and long is the night, and long is the waiting of Arawn.*

I get up and wash my hair in the stream, then wring out as much of the water as I can, twisting it tightly so that drops rain back down. I have no brush, so I scrape my fingers through the worst of the tangles and then plait it as tightly as possible to keep it away from my face. That will have to do. It's not as if I was ever going to have a big party today with lots of friends: I am not Diana. It will soon be her birthday too, and I was supposed to be helping set up for that. She will have to find someone else to make centrepieces for the tables.

This morning I will go and pick elderberries for my breakfast.

Later, I will treat myself to one of the tins of soup I took from Diana's house. It is my birthday, after all.

Lleu swoops into the clearing just in front of my house and alights in front of me. He gives me his usual expectant stare.

"I don't suppose you've come to wish me *penblwydd hapus*, have you?" I say. The hawk starts towards me, expecting me to offer my arm as a perch, but I shake my head and stay put.

"Not today," I tell Lleu. I am probably imagining the indignant look in his eyes as he alights in a nearby tree instead.

I might try to avoid Callum for a day or two, after our fight. I know we reached a kind of agreement in the end, but I still feel like keeping some distance between us, in case he is still angry with me. I will quickly go to say hello to Adam and Grace when they come to the woods today, but then I will come back to my house.

It is late morning when I hear voices in the distance to tell me that they must be here. I go to the road, followed at a distance by Lleu, where I find Grace and Callum talking, but there is no sign of Adam. Grace is holding a shoebox. I hesitate, seeing that Callum is there, but Grace has already spotted me.

"Morning," she says. "This is for you." She hands me the box, but I do not understand.

"What is it?"

"A birthday present," she says. Has she bought me shoes for my birthday? My current pair may be caked in mud, but they are still in one piece and it had not occurred to me to replace them. I was planning to go barefoot next summer when the ground is dry. Grace continues, "It isn't the most conventional of gifts, but I hope you'll find everything in there useful."

I lift the lid. The box is crammed full: I can see plasters and bandages, dried food packets, a ball of string, a box of matches, and that is just the top layer. Further down, a brand new pair of socks sits half hidden under a bar of chocolate.

"Thank you," I say.

"Adam is on his way. He had some things to pick up. Oh, there he is." Grace points as Adam comes marching up the path. Over his shoulder he carries a piece of timber a little less than a metre long, and a length of rope coiled around his arm.

"Right," he says, not stopping as he reaches us, "come on. This way!"

"What's happening?" Callum asks, but Grace does not explain. My plan of returning to the mill evaporates as curiosity takes over. I glance over my shoulder to where the hawk sits watching. Lleu makes no move towards us, and somehow I know he will not come wherever we are going. With a last look back to the sparrowhawk, I turn my attention to the group. Bewildered, we all follow Adam further into the woods, until he stops at Owl's Ledge. This is where the stream becomes a waterfall, pouring over the drop in the land. I am always afraid of coming this way at night, in case I lose my way and tumble down over the edge. But in daylight this place is incredible. The water is so clear, and after it has hurtled over the rocks, it becomes tranquil again so that you can see the trees reflected in the stream.

"Come and give me a hand here, Callum," says Adam. He picks a beech tree near the water and starts to climb up it.

"I still don't get what's going on," Callum protests as he stands at the foot of the tree. I glance over to Grace to see if she looks concerned. She seems to be the one who keeps Adam in check. She is smiling, so I think that means everything is under control. When she starts to look worried, I will know there's a problem. I try to guess what they are planning: something useful for Callum, no doubt. Perhaps a pulley system for collecting water, or a trap for hunting small animals.

"Simple," says Adam, pulling himself up onto a higher branch. "While we've been helping you out here, we've sorted out the essentials – food, shelter, water, warmth – but we forgot one very important thing. Throw me that rope, would you?"

He is sitting on a branch hanging over the stream, his legs dangling in the air above us. Callum tries to throw the rope up to him, but it falls far too short. The second time, he throws it higher and Adam catches it. He ties one end of the rope around the branch.

"This here's a bowline knot," he says. "Should be strong enough to hold."

"So what did you forget?" Callum asks.

Adam slides back down to the ground and takes up the piece of wood. It has a piece chipped out of the middle, so that when he ties the rope around it, it does not slide to either end, but holds. He pulls sharply on it to test its strength.

"That even when things are bad, there's still room for some fun," he says. "So, who wants the first turn?"

He has built a tree swing. My first thought on seeing it is that we will have to take the whole thing down before the end of the day, otherwise someone might see it and it could lead to further search parties in the woods. I'm always so careful not to leave anything behind when I'm outside of my little portion of land, in case it gives away my location.

"Go on then," says Grace, seeing that Callum and I have not moved. To my surprise, she takes a run up to the swing seat and launches over the water. It's strange to see her behaving like this when I always think of her as the sensible one next to her brother.

Callum seems to accept the idea of the tree swing very quickly, and as soon as Grace jumps down, he declares it is his turn. I am becoming more and more uneasy though. What if I fall off? What if I am not even tall enough to reach the swing seat in the first place? The trouble with situations that are supposed to be fun is that there is a high risk of everyone laughing at you. I think of all the practical things I need to be doing today: gathering food and firewood, washing and drying out some clothes, repairing the boundary to my land where it is starting to fall in on the north side.

Then a picture pops into my head, of my mum and Diana when they were younger. Faced with a situation like this, Diana would be the one to react like I am now, and Elin would already be laughing and shrieking as she flew out across the stream, trying to see how

206

high the swing would go. I have never thought that I had anything in common with my aunt: I always assumed she disliked me so much because I reminded her of her sister. I have certainly never wanted to be like Diana. Well, if Elin would have chosen to have fun, then so will I.

"Rhiannon?" Grace looks over to me when it is my turn on the swing. I can already see Callum opening his mouth to tell her that there is no way I will appreciate something that isn't meant to be taken seriously, but I march past him and take hold of the rope. Adam holds it steady for me as I jump up onto the wooden seat, and then I kick back against the ground and am propelled forwards. I had forgotten how much this feels like flying! The air rushes past my face as I am suspended above the stream. If I fell now, it would be straight into the water. My feet almost touch the branches of the trees on the opposite bank before I start swinging backwards. I hear a voice ring out with loud laughter, filling Owl's Ledge with the sound. A second later, I realize that I am the one laughing.

"OK, I'm going to go for a proper run-up," says Adam when his turn comes around. He pulls the swing back as far as it will go. "Did anyone ever figure out, as a kid, if it's possible to swing all the way around the top of a tree if you go high enough?"

I smile to remember it: that was what I always used to try to do. I think there was a swing in the back garden when I was younger. I made it quite high, too.

"No," says Callum, "but one time I tried to kick the top of a tree in front of the swing, and my shoe flew off into the next garden! I had to hobble over there in one trainer to collect it."

Adam begins his run and jumps out across the stream at high speed. We shout encouragement from the bank. He makes it across the water, and the rope is close to horizontal before he loses momentum and starts falling back.

"Not quite high enough," Adam says, smiling as he jumps to the ground.

Next, Callum decides he will try standing on the swing seat.

Halfway across, he nearly lets go of the rope, and struggles to regain his balance. He laughs as he wobbles and almost falls into the stream, which seems to make it fine for the rest of us to laugh too.

I wish I had a camera and could keep a picture of this: everything, from the sunlight glinting on the waterfall, to the childlike fun we are having under the autumn-coloured trees, is just perfect. I wonder if Adam and Grace meant for this to be their real birthday present to me. As if guessing what I'm thinking, Adam hands the swing over to Grace and comes to stand next to the rest of us, and as he does he says, "Happy birthday."

"Thanks," I say. "It's a much better birthday than I could have imagined."

And I make a promise to myself that even though I don't have a camera, I am going to capture this moment in my memory and never forget it.

PART THREE

BOOK

CHAPTER ONE

LLANDYMNA

The church hall has been booked for months in advance. Diana's birthday party will be all that anyone might expect it to be: meticulously organized, thoughtfully detailed, and implicitly compulsory. Two days before the event, Adam and Grace find they have been delegated tasks along with the rest of the village.

"It's a compliment, if you can believe it," says Tom, who has come to the cottage to bring them their instructions. "It means she wants you to feel like you belong here."

"I don't know the first thing about table centrepieces," says Grace from behind her pile of books.

"Well, I guess she interpreted the fact that your research involves looking at plants as basically meaning you arrange flowers for a living."

"If anyone wants a vase full of hemlock and acorns, I can certainly oblige."

"Always good to have an excuse for a party, though," says Adam. "I don't mind helping set up the room, if you let me know what time to get there."

Tom thanks them for being so gracious about the fact that he has just turned up at the cottage with these instructions from Diana. He half turns to leave, and then lingers in the hallway.

"Actually, there was something else I wanted to talk to you about," he says. Grace motions for him to sit down.

"Callum?" asks Adam.

Tom nods. "I'm assuming you passed on the message that he wasn't going to be prosecuted over the fight with Ifan?"

"I did."

"Well then, I don't understand why he hasn't come back."

"You and me both!" Adam mutters, then adds, "Sorry, that's not helpful. Callum seems worried that even without legal consequences, there might still be trouble waiting for him if he comes back to Llandymna at the moment. He takes the opinion of his neighbours very seriously."

"What does he think will happen? That we'll form an angry mob with pitchforks and flaming torches, and chase him down?" Tom exclaims crossly.

Adam and Grace exchange a look across the room. Evidently Tom does not know his village's history, or he might think that scenario less improbable.

"There has been a fair bit of gossip," Grace points out.

"But that won't amount to anything real. What if I went and talked to him? You still know where he is, right?"

"We do," says Adam, "and I think it might be a good idea for you to speak to Callum. You might have more success than we have in convincing him to come back. But at the moment he may not want to see any of his old friends."

"Why not?"

"He's angry. He feels… well… let down by all of us for not speaking up for him more."

Tom looks away.

"It'll pass," says Grace. "Give it time."

They invite Tom to stay for dinner, but he declines and instead makes his way back into the village. He finds himself outside a house he has not visited since the day Rhiannon disappeared. Maebh does not ask him why he has come; she simply invites him in.

"I'm sorry it's been a while since I've come to see you."

Maebh does not seem to consider the apology necessary, as she offers him every kind of biscuit and cake in her house.

"I wanted to speak to you," he says. These are words she has not heard from Tom since he was much younger, and she grants him her complete attention now.

"What is it?" she says, taking on the grandmotherly tone she once used in talking to this young man, and still uses with all the children.

"You always seemed to think well of me, to see some promise in me, when I was younger," he says, "even when others didn't. You encouraged them to trust me and listen to me, and I wanted to thank you for that now."

Surprised and smiling, Maebh answers, "Why would I not have told people to pay attention to you? You always had a wise head on those shoulders. It was clear when you were a child that behind the serious face there was a lot of thinking happening."

"I know that I started trusting my own head above anything else after a while," he replies, "and I'm wondering now if I've really reached the right answers. I don't know who else to tell this to, but I think I made a mistake letting Callum get away."

"Do you, now?" Maebh says, interested.

"I meant to protect a friend, but now he isn't coming back, and I've just learned tonight that he blames me for not speaking up for him sooner. I thought that by just doing nothing I could help, but I don't know any more. And I wonder about Rhiannon too: if I should have done something sooner; if intervening after the incident at the school would have kept her here."

"You've been doing a lot of thinking, it seems," Maebh remarks, "but the question is, what are you going to do now?"

"Nothing, really," says Tom. "They're gone, and neither wants to be reached, and I don't see what I can do without making things worse."

Maebh looks disappointed. "Thomas Davies," she says, "you are a policeman. If anyone has the authority to take action and sort this mess out, surely it is you. There are a thousand things you might do. You could have a message delivered to Callum, as it sounds like you know how to reach him now. You could tell Diana her niece is alive."

Tom starts. "You know about Rhiannon?"

"I do. And I hope you haven't been keeping her situation a secret simply to make life easier for yourself. You are a thoughtful, sensible young man, and there are much bolder characters than you in this village. But you cannot avoid the difficulty they may bring you, if it means being unkind to them."

Tom pulls a perplexed face and stares at the wall as he contemplates this. Maebh sighs with exasperation.

"I shall have to take matters into my own hands at this rate."

"I thought you already had," says Tom, snapping his attention back to her. "Don't think for a second that I believe Ifan was persuaded to drop all the charges against Callum purely because I made a case for it to him! Nia told me you went over there."

Maebh pulls a face. "Someone has to sort this village out."

RHIANNON

It may be cold, but the sun shines on the forest, or at least the part where we are sitting. We all agreed that it was time to break from work and have something to eat. Grace has been teaching me to recognize more plants today, and now she points to a clump of tall pink flowers.

"That's rosebay willowherb. It's also called fireweed, because after a forest fire it's the first thing to grow back."

I prefer the name fireweed. I like the idea of this resilient plant bouncing back from disaster with swathes of bright flowers.

"Is it edible?"

"Yes, but it'll taste bitter. I think if you peel off the outside of the stem, the inside is good. Not that I've ever tried it, of course. This is all just from research reading."

"I'll stick to sandwiches, thanks," says Callum through a mouthful of cheese and ham.

Callum and I never speak of how we fought: it would mean

admitting a degree of defeat on both sides, and we have no intention of becoming friends enough to do that, though I think Callum is a little less intolerable now. Every day Grace teaches me about new plants that are good for curing illnesses or eating, and Adam tells us that we work harder than most adults. I'm not used to trusting compliments, but he always makes such an effort to find something good in everything that I find myself walking home a little taller at the end of each day.

Grace starts telling us about the plans for Diana's birthday party. Callum looks resentful at the mere mention of Diana, and I think I would have reacted the same way back in the summer. But somehow I can bear to hear her talked about these days. Perhaps it is just good to be talking with anybody at all.

"We've all been roped in to help with the day."

"I bet she won't let Nia be part of it though," says Callum.

"Even Nia," says Grace.

Callum splutters and almost chokes. "So Diana forgave *her*, but not me?" he says, indignant enough to stop eating for a moment. "Besides, what on earth would Nia ever add to a party?"

He casts a look at me as he says this, presumably because he knows that Nia and I were sort of friends before I left. I decide to confuse him by saying nothing. A squirrel bounds past and leaps up a tree, chattering crossly at us. I watch it intently, deliberately not turning back to Callum.

"So you agree," he says, drawing whatever support he can from my silence, "that Nia is just about the most boring person in Llandymna, and that her whole nervous and feeble act just makes people feel like they can't have any fun around her in case they step on her and she breaks?"

Slowly, I turn back towards him. "Not at all," I say. "I think she's far more considerate than most of us, and that no one ever really gives her a chance to say what she thinks. She might be interesting, if you bothered to listen to her. But that's beside the point, because really I think you're only goading me into criticizing her because you'd like to feel that everything that has happened to you is unfair, and having a go at someone else is the only way you know how to stop blaming yourself."

The stunned silence only lasts as long as Adam is able to hold back his laughter. I turn sharply towards him, but his face says that he is not laughing at me.

"I think she's got you there, mate," Adam says. Callum scowls.

I watch as a small flock of sparrows lands not far from us and starts pecking at the crumbs we have left from our lunch. I used to think they were horrible drab little things and prefer majestic birds of prey like Lleu, whom I have not seen since the day we went to Owl's Ledge. I don't know exactly why, but his absence doesn't surprise or worry me very much. I think I always knew he would leave eventually.

"I think I've come to like sparrows," I say out loud. Adam tears off a small chunk of bread and starts throwing pieces to them.

"Why's that?" he asks, keeping his voice low so as not to scare them away.

"They're friendlier than hawks, even if they're a bit scruffier too. And they're brave, when you consider how small they are. I think that's better than being imposing and elegant like a hawk."

One sparrow ventures so close to me in its quest for food that I could probably reach out and pick it up if I wanted to, but I leave it alone. When they fly away, I feel disappointed.

"Maebh used to tell these stories," I go on to explain. "She still does, I guess, about the Sparrow Girl and the Boy Who Shone. I didn't understand before, why she called her the Sparrow Girl. But I think she wanted us to see what was important about the character."

"What did you say was the name of the other one?" Grace asks.

"The Boy Who Shone. Why?"

"Nothing. It just reminded me of a story our dad used to tell. But the name of that character was different."

"What was it?"

"The Boy Who Ran."

I feel there is something important in her words, if I could just fit all the pieces together.

"Can I borrow a knife from one of you?" asks Adam.

"Here, take mine," says Callum. "Might as well put it to some better use."

Adam takes a stick and cuts a small part off so that he has a lump of wood not much bigger than a two pound coin. With Callum's penknife he starts to cut away at it, carving something small. I wonder if this is another survival mechanism, or just idling away the time.

"Can I ask you something?" I say to Adam and Grace.

"Of course," Grace answers.

"You said that your dad used to live in Llandymna, but he left. Did he decide to move to another village, or did he run away?"

Adam pauses in whittling the piece of wood.

"He ran away," says Grace.

I wonder why I never knew his story. Llandymna is a quiet place, or so I thought; I would have expected the gossips to thrive off the legend of a man who ran away. Why do we not have stories of the Boy Who Ran, like the ones Adam and Grace grew up hearing?

"Did he come out this way too?"

"Perhaps. He told us stories, long ago, of sheltering under bridges and in ruins, and of making his way through a vast forest. It would make sense for him to have come this way at some point."

Sheltering in ruins. But I have only come across one ruin in all my time out here. Surely she does not mean my house? Then I remember something that has sat untouched since the day I found it.

"Did he lose something while he was out here?"

"What do you mean?"

"A pocket watch – did he ever mention one?"

"D'you know, he did talk about that, yes," says Adam. "He inherited a watch from his grandfather and carried it everywhere with him when he was younger." He frowns. "But how did you know that?"

I jump to my feet. "I'll be back as soon as I can," I say, and start to run towards my house. If the watch is their father's, that must mean he was the one who sheltered there before me, the last runaway to hide in the abandoned mill house. I race along the path that only I know, and push aside the ivy tendrils concealing the way to my land. The watch is still lying in a corner of the house, behind my dried food rations. I pick it up and run all the way back to the clearing where the others are.

I am slightly breathless, but able to say "here" and thrust the watch towards them. Grace takes it from me and turns it over to examine, before passing it on to her brother. Adam tests the weight of the watch in his hands, and then stares at it.

"Do you think it's his?" I ask them.

"It has the right initials engraved," Grace replies. "R. T. – that could be Robert Trewent, his grandfather. But where did you find it?"

I wonder what to tell them so that I don't give away the location of my house.

"It was when you mentioned ruins," I say. "There are some in the woods, where I found that when I first came out here. I always wondered who it belonged to."

"A ruin?" Grace sounds interested. "I'd like to see that, as much for my research into this area as anything else. Could you show me?"

"Maybe one day." I give a non-committal answer. Adam still hasn't taken his eyes off the watch. He seems to be drinking in every detail, taking in all the scratches that speak of its history. I suppose if someone brought me something that belonged to my mother, I would be the same. Grace leans over his shoulder to take another look.

"I'm pretty sure it was his," she says.

"Thank you," says Adam. His voice is controlled yet somehow emotional too. I feel brighter at the thought that I made this moment happen.

"Does it still work?" asks Callum.

"Let's find out," Adam replies, winding the dial and listening out for the ticking sound. "There we go, like new! I'll set it to the right time."

It takes him a minute to open the watch up, but he manages it in spite of the object's age. The watch face is intact, with Roman numerals all around its edge, and two hands currently pointing in the wrong directions.

"It must be getting late now, and weren't you supposed to go with Tom to collect some equipment for the party?" says Grace. It is days away, and Diana already has them running her errands.

"So I was," says Adam, rising to his feet and groaning like an old man as he does. We say our goodbyes, and as soon as Adam and Grace have gone, Callum and I also part ways.

"Right then," he says, "I should go too."

"Yes, and me."

We have little to say to one another when there is no other company present, and we seem to have both silently acknowledged this, so we never seek one another out when the other two are away. I go back to my house empty-handed.

It is peaceful here. Leaves that have come loose drift lightly, catching occasional shafts of sunlight, which cause their colours to shine brilliantly for a few seconds before they fall to the floor. The oak trees all around blaze orange, clutching rich heavy handfuls of acorns. I stand at the doorway of my house and imagine a young Emrys here, seeking refuge in the woods.

I don't know what kind of man he was, but I know that we are from the same place, and that we both ran away, so I feel I have something in common with this stranger. I wonder why he left and if he ever wanted to come back. I wonder why I have never heard of him. Surely Maebh would have remembered something like that, and told his story to us? I picture him as fairly young, maybe Callum's age, sitting beside the stream and watching the squirrels chase one another up a tree, while he whittles a piece of wood in the way that Adam did this afternoon.

I sit down in the doorway and look out towards the trees. *Well,* I think, *you and me and Callum – we've got a lot in common really. All of us runaways – all of us ending up in these woods.*

And then, because not many people know what it is truly like to live alone in a wild place, I stay sitting here for some time in silence, while the oak leaves drift and settle all around.

CHAPTER TWO

LLANDYMNA

Ifan sits up and looks outside. It is an overcast day, the sort he hates. But he has decided that this will be the day he gets out of bed. He suspects that he should have gone back to work sooner, but that the combined insistence of his worrying wife and the power of his painkillers to make him drowsy have prevented this.

When he stays still like this he can barely feel his wound with its careful stitches. Instinctively, he prods at it and immediately feels the twinge of agony that tells him he did not dream the whole episode. The pain is proof that all is not right with the world, and Ifan has no intention of letting go of that reminder.

While he is in pain, he can remember, instead of falling into the fog brought about by the drugs. And he wants to remember every detail: the fight, the sight of the knife in Callum's hand, the news that his attacker had run away, the police's failure to catch him, and his so-called friends' betrayal in pressuring him to drop the charges. He needs a clear head to process all this.

Ifan has always considered himself an honest, hardworking sort of man. He has been on the farm all his life, first helping his father and then taking it on with his wife and a few extra workers. He has never had the opportunity to be lazy or to cheat, because you cannot cheat the land or the elements, who are his bosses. Either you work hard or you fail. In return, Ifan has never asked for much, no special treatment or awards, but he has assumed a certain level of respect from his neighbours. Yet when it really matters, the people around him have turned their backs. The police have been nothing short of useless; his friends have mumbled platitudes but done little to help. And now that he has dropped the charges against Callum, he fears what others may be saying.

He shifts his weight so that his arms support him as he swings his legs off the bed and his feet touch the floor. So far, Nia has helped him walk everywhere, but he does not call her this time. He pushes himself up from the bed. As he does, the area around his stitches flares with pain, but Ifan straightens up and waits for the feeling to subside. He will not be beaten by this. He moves to the wardrobe and picks out some clothes to change into. Dressing takes a long time, because it hurts with every stretch to reach a button or pull on a sock. Eventually Ifan stands, looking like himself again. He checks his reflection in the mirror. Now he does not look like a victim any more.

The door swings open and Nia enters carrying a tray.

"I brought you some soup – oh, you're up! And dressed."

"I've been in bed long enough," Ifan tells her.

"Are you sure? The nurse will be here to change the dressing later today. I'm sure she'll say you should still be resting."

"Nothing good ever came from sitting around doing nothing," Ifan mutters as he pushes past her and marches downstairs, leaving her still holding the tray.

RHIANNON

I have been laughing all day – we all have. I sit cross-legged and look up, noticing that the fallen leaves mean I can now see more of the sky. This is what freedom is: not the space around you or no rules restricting you; it is being able to throw back your head and laugh out of happiness, and not worry about what anyone else thinks. Grace has built a small fire at the centre of the clearing so that we can stay here and be warm rather than trouble with the walk to

Callum's shelter. I extend my arms towards it and warm the palms of my hands against its quiet crackling, entranced by the sparks that drift upward and then transform, mid-air, into grey ash. Adam is carving something out of a small piece of wood again. It's starting to take shape and I think it might be some kind of bird. I wonder if it will be Lleu. I haven't seen him since my birthday, though I thought once I saw the shape of a hawk flying away between the trees. But I knew he wouldn't stay forever.

"You know, I think you may have started a new trend in leaving the village," jokes Callum.

"If anyone else leaves, it will make more sense to move those remaining into the forest and send the runaways back to the village, where there is more room!" I say. I glance over to Adam and Grace. I know that their father ran away, but so far they have said nothing more about him, and I think it best not to ask. If they ever want to explain, I expect they will.

"But you could go back," says Callum. "I can't."

"What makes you think I can go back?" I ask, knowing not to argue with him over whether he can return. We have all given up on that by now. Callum clearly hates living out in the woods: he complains constantly of being cold, hungry, and uncomfortable, but none of that is enough to drive him back to Llandymna.

"You never injured anybody."

I have been thinking this over for a couple of days, but only now do I feel ready to articulate it. "Not like you did, no. But I was unkind to a lot of people. I feel sick just thinking about some of the things I said."

"People can forgive each other far worse things," says Grace. I expected a sterner response, something that affirmed just how much I have to regret. When I lived in Llandymna, I used to swoop in on people's imperfections and rail against them. I wanted everything to be better than what I saw around me, but I must have been unbearable company because of it. No one here reprimands me for it though. Perhaps they sense I need no further rebuke to wish I could change the past. Perhaps even this revelation is their doing.

With Grace's gentleness and Adam's unshakable good cheer, these two balance one another out. There is something about them that I find hard to express. It's the effect of their company. Being around them seems to make Callum calmer and more considerate towards others, a definite improvement in my opinion. And I find that when they are in the forest, I feel able to face what lies outside my fairy tales. I feel maybe there's some good for me to do in the real world after all. Yet they seem completely unaware of what they're doing every time they come and spend an hour or two with us. It's as if their ordinary lives simply happen to dispense goodness to the people they encounter, and none of it is deliberate or premeditated. That's how I shall describe them: accidentally wonderful.

As I think over what Callum has just said, I realize that technically it is true. On any given morning, I could wake up and resolve that this is the day on which I shall make the walk up the hill and go back to the people I left. I wouldn't have to fear the same kind of punishment that might face Callum if he were to attempt the same thing. And yet there would be some kind of retribution waiting for me as I faced those people again, and I fear it would be humiliating. Some days I wonder if I would like to go back: to be among friends and family again; to make amends for some of the cruel and childish things I said when I was last there; to see if I could repair some of the relationships I left behind. At other times I think that life is much simpler here, and more beautiful in some ways. Often the truth is that I do not know if I would be able to find the strength to leave the simplicity of a solitary life for all the complexities of community, where apologizing and considering the feelings of others would be necessary. I wonder if I could be trusted to do what's right in those surroundings.

"I brought some coffee for us to brew, but it looks like we're out of water," says Grace, checking the bottles. "Callum, can you pass me the flask from my rucksack over there? There might be some left in there."

Callum reaches into the bag and pulls out a metal flask. He shakes it close to his ear.

"Sounds empty to me. Here, you check it." He throws the flask, but misses his aim and hits Adam instead. "Woah! That went wrong."

The impact causes Adam's hand to slip, and he draws the knife across his palm instead of the small wooden animal he has been carving. He closes his hand into a fist, but not quickly enough to stop the rest of us seeing the dark red line of blood.

"Let me see that," says Grace.

"It's fine," Adam insists as she examines the cut. He is as off-hand and careless as people always think they should be about this sort of thing, but I know that even a small scratch can get infected and become more serious.

"You ought to do something about that," I say.

"No need," he assures me.

"Grace, will you please tell him?" I ask, trying not to sound annoyed or impatient.

"It's quite deep, and the knife wasn't clean. You should at least wash it. Except, of course, we've just established there's no water left."

Adam groans at the thought of walking all the way back to the stream by Callum's shelter, or making the treacherous climb down Owl's Ledge. Callum looks at me, hoping that I will be either horrified or disgusted by the sight of blood. Obviously, I am not.

"Something like plantain would be good too," Grace adds, "for cleaning the wound so it doesn't get infected."

"I know where we can find some," I say suddenly, "and it's right next to the stream."

For an instant I wonder if I should regret saying this, but we seem to be already walking, quite quickly, towards my land, with me leading the way.

"Sorry about that," says Callum, as he strides alongside the others.

Adam shakes his head. "Don't beat yourself up about it," he says. Here we are, at one of the gaps in the boundary.

"There's no way through," says Callum. "Can we go around?"

"The plantain's the other side of these brambles," I say, "and there are ways in, if you know where to look."

I go to one of the gaps and pull back a curtain of ivy that conceals the entrance. I cross through first, and they follow, turning sideways to fit through the space.

"Perfect," says Grace, seeing the stream before us flanked by shallower banks than elsewhere in the wood. Adam washes the cut in the stream until any traces of rust or splinters from the knife are gone. I point Grace towards the clump of plantain next to my house, and she picks a handful of the leaves.

"Do you need anything else?" I ask.

"A bowl – and do you have any bandages left in the box I brought you?"

"There's still one," I say, and I go to fetch it, along with my cooking pan, which will hopefully do in place of a bowl. Grace starts to crush up the leaves in the pan, mixing them with her hands until they form a paste. She then gets Adam to apply it to the wound, and winds the bandage over the top.

"This will help it heal faster," she says. Sometimes I think Grace would be much better at living my life than I am.

"Is that your house?" asks Callum, pointing past me to the ruins of the old mill house. A pile of firewood sits by the doorway. My staff leans against the wall. It looks almost homely. I nod, and he looks impressed.

"Was it there when you arrived?"

"No, the sparrows built it for me," I say solemnly. It takes him a moment to be certain that I am joking.

"A house in the forest," Grace murmurs. She and Adam both stare at my house as if it is something out of a dream: familiar and yet impossible. They must have made the connection that this is the place where I found Emrys's lost pocket watch.

They are here. There are people sitting by the stream, commenting on my house. It's strange that I don't mind as much as I thought I would. After all, the whole point of the fence was to keep the world away from me. But lately I haven't worried so much about checking it for damage and repairing the gaps. Most of the people in the woods these days don't mean me any harm.

I watch as Callum stands behind Adam and visibly debates with himself over whether or not to push him into the water. He is just about to, when Adam moves aside, completely oblivious to the scheming that has taken place, and Callum has to leap forwards to avoid hitting the water. As I laugh at him, Adam seems to be looking at me seriously.

"How did you get those marks on your arm?" he asks quietly, so that Callum, still staggering to regain his balance, does not overhear. I have to look down to see what he means. The remains of claw marks criss-cross over my skin, leaving thin pink lines that I have neglected to bandage lately. I have managed very well so far in ensuring that nobody notices the cuts, and had even forgotten them myself until now. I expect it is my own fault for turning his thoughts towards injuries of various kinds. I explain that the scratches are due to Lleu, but they are healing well now that he has disappeared. Adam nods, accepting this answer almost entirely.

I feel I ought to fetch my guests something to eat, so I run into my house and put together a selection of what I have, which feels meagre now that I have to put it in front of friends. Yet when I emerge and offer them crab apples and hazelnuts they thank me as heartily as if I had cooked a Sunday roast for them. Even Callum seems appreciative. I think the realization that he was wrong to throw the flask has silenced his usual sarcasm.

"What's the time?" asks Grace. "We need to be back by three to help Tom and the others start setting up the church hall."

"Of course," says Adam. "Only a day to go until the big event now." He takes out the pocket watch and checks it. It is just after two o'clock.

227

"Is that Diana's birthday you're talking about?" asks Callum.

"Yes," says Adam. He seems reluctant to put away the watch, as if it might not stay in his pocket if he lets it out of his sight.

"Do you miss him?" I ask.

"Who?"

"Your dad," I say, with a nod to the watch.

"Yes," he replies. "Reckon I will for a long time too."

"Some days are easier than others," Grace adds.

"Like you think you're doing fine for a while, but then sometimes it hits you again, and you wonder if you were just so distracted that you forgot to feel sad?" I say.

"Yes, exactly like that," says Grace.

"I think it takes longer than anyone realizes, to be OK again after you lose someone," I say, "and everyone stops asking how you are or thinking that you might still be grieving long before you stop."

"I think you are probably right," says Grace.

"Do you still miss your mother?" asks Adam. Grace gives him a sharp look, the only time I have ever seen that kind of exchange between them, as if she thinks he is being insensitive. But the truth is, I am glad to be asked this question. Most people are too afraid of the answer. Of course, now I have to decide what to say. Should I reassure them that it is all right; that I am never sad about this any more? Should I smile graciously, in the way that admirably tragic women always do when they are reminded of loss? I almost wish I were able to, but if these people are half as accepting as I think they are, then I need to respond more honestly.

"Yes," I say, with neither false lightness nor melodramatic gloom. "Not every day. I was very young at the time."

I suddenly realize that I want to tell somebody what I can remember. It is a story I have never told before, because of course I grew up surrounded by people who already knew it. Diana was there, at the funeral and the aftermath, and she did not need to hear my version of events. But maybe it's because I have never told this story that I have spent years replacing it with others.

And so I tell them what happened. I tell them what I remember of Elin Morgan: her smiling face and the voice that used to sing to me. I tell them about the night my mum went out when she thought I was asleep, and how later my aunt and uncle came over and told me I was going to have to stay with them for a while, and how I overheard them arguing in the kitchen about what exactly they were going to tell me about where my mother was. Uncle Ed had wanted to tell me the truth, as kindly as possible. Diana had thought there was no way a child my age could understand or deal with that.

I do not cry as I speak. It has been more than ten years, and though I am aware of the absence of someone who really ought to be here, I am also conscious that I have grown used to this being the way things are. Diana became my guardian after that. Now that I think about it, I see just how young my aunt was back then, and what a responsibility must have fallen on her shoulders that day. Did it frighten her, the prospect of raising her sister's child?

"I've never talked so much about what happened," I admit.

"Then it's an honour to hear it," says Adam. I acknowledge that I have made everyone's mood very serious. Even Callum does not make any jokes at my expense. They don't say anything sympathetic either, as people normally would in this situation, but I am actually glad they do not. I would not know how to answer, and their listening has been kindness enough.

"You mentioned that Ifan was better?" I say, deciding it is my responsibility to change the subject.

"Yes," says Grace slowly. "The wound wasn't so bad after all. He seems to have returned to his old temperament."

I smile, knowing that Grace means the injury and the fight have done nothing to ease Ifan's fiery pride. Then I think of Nia, and my amusement fades. She will bear the worst of his temper, I'm sure.

CHAPTER THREE

RHIANNON

Adam and Grace arrive early the next day, because they need to be back in the village to help get ready for Diana's party. They bring the usual supplies for Callum, and when I hear them on the path I go to join them. This is my favourite part of the day. The time I spend alone feels dull, even when I spend it on vital things like gathering food and firewood.

However, when we find Callum today, he isn't impatiently awaiting the arrival of his first meal of the day. He is packing everything he has into a bundle.

"What's going on?" asks Adam.

"Good, you're here," says Callum. "I can say goodbye then."

"Are you going somewhere?"

"Yes, away from here," he says, and then launches into a speech that sounds rehearsed. "I've realized that even if I can't go back to Llandymna, the police aren't looking for me any more, so there's no reason why I shouldn't go somewhere else and start a new life."

"Right." Adam puts down the bag of food he has brought for Callum. "So what's the plan?"

Callum looks taken off guard by this question. "I thought I'd hike south for a bit until I get to another town – one where I won't bump into anyone I know. Then, uh, I'll get a job, find somewhere to stay, and forget I was ever here."

I wonder if Callum has really thought this through. I doubt it.

"You realize you might need to shave or shower before anyone will offer you a job, right?" I say.

"And what about your family?" says Grace. "Will you say goodbye to your mother before you go?"

Callum falters. I guess he planned to leave without saying anything to Angie.

"Here's a thought," Adam adds. "If you're set on going somewhere new, let us drive you there, rather than walking. Come back into the village, say your goodbyes to everyone, explain all this to your mum, pick up some fresh clothes and any money or documents you need to start fresh, and then we'll take you to a town and get you booked into a bed and breakfast until you can find your own place."

"That's a good plan, and I wish I could," Callum answers, "but I can't risk showing my face in Llandymna."

"Why? What are you afraid of?" Adam sounds incredulous as he blurts out the question. And I have to say, I think his plan sounds much better than Callum's, but I never expected him to agree to it.

"I'm not afraid of anything," Callum snaps back, and for a moment I think he and Adam are about to start shouting at one another.

"All right," says Grace, "point taken. Let's have something to eat together before you go then."

She starts to unpack the bag, and we all sit down on the forest floor together, Callum still shooting glares towards Adam for his accusation. Grace hands out plastic mugs and then pours tomato soup from a flask into each one. We all fall quiet for a while as we drink, no one looking particularly happy.

"You know," Grace says after a pause, "you were asking about our dad yesterday, Rhiannon. Do you know why he left Llandymna?"

"No," I say, thinking: *How could I possibly know this?* But then it occurs to me that in a village where everyone knows one another, perhaps the fact that no one has ever told me is the real mystery.

"Maebh told us that no one talks about him these days. But he ran away because he was wrongly accused of a crime."

"Just like me then," Callum mutters.

232

"Except that in your case, you did actually stab someone," I point out. Sometimes I think Callum is starting to behave like an adult, but then he says something self-pitying again and I wonder how long it takes a person to really change.

"Thanks for that reminder," he says crossly.

"He never came back, but he never put Llandymna behind him either. How could he, when there was so much left unresolved here? He missed his old friends, even if they were very few, and he felt the sting of never having reconciled with the people he left behind. At the very end, when he was too weak to travel, we found out how much he regretted it. Callum, I'm saying this because I don't think you fully understand the implications of your plan. Adam and I have done a lot to help you, but I think you should go back home now."

"Look, I appreciate you passing on your dad's wisdom or whatever, but this is different. I can't go back."

"It's your best chance of surviving once these two have left," I say. "You're not exactly self-sufficient here, and I don't think you're going to land on your feet anywhere else immediately. When Adam and Grace leave, you'll need to be at home or you're going to starve to death."

"Actually, Rhiannon," Grace continues, "I was about to say the same thing to you. I know you don't want to hear it, and you're very capable of looking after yourself, but I think you need to go back and face your friends and family again."

"And why exactly do I *need* to do that?" I ask. I feel torn, between the strong loyalty I feel towards my friends and my instinct to defend myself against any attempt to send me back to Llandymna. Everything in me hates the tone I am using towards Grace right now, but I cannot make sense of her suggestion. Doesn't she understand how awful it was – both my behaviour to others and theirs to me? Does she think everyone will have forgotten and welcome me with open arms? It would take something more than a cautionary tale about her father to make me willing to face what waits for me in Llandymna.

"The thing about running away is you won't actually escape

anything," says Adam, "but ultimately it's up to you. If you're going to leave, Callum, we'd like you to do it as properly as possible."

"What d'you mean?" Callum cannot object to what sounds like it might be a supportive remark.

"You'll need things to start out in a new place: ID and paperwork, for example. So you can get a job and somewhere to live. Those are all at your house, right?"

"Yeah, but I can't go and get them. Can you go for me?"

"You want us to go to your mum's house, tell her that we know where you are and that you're leaving for a new start somewhere else, but that you won't come and tell her yourself, and then ask her to hand over all your belongings to us?"

"Well, I know it sounds bad if you say it like that, but yes."

Adam and Grace look unconvinced, but they say that they will think on it and come back with an answer after the party. Then they pack up and return to the village to celebrate Diana's birthday. I half entertain the thought of sending them back with a message for my aunt, but then I realize I'm not ready for the consequences of doing that. They leave, and I wonder if this is the last time the four of us will all be together; if by the time they return Callum will have gone for good.

I sit beside the stream, my bare feet in the water, mud curling away from them as the little current cleanses my skin. Callum is on the opposite bank, sorting through a handful of small stones and throwing them into the water one at a time.

"Can you believe them?" he asks.

"You can't blame them for trying," I say. "From a practical perspective, they're right. It would make sense to go back, especially before winter. I don't know what I'm going to do for food once the harvest dries up."

"I guess there won't be much on the trees soon, right?"

"Exactly."

"Still, I can't go back. I'll wait to see if they come back later with the stuff, and then I'm going, either way."

It is strange to think that Callum will be leaving. I can't say I've exactly grown to like him, but I have become used to him being here.

"What if they don't come back?"

"Then I'll need you to say goodbye to them from me. And thank them for everything. I wouldn't have managed without their help."

"They're good people," I say. "It's a shame to think that if their dad hadn't been driven out, they might have been born in Llandymna and then we would have known them all our lives. I wonder if things would have been different then."

"Different how?"

"They're so... so reassuring. They make you feel as though you're doing OK at life rather than falling flat on your face all the time, which is what Diana seems to think."

"Don't feel bad. She doesn't reserve that just for you."

"It's like they look at someone and see everything about them, understand them, but then choose only to talk about the very best side of that person. I wonder how you learn that, or if it's something you're just born with."

"I've said it before, Rhiannon, but you think way too deeply. It's what makes you so angry all the time."

I don't resent this comment any less than before. "As opposed to someone who doesn't dare look below the surface, because it complicates life too much?" I retort.

He doesn't snap back. After a pause he says, "You were right, in what you said about Nia the other day." I am glad to be sitting down, or I might have keeled over in surprise at hearing those words escape his lips. "She's only ever been kind to me. She's like Tom – she thinks before she speaks. I know I don't do that."

I have nothing insightful to say, so I respond with, "Really?"

"And if I'm honest, I hate that. I remember when we were younger, when we used to go to Maebh's after school and listen to her stories, she would always single Tom and Nia out for being thoughtful, while I'd be starting a fight with one of the other kids in the corner and arguing over whose dad was tougher."

I suddenly feel pity for Callum, the boy who grew up copying Ifan and hoping to be admired for his efforts.

"It's not as if Nia and Tom have all the good qualities and you have none," I say. The kindness feels a little stilted in my throat, but hopefully it doesn't sound that way. "I heard you apologize to Adam yesterday for what happened to his hand. Someone like Ifan would have been much too proud to do that."

"Living in the forest does strange things to people, doesn't it?" he says, and I think that for the first time he may be acknowledging that we have both been changed by our time in Dyrys. I think about how differently I view others now, about how much less Callum and I both find to resent in other people these days.

Maybe it is the fact that we are finally agreeing on something, or maybe the peculiarity of our situation, but our eyes meet and we both start to laugh together. It is strange, this shared moment of incredulity and mirth – perhaps a reaction to the underlying worry of what will become of us next.

LLANDYMNA

Diana stops on her way to the party to collect some cakes that Maebh has baked for the occasion. She does not want to risk not having all the food ready at the start of the event. She brings Eira and Owen in with her, and sends them into the front room while she and Maebh go to the kitchen, where lemon drizzle slices and shortbread are cooling on wire racks, halfway to being packed into their boxes and tins. Diana sighs as she sees that Maebh is not ready for her yet, and rolls up her sleeves to help get everything prepared.

"And I hope you'll be coming to the party too," she says, prising the lid off an old tin.

"Of course I will, dear," says Maebh. "It's a special occasion."

"Oh, it's just a little get-together, really. I'm so touched at how much effort everyone has put in."

Maebh gives a wry smile, knowing full well that everyone has worked exactly as hard as Diana has instructed.

"Well, dear," she says, "you work hard for this village, and I'm sure people are looking forward to thanking you for all your efforts."

Diana looks gratified, and Maebh sees she has articulated exactly what Diana was hoping the party would represent. But Maebh has another agenda today, so she continues, "And you know, I've been thinking about all the things that might drive a person to work as hard as you do."

"There's no mystery to it," Diana says, going to the kitchen drawers to look for a utensil to help her lift the smaller cakes. "It's for the good of Llandymna and its people."

"Of course. But I know that a lot of people who work like you do would be motivated by something else." She pauses, easing the lid off one of the tins where it had stuck tight, and then looks back up at Diana. "Maybe the idea that they could forget what hurts them if they keep busy enough. Or that by doing enough good, they would be making amends for something else."

Diana selects a cake slice and returns to the kitchen table, but now she looks uneasy. "I don't know what you're talking about."

"You do, my dear, or you wouldn't have just used that tone with me. And I think, if you're honest, you want to talk about it to someone."

"What do you know?" Diana asks, her voice now quivering with a blend of fearfulness and anger.

"Only that you've been carrying a lot of guilt around on those shoulders of yours for a long time now."

"Maybe," she says, and keeps her eyes fixed on the task in front of her. "But I can't talk about it."

"Well, not talking about it hasn't done you much good so far, has it? Why not try another option?"

"You do know, don't you?"

"Try me," says Maebh. Diana checks the children are occupied in the front room before she puts the cakes aside and faces Maebh. She looks frightened and relieved all at once as she takes a deep breath.

"The night Elin left – for the last time –" her voice wavers, "it was my fault."

"Go on."

"I'd thought when she came home pregnant that would be it – that having a baby would force her to calm down, to start thinking about the consequences of her actions. And for a while I think it did help. She stayed, after all, and took care of Rhiannon. But then her old ways started creeping back in. She'd leave the child with me and go out all night. She'd leave Llandymna and not tell anyone where she was going. And I wanted her to understand that people were going to get hurt if she carried on.

"So one night, I told her about what happened when she was four years old, when she wandered off one night and everyone thought she was lost. How that man Emrys was blamed. Yes, I'd known about that for a long time, even if I was too young when it happened to remember it. When you're a quiet, serious child, adults forget themselves in front of you. They discuss things they don't mean to, let you overhear secrets before they even remember you're in the room.

"I told her it was her fault that man was beaten and attacked and driven away. That he was probably dead now because she had been too self-involved to think about anything except what she wanted to do. I thought if I could just shock her enough, she'd stop and actually listen to me.

"I shocked her all right. She went white as a sheet. She didn't say anything. She just picked up her keys from the table and walked, like she was in a trance or something, past me and out of the house.

"That was the night she crashed the car. I've pictured her a thousand times, driving out into the night under the burden of all I said, too distraught to pay attention to the road. And I – I'm almost certain that if I hadn't said all of that, she would never have lost control of the car. She'd still be here." She buries her head in her hands, instinctively trying to conceal the pained expression on her face.

"Diana, my dear, you can never know what was going through your sister's head at that moment. You can't be sure of that."

Diana looks up. "Not being sure is somehow just as bad as knowing. I keep thinking, what would people say if they knew the truth? It isn't easy to keep a secret for ten years, but I can't seem to do enough good to insure against the backlash."

Tears stream down her face, and Maebh remembers how uncertain Diana was as a child, always desperately trying to do the right thing, reading every situation to find out what was expected of her.

"But that's the awful thing about not knowing everything, isn't it? I try not to think about that poor man Emrys. Because what if he really did die all because Elin wandered off? And then there's –" she exhales and steadies herself to say what follows – "there's Rhiannon. What if something similar has become of her? She always had so much of her mother's character – the daydreaming, the stubbornness."

"Elin was a dreamer, and she made many mistakes with bad consequences, but what happened to Emrys was not her fault. Emrys was driven out by people who were frightened into cruelty. And he did not die that night."

"How do you know this? Have you heard from him since? I thought he vanished without a trace."

"He did, but two weeks ago his children returned to the village."

"What? Who? Wait, two weeks ago… Not Adam and Grace?"

Maebh nods. "No one else in the village knows who they really are."

Diana gasps. "They must be so angry with us all!"

"I think they are able to forgive the people who hurt their father."

Diana sits and reconsiders everything she knows about these two visitors to her village. She goes through each interaction she has had with them and realizes that all this time they have been showing even more kindness and grace to the people of Llandymna than she ever understood.

"I recruited them to help with setting up for the party," she remembers with a groan, "and they never complained once."

"There is more," Maebh continues. "Something I know Tom Davies is actually coming to tell you later, but given our conversation I think you need to know now."

"It's about Rhiannon, isn't it?" Diana tightens her grip on the arm of the chair.

"She is alive."

Diana exhales a breath she feels as though she has been holding for a long time.

"She is living in Dyrys, a long way into the forest where the police search parties could not find her. But Adam and Grace have been helping her."

"And Callum? Is he there too?"

"Yes."

"All this time. Why didn't they tell me before? Don't answer that – I imagine I'm the villain in all this, aren't I? The cruel aunt whose niece runs away from home. Do you think they would take me to her? Do you think she would want to see me if I went?"

"I do not know."

Diana stands up. "Then I have to find out. What's the time? Oh goodness, the party's due to start soon! At least that will make it easy to find the others. Maebh, can I drive you to the church hall?"

"Thank you, my dear. I would be glad not to walk."

Eira is delighted that Maebh is coming with them. They pile into the car with more chaos than usual, due to the excitement of the party.

"Do you like my dress? It's swooshy," she says, demonstrating by trying her best to twirl as Diana fastens her seatbelt.

"Eira *cariad*, that's not helpful," her mother reasons. It is a short drive to the church hall from the house, but easier than walking with two small children and an elderly woman.

"Are you going to find Rhiannon?" Eira asks suddenly. Diana stops so abruptly she almost hits her head on the car roof.

"What makes you say that?"

"I heard you and Maebh say that she's in the woods. Are you going to see her?"

If there were one thing Diana did not want, it was for her children to be dragged through the turmoil of what is unfolding today, and yet she is suddenly reminded of how she too as a child used to sit quietly and listen to the adults, so that she always understood more than they realized.

"Yes, I am. Now I don't want you to worry about any of it. We're going to go and play at the party, and Maebh is going to look after you while I go and see if I can find Rhiannon."

Eira smiles and nods, as if this makes complete sense to her.

"I'm not worried, Mummy. I'll be like the fox on the bridge."

"The what?" Diana wonders what her daughter has imagined up this time. Maebh looks pleased.

"Maebh told me about him. There's this little fox, and he wants to be at home with his family instead of lost in the snow, and there's a magic bridge, and he has to tell someone what he's worried about. And then suddenly he's not worried any more. So me and Owen can be like the fox and the fawn, and then we won't be scared of anything."

Diana looks at her children in amazement, then turns back to Maebh.

"Never underestimate the power of stories," the old woman says with a shrug.

They pull up outside the hall, and as they do, a teenager loitering on the steps outside runs into the building with a shout of "She's here!" There is a scuffle of chairs and bodies rearranging themselves inside, and as the group enter the hall they are greeted with a cheer.

The hall is decorated beautifully, with pots of lavender on every table, while bunting and fairy lights hang from the ceiling. A banner wishing Diana happy birthday hangs over a raised platform intended to work as a stage for speeches.

"You two stay with Maebh now. Mummy has to go and have boring conversations with grown-ups," Diana tells her children, as she scans the room for the people she needs to find. Crossing the hall is difficult, as every one of her guests approaches with cards, gifts or an inquiry as to when she will be making a speech. She makes her way to the far side in a whirlwind of platitudes.

"Thank you... So kind of you... So glad you could come... How is your husband now?... I'm just so touched that everyone has gone to so much effort... Would you excuse me?... There's something I need to see to first."

She selects a side table to hold all the cards and presents she has received so far, and then finds Grace making some final adjustments to the layout of the buffet table.

"Happy birthday, Diana. Thank you for inviting us to your party."

"Is it true?" Diana asks. "Do you know where Rhiannon is?"

Grace's whole expression changes. For a moment she looks troubled and then turns solemn as she answers, "Yes."

She waves to Adam urgently as he walks past with folding chairs under his arms, and he stops.

"What's this?" he asks.

"Diana knows that we've seen Rhiannon," Grace updates him, before turning back to Diana. "I'm sorry we didn't tell you. We've done what we thought was best for her, but –"

"Yes, never mind that. Can you take me to her?"

"Um, yes. At least, we can take you to the part of the woods where she is. But we wouldn't be able to make her come out of hiding to meet us if she didn't want to."

"Of course," Diana nods, "and she may not want to see me. Perhaps if we were accompanied by someone she would talk to..."

Adam and Grace look on in bewilderment as Diana considers her options, rules out Maebh as not being sufficiently mobile to make the journey out into Dyrys, and fixes on her best chance.

"Do you know where I can find Nia?"

They direct her to the little kitchenette, separated from the hall by a hatch that is currently lowered so that food can be prepared out of sight. Diana finds Nia opening the oven door and releasing a mushroom cloud of steam into the room. She removes two trays of quiche and then turns around to spot Diana.

"Oh! I didn't realize you were there. I'm sorry – the food's almost ready to come out. It's taking a bit longer to prepare than I expected."

She looks around frantically at the trays set out on the counters and counts them again. She starts muttering under her breath about timings for the oven. Diana is tempted for a moment to step in and help Nia work out her timetable properly, but stops herself.

"There's no hurry. I wasn't coming to chase the catering. I have something else to ask of you. But before that, I need to apologize first."

"You – you do?" Nia stops and looks puzzled.

"Yes," Diana says firmly, determined not to be talked out of her resolve now. "I have behaved very badly towards you. As my daughter wisely says, grown-ups are not supposed to be rude to each other, but I have been unkind to you. I even tried to blame you, and the interview you gave, for the fact that Rhiannon hasn't come home. I never really believed you had anything to do with it; I just wanted someone else to point the finger at. I know you only did what you thought was best for her."

"I don't know what to say." Nia leans back against the kitchen counter, now looking shell-shocked.

"I hope that you won't hold it against me –" Diana is trying hard not to revert to her usual brisk tone, even though anything gentler feels unnatural – "because I need to ask for your help again. You see, I know where Rhiannon is."

"You do?"

"Yes. Or rather, Adam and Grace have found her. They have agreed to take me to her. But I'm afraid she won't want to talk to me. I hoped you might come with me, so that there's a friendly face for her."

"Of course, anything I can do to help!" Nia cries. "When are you going?"

"As soon as possible. It's terrible timing, but I'm going to have to try to slip away from the party without offending anyone."

"Is she nearby?"

"Yes. She's in the woods. So here's the plan: I'll go out and show my face quickly, then when people are occupied with eating, I'll come and find you, and we can leave while no one is watching."

Diana leaves Nia to finish putting food on trays as she goes out to mingle with guests, though her mind is not on the party. She is quickly ambushed by Joan Perry and Elsie Jones, who want to update her on their respective families.

"Diana, I've just seen Eira playing over in the corner. Hasn't she grown? She reminds me of my brother's youngest, you know – they're about the same age. Of course, I only get to see pictures of her that he emails over from Vancouver."

"Of course," Diana smiles, and takes her cue perfectly, "and how are your brother and his family? Are they preparing for another severe winter?"

"Oh, they're well, thank you," Elsie answers with delight, "though you know Sara was ill for so much of the summer that he had to look after the children himself!"

Elsie seems to be blaming her sister-in-law Sara for being selfish enough to fall ill during the school holidays, but Diana is only half paying attention.

As the clamour for food sets in, she catches Nia's eye and gives a nod. Nia, Adam, and Grace gather by the side door of the hall.

"So what's the plan?" asks Grace.

"We can leave now and no one will notice. If you two can get us as close as possible to where you think Rhiannon will be, then Nia can talk to her first. If nothing else, I just want to see her, to know that she is all right."

"OK," says Adam, "there are a few places in the woods we can

244

try: there's a clearing where we've met before, or where Callum's staying –"

"You're going to find Callum?" exclaims another voice. The four of them look around to see Ifan standing nearby. "Good, I'll come with you. I want to have a word with him."

"Ifan, please –" Nia begins.

"Look, clearly you all know where he is. You've been hiding him, haven't you? Is that what the four of you have been scheming about all evening? I've seen you all talking together in a huddle. That boy nearly killed me and he thinks he can get away with it. Tell me where he is!"

"Ifan," Diana reasons, "you already dropped all charges against him. Even if anyone tells you where he is, what do you suppose the police are going to do about it? Leave him be."

Ifan snorts. "As if they would do anything either way! You have to take care of these things yourself. My father and his brothers, they never called the police to fix any of their quarrels. They resolved things properly."

"Ifan, we are not going to tell you where Callum is, especially if you're planning a rematch against him," Adam says firmly.

"You've already told me he's in the woods. That's a good enough start for now," Ifan says, and he strides over to a table where Simon and other local farm workers have started to eat. They watch as he gestures wildly with his arms while addressing them. His friends' faces start out puzzled, but then one man stands up abruptly.

"Oh no," says Nia, "he's gathering a search party!"

"Well, now we can't go to find Rhiannon," whispers Grace, "or he might follow us."

"Not if you have a head start," says Adam. "I can delay them while you find her and then warn Callum that Ifan is looking for him."

"I'll help you," says Diana, to everyone else's surprise.

"But I thought you wanted to see Rhiannon?" says Grace.

"I do. But I don't want that man anywhere near my niece while he's in such a state. Nor do I want Callum to get hurt – the boy seems to keep on paying for his stupidity and it needs to stop. I can use my influence here far more than I would be any help in the woods. Nia and Grace, warn them to hide. I don't know what exactly Ifan is capable of when he's this angry."

Nia gives a look that suggests she might have some idea, and agrees to the new plan. Adam and Diana block the doorway behind them as Nia and Grace slip outside.

Ifan's raised voice has drawn some attention now, and Tom walks over to see what the matter is. "Everything all right here?" he asks.

"Tom Davies, I'd like to report the whereabouts of a wanted criminal – not that you'll do anything about it, as usual."

"Go on."

"Callum is in the woods. We're going to find him for you!"

"Ifan, you can't just take the law into your own hands. Tell me what you know, and the police will take care of it."

"Like you did when he got away before? No, I think it's time we actually got something done around here."

There is a general rumble of laughter and agreement from the farmhands and friends of Ifan gathered around him. Others, particularly the families who have come to celebrate Diana's birthday, look disapproving and uneasy at the disturbance taking place.

Diana marches up to join the conversation.

"Ifan, that's a police officer you are talking to, and don't forget it!" she snaps, like a parent irritated by a child's bad behaviour. "Besides, you're making a scene. I invited you here as my guest."

"She's got a point," says Ifan. "I guess we'll take this outside then."

He starts walking towards the door and then falters for just a split second, turning back with his own invitation to his friends: "So who's coming with me?"

Tom ignores Ifan and addresses the others, sensing that there is more hope of reasoning with them. "Stay where you are," he warns them. "If you go with him, I won't be able to protect you from the consequences."

"Consequences?" Ifan repeats. "Where were your precious consequences when I was being sewn back together in hospital? Or when you had the opportunity to arrest Callum in the first place?"

Ifan's furious speech seems to draw others in, and though a few men stay seated in response to Tom's plea, several get up and follow Ifan to the door. As they reach it, Adam steps forward. At first they think he has come to join them, but then they realize he is blocking their path.

"You should listen to Tom," he says. He stands where he can bar their way out, and shows no sign of moving.

"Out of the way," Ifan cautions, "before this gets ugly in front of all these children."

Adam glances from Ifan's tight-knuckled fist to the many faces fixed on them. Parents, children, and the elderly are among Diana's party guests. Reluctantly, he steps aside to let them leave, realizing that once he loses the advantage of the narrow doorway, the group going with Ifan will be too many for him to stop them all. He grimaces at his decision as he lets them all walk out of the hall, knowing they are on their way to Dyrys.

CHAPTER FOUR

RHIANNON

Callum asks me what time I think it might be. I look up at the gaps of sky visible through the browning canopy and try to guess. We have been waiting here for hours. Callum has finished packing all his belongings away. I've begun to build a fire to keep off the evening chill.

"It'll be dark in about an hour," I tell him. "That won't make travelling easy. Maybe you should leave tomorrow instead, to avoid losing your way."

"No," says Callum, rising to his feet and fastening his coat. "I said I would leave today, and so I will. I've waited long enough. Can you say goodbye to Adam and Grace for me?"

I think about this for a minute as I stoke the fire. "No."

"What?"

"I think you owe them a proper goodbye, after everything they've done for you. You'd have starved if it wasn't for them. It's not like I would have fed you – not for the first few days you were out here at least."

Callum sighs. "You're probably right."

"Wow! Can I have that in writing?" I tease. He laughs.

A noise up ahead catches my attention and I run to the other side of the clearing.

"What is it?" asks Callum.

"Someone's coming."

"At last," he says.

"No, something's wrong. It sounds like people running."

"Why would Adam and Grace be running?"

"Wait here," I say, and I duck low to the ground and edge forward, trying to get a glimpse of whoever is coming. Callum falls silent behind me, finally picking up on my unease. It is definitely more than one person, and heading this way. I creep forward and in the distance I can see two faces. I try to block out memories of that day, months ago, when men and dogs raced through these woods in search of me, and I ran wildly and blindly away from them into the depths of the forest.

"It's Grace!" I hiss back to Callum. "And someone else is with her – I think it's Nia!"

"Nia?" Callum repeats. I can't guess what she could be doing here, or why is Grace leading her straight towards us. "You don't think Ifan sent her? To find me?"

"Hardly," I say, but this is more to reassure him. I don't understand what's happening. My first instinct is to run, in case this is some sort of trap, or a ploy to bring us back to Llandymna. The last conversation we had with Adam and Grace was them trying to convince us to go home. But I trust them, and I want to know what is going on.

"I'll find out," I say to Callum, and I go to meet the runners.

"What is it?" I ask, as I reach them.

"It's Ifan," Grace says, trying to catch her breath. I wonder how far they have run. "He's coming to look for Callum. When we left, he was trying to round up others to help him. I think he wants to finish off the fight."

Nia stares at me. "It's really you, Rhiannon? You look so different!"

"Is Callum still here? Did he leave, like he was planning to?"

"No," I say, ignoring Nia's comments for now, "he waited. He's back there. You don't think… Ifan wouldn't actually *kill* Callum, would he?"

"No, but he's not in his right mind. He thinks Callum got away with injuring him because the police didn't put enough effort into finding him. Conveniently forgetting, of course, that Ifan himself dropped the charges and so ended the search. But he's angry and feels he's been wronged. I think he plans to confront Callum and do whatever it takes to drag an apology or admission of guilt out of him. We need to warn him!"

The three of us run back to Callum. When we arrive, I quickly stamp on the fire that was starting to take hold.

"What are you doing?" he protests.

"There are people out looking for you," I tell him. "The light would have led them straight here."

"Who?" he asks.

"Ifan, and probably some of his friends."

"I'm sorry I couldn't stop him. I couldn't make him see that you never meant to insult him," says Nia.

Callum frowns in confusion. "You tried to explain to him though. Why would you do that? You don't owe me anything."

She seems surprised at this question. "I know what it's like to feel frustrated at how people see you, what they think of you. Besides, you and I both stood up to Diana in different ways, but you paid for it much more than I did."

Callum looks more ashamed than I have ever seen him.

"How long till they get here?" I ask.

"They'll be in the woods by now," says Grace, "unless… Adam and your aunt were going to try to stop them, or at least slow them down."

"OK," I say, "Callum and I have both managed to hide from people in this forest before. It's getting dark, which is to our advantage. If he goes deep enough into the woods, they shouldn't be able to find him."

"Knowing my luck I'll get lost and circle back around to meet them by mistake," says Callum.

"Then I'll be your guide. I know the way, even at night. I've been running around Dyrys for months now, after all."

"It's a good plan," says Nia. "Eventually they'll have to give up looking."

I turn back to her and Grace, knowing what I must say next. "Thank you for coming to warn us. You understand, though, that the more of us there are, the more likely we are to get caught? An extra voice or set of footprints makes it easier to track us."

"You're right," says Grace, "but I wish there was something we could do to help."

"If you can get back to the village," says Callum, "you could give the police directions to help them navigate these woods. I assume Tom will have called for some help by now."

"But if you can't," I add, "if it's not safe to go back the way you came, for any reason, go to my house and wait until everything's died down. You remember how to find it, Grace?"

"I think so. You did hide it very well though."

I suddenly regret this. A flag or sign over the mill house would help us all right now. I kick the cooling ashes from the fire to spread them across the ground and reduce the signs of life.

LLANDYMNA

"D'you know where they are?" Tom asks as soon as the others are gone. Adam nods grimly as Tom phones the station for back-up.

"If only Ifan had realized Callum wasn't trying to start a fight with him," Adam mutters to himself, reflecting on how far this feud has gone.

"He did," a voice rasps. "I told him myself."

Maebh holds herself up against the doorframe while Adam rushes over to her. She looks strangely frail tonight, and so much older than she had seemed in her own home. He supports her thin form and ignores the urgent tactical conversation Tom is holding over the phone, so that he can properly hear what this old woman has to say.

"Adam, you mustn't let this happen," she croaks. "Llandymna has been here before, even if no one out there chooses to remember it."

Adam finds somewhere for her to sit down. The effort of her petition seems to have drained her of energy, and all the wry knowledge and sparkling wit is gone from her face, so that she is left looking softer and more fragile. It is as if the cynicism of the ages has been washed away and all that remains is a simple, desperate hope.

"I loved your father, and I wish I could have saved him," she says. Adam looks at her and sees suddenly another path that their lives might have taken. If Emrys had stayed, he might have married Maebh, and this storyteller would now have a clan of children and grandchildren to care for her, instead of living alone. But then, would Adam and Grace have ever been born? He glances over to Tom, who is still on the phone, and calculates that he has a little more time before they need to act.

"Can I ask you something, Maebh?" he says. "Why didn't you leave? After they drove Emrys away, and covered it all up, how could you bear to stay in this place?"

"I did think of leaving Llandymna. For a time, I didn't think I could live here any more, when it had caused so much hurt. It felt as if my neighbours had taken everything from me. But you know, I do still love these people, for all their failings. At times it has been more through choice and perseverance than because they made it easy. But our lives tell stories when others look at them, don't they? And I decided a long time ago that by staying here I could tell these people a better story than by leaving them all behind."

Adam shakes his head. "I hope they know, one day, how much you've given them all. Tom's signalling to me – I have to go now. But I promise you I'll do everything I can to help our runaways."

Contented, Maebh sits back in the dim light of the candles and thanks him.

"He would be so proud of you," she says, smiling faintly.

Adam rejoins Tom as he hangs up the phone.

"Back-up is on the way," Tom says, "but it will be about half an hour before they get here. I've been instructed not to do anything until then, aside from handle the situation here."

"In that case, I'll go after Ifan now," says Adam. "If we let them go for long, you'll struggle to track them down again."

"You mean to follow them right now? Without waiting for the others?"

"I've already done everything I can here. I'd hoped to stop them setting out at all. But now I need to make sure nobody gets hurt."

"Callum may be young, but he isn't defenceless."

"No, but he isn't the only person in the forest tonight who Ifan might find. Rhiannon, Nia, and my sister are all there too, and might get caught in the crossfire."

Adam is resolute, so Tom does not press the matter any further. The policeman watches as this visitor who has become so involved in local affairs leaves the hall, turns down the street leading out of the village, and starts to run towards the woods.

RHIANNON

Parting ways with the others is hard. I don't think any of us really like the plan I have proposed, but no one can come up with anything better that guarantees our safety.

There's so much I could say at this moment. I suppose if I'd imagined today as a story, back in the days when I would dream up such things, we would be suddenly blessed with the ability to speak succinctly yet movingly some words that would express what all our friendships have amounted to, and how much we care for one another's safety. But Ifan may be getting close even now, so Grace and Nia leave in one direction as Callum and I go in the other. A last glance back puts an odd thought into my head. Nia looks taller. Perhaps I have only seen her beside Ifan before now, at least ever since they were married. We were almost friends when I was a child and she was still at school, long ago. She shouldn't be able to surprise or confuse me the way she has done today.

Darkness is gathering as we hurry deeper into the woods, towards my house. I lead the way between the shadowed boughs, followed by Callum. I am used to this fear of being found, this desperate escape, and Callum must be growing familiar with it too. He'd never admit to being scared, even now, but who can say what might happen if Ifan catches any of us?

"I wish it wasn't so dark," Callum says as he stumbles on the uneven ground behind me. I wait for him to get back up again before we carry on walking.

"You'll get used to it soon enough," I say. "Just follow me."

I know this way well. I walked here in the dark one night, holding a torch and wishing there were a procession to follow me. Two people don't quite make a procession. The ground slopes a little, and I hold on to tree branches to stop myself from slipping as we descend.

"I don't understand Adam or Grace."

I ask him what he means, not stopping this time, barely listening for his answer.

"All this. The warnings, helping me get food out here, running back and forth trying to make sure I'm not killed by Ifan. Why do they do it? I mean, I'm nothing to do with them."

"They're the sort of people who believe that friends look after each other," I say to him. He is not silenced by this.

"You know what Adam said about running away? That it doesn't really help you in the end."

I say nothing; I am wondering whether the left or right path will take us further away faster.

"I think he was right."

Right? But the left path will take us over flatter ground.

"Rhiannon, are you listening to me?"

I nod, a pointless action in all this darkness, and lead the way down the left path. Before I can take more than a few steps, he grabs my shoulder to stop me. I spin around to face him.

"I think Adam was right," he repeats. There is going to be some implication to this that I won't like. He persists, "I think we should go back."

"Go back where? To my house? Nia and Grace may not even be there, but they will be in danger if we are with them. After everything they've done for you –"

"No, I mean I want to go back to face Ifan. To see if I can put a stop to all this."

For some time I am speechless. I can hear his sincerity.

"Callum, have you lost your mind? He'll want revenge. He'll try to fight you. And you know how that went last time."

"What's the alternative? Running away forever?"

"Not forever! You can go back some other time."

"When, exactly? When Ifan has had even more time to dwell on his injuries? After he's taken out his anger on someone else in Llandymna, who didn't deserve it but was just there at the wrong time? Or when Ifan is dead, and I'm safe from him? Or when everyone has forgotten me and means me no harm? Or when I'm too old to walk back up the hill, and become a figure of legend alongside Emrys?"

There is something new in his voice now. I hear no defensive anger, only a kind of resigned honesty. It is strangely refreshing. What's more, he is right. He could well hide from the village forever. He could go somewhere far away, create a new life, and try to forget everything he left behind here. He could be like Emrys, someone our grandparents' generation lost because they misunderstood him. None of these things is impossible, but I know Callum does not want that life. I know it would weigh on him forever: all the words he should have said to his family and friends, all those words racing round and round his head every night as he tries to sleep. I think I understand why he has to go back.

"All right, if you want to face Ifan, I think I can find him."

Abandoning the left and right paths, we go a different way.

We make our way back through the darkness of Dyrys. Twigs and boughs scratch at my face and arms as we try to follow the same route back. There is no light anywhere around us. That reassures me. I know that when we see light up ahead, we will be near our destination.

After months of avoiding being sighted by anyone from the village, here I am leading a fellow runaway straight towards those very people. If I had the chance, I would go back in time and stop myself from causing so much damage to the people around me. Callum is just like me. He wants to set things right, by facing Ifan and putting an end to the quarrel he once fled. If I cannot make amends for my own mistakes, at least I can help him fix his. All this flits through my mind with startling alacrity as I try to judge the way towards Ifan.

"You do understand, don't you?" asks Callum, as he keeps pace alongside me.

"I wish I didn't. Then I could tell you to turn back and keep running, and then we'd both be heading away from danger, not into it. But yes, I understand you."

We take a few more steps, and then I catch sight of it: a flickering yellow light in the distance. I stop without signalling, so that Callum, realizing too late, bumps into me.

"What's that?" he asks, catching sight of the glow. I judge the distance and estimate where the light is coming from.

"I think they found the remains of the campfire after all."

My guess is that Ifan has stumbled across the last embers I tried to stamp out, and that has led him to find Callum's wattle and daub shelter. They must have stoked the fire again for it to be visible from here.

"Come on," I say, "but stay quiet. Let's find out what they're up to first."

We keep to the cover of the trees, but start to move forward for a better viewpoint. About ten metres away, I stop and duck behind a clump of holly. From here I can see half a dozen men standing around the fire. Ifan is speaking to the others.

"He was here, and not long ago. He must have run away when he heard us coming. We should be able to find him easily if we split up."

"But it's pitch black out here now," protests one of the others, who I think I recognize as Simon, who works on Ifan and Nia's farm. He is right: their eyes will have adjusted to the low firelight, and the woods will seem even darker to them now. We have that advantage, at least, if we need to run again.

Ifan is not deterred by this. He grabs some of the branches that hold up the roof of Callum's house, wrenching them free, and dips the end of each one in the fire. Flames jump out of the ashes, revitalized by the movement.

"Here we go. Torches!" he says. I smile with relief, knowing they are unlikely to work. They will probably either burn up too fast or go out by themselves before long. Fire is a tricky thing, as I have learned while I have been out here. It will not always do what you want it to. I seem to have guessed rightly too: only one of the branches has really caught. Frustrated, Ifan drops the others to the ground.

"Look, mate, I'm all for you teaching this kid a lesson, but we're never going to find him like this."

"CALLUM!" Ifan roars his name. The sound is angry and desperate all at once. The others look ready to go back home, but Ifan is only enraged more by the disappointment.

Before I can stop him, Callum is walking past me towards the gang and their furious leader.

"I'm here, Ifan!" he calls. Ifan turns towards the noise, the burning branch slung over his shoulder like a garden spade.

"You!"

"Can't we put an end to this?" Callum asks as Ifan advances. "I'm sorry about what happened. I didn't mean it to turn out like it has."

"I bet you're sorry. But you'll be sorrier when you've paid for what you did."

"All right," says Callum. "I won't run away this time."

It looks as if they are about to repeat themselves. I wasn't around for the first fight between these two, but if one of them ended up in hospital and the other on the run from the police, I can only assume it is not something to revisit. I have no plan, except to interrupt them long enough for us to figure out a better solution. I jump up and run to the clearing so that I am visible in the light cast by the fire.

"Wait!"

Ifan looks annoyed at first by this interruption, and then surprised when he sees me. Behind him, I see recognition dawn on the faces of his friends.

"Rhiannon Morgan. You're alive, then."

I wonder how many of them thought I was dead. A murmur passes round the group, perhaps as they acknowledge they had guessed wrong.

I know I have to speak quickly, to keep Ifan's attention away from Callum, but fear takes over and I hesitate. We are outnumbered. I wonder if I might be able to talk some of them round, and convince them to help me stop this fight breaking out. Or would they join in, and all set on Callum together? Would they attack me too? The surprise of seeing me is wearing off, and I think Ifan will turn on Callum soon if I do not think of something fast.

"Yes, I'm alive. But that's a story for another day. Ifan, Callum's apologizing to you. Isn't that what you wanted?"

I don't really expect this to talk Ifan round. He has never valued words as highly as actions, and a spoken "sorry" probably won't be enough for him now. But it might be enough to get the others to relent. They can't all be here just to see how many punches Ifan can land, can they? I feel their eyes on me, and realize this is something I have not missed at all – that sense of everyone staring, sussing you out as they decide how seriously to take you. I decide to try again.

259

"You can do whatever you like, Ifan, but you're still going to have to go home and live with everyone afterwards. Don't do something you don't want to be known for."

Like interrupting a fundraising event and destroying school property, I think. But maybe I've judged this wrong. Maybe Ifan is more afraid of being known for letting this slide than for teaching Callum a lesson. Either way, he isn't backing down. I hope Callum is glad we tried.

"OK, everyone, let's take a step back for a moment!" a new voice calls as Adam arrives in the clearing. He is out of breath, and I can only guess that he must have run all the way here. Now he stands between Callum and Ifan, his hands open in an unthreatening gesture.

"You again," says Ifan.

"You need to stop. The police are on their way, and if you don't stand down now you will all be arrested. Go home and put this behind you!"

"What good is a law if it doesn't allow a man to defend himself? This one attacked me, and insulted me too."

"For the hundredth time, Ifan," Callum shouts, "there was no insult to you! It was Diana I was fed up with. Even Nia could see that, and she tried to tell you that's what really happened."

I see what flickers across Ifan's face. He's working out when he last saw Nia, which will be before she and Grace came to warn us. His expression contorts with the self-righteous anger of someone deciding that everyone they know is turning against them.

"You persuaded her to take your side, to help you!" he rages, reaching a conclusion that is both true and deluded all at once.

"If you learned to listen, there wouldn't have to be any sides," I snap, because I am getting really fed up with Nia being blamed for everything around here.

"And you," he rounds on Adam. "You were helping this one from the start, weren't you? All those days of going into the woods for your sister's research were a cover, weren't they? You come here as a stranger, you stay in my house as a guest, and this is how you repay my hospitality?"

A change seems to have come over Adam. Before now, I've noticed that he can look content while he secretly contemplates serious things, and equally appears solemn if you don't know to look for the glimmer of mischief. Now I think his face shows exactly what he feels. He looks directly at Ifan, the firelight casting sharp shadows around his eyes, and he seems both weary and angry at once. Ifan somehow manages not to back away from this expression.

"I am not as much an outsider as you like to think," Adam says. "I was almost one of you. My father was born here in Llandymna, and lived here until people like you drove him away and forgot him."

For a while, Ifan does not know what to do with this knowledge. After a few stuttered moments of uncertainty, an idea comes to him.

"So that is why you are doing this! You have created a nice little war between us here, encouraging Tom to use his authority against us, keeping Callum here as bait, and now you'll watch as we destroy each other, and you will have your revenge, satisfied to know that all your father's enemies were beaten through your own actions."

This is surprisingly well thought out for Ifan, and worse still it sounds almost plausible. If someone wanted to hurt Llandymna, that would be a sure way of doing it. Can we have been deceived all this time? For a horrible moment I wonder whether it could be true. Then I remember that revenge is the only motive Ifan understands at the moment. Of course he would assume that everyone else wants it too.

"That can't be true, can it?" Callum asks me.

"Of course not," I assure him.

"But they did tell us not to avoid the fighting. It's because of him we're here, isn't it?"

"No, moron," I hiss, not wanting Adam to overhear us. "They told us we couldn't run away forever, but they didn't want us to get drawn into a fight. That was your choice, remember?"

"I don't want revenge any more," says Adam. The "any more" startles me. How strange to think that he of all people might once have been a little like Ifan.

"Then you clearly don't care that much about your father, or what happened to him. Or maybe he brought you up to be a coward."

Adam laughs at the conclusion Ifan has reached. "You didn't know him, and that's entirely your loss. He could have come to pay back the people who drove him out. He chose not to. Because at some point it stops being about justice, doesn't it? Your measure of what's right and fair gets twisted up and stained with anger so that you can only think about the retaliation that will make you feel better, make you feel less wounded. Except it never really helps – you just have to pretend the act of vengeance was enough, because if you don't, you might go mad trying to feel the world was fair again. Emrys managed to break free of that."

Ifan's look of defiance and contempt barely wavers, but to me it is as if Adam's words have lifted a curtain off the man, and I see him, and everyone like him, so clearly for the first time. Those words must have been Emrys's – Adam has never come close to uttering a speech like that before now. I scan the faces of all the gathered men opposite and wonder if they feel trapped.

"What will you do?" Ifan sneers. "Stand there and preach at me instead?"

"If you're set on proving a point tonight," he sighs, "at least let it be fair. Fight someone more your own size than this lad."

"You think anyone would face me in Callum's place?"

"Yes."

"Who?"

"Me."

They certainly look more equally matched. Callum's foot still hasn't quite mended; lack of medical attention means he's got used to hobbling slightly wherever he goes. Unlike last time, Ifan is sober and alert today, and easily the stronger of the two in spite of his own injuries. Adam, on the other hand, is almost as broad-shouldered as

Ifan, and has spent his life hauling wood and repairing fences, not sitting around in pubs on match days. I wonder if Callum will be insulted by Adam's offer to take his place; if his pride will refuse to allow anyone to protect him. But he does not look offended. He looks astounded and confused.

"Why take his place? The brat doesn't deserve it."

"No, he doesn't," Adam replies simply, as if this were not the important point at all, "but you will still have your fight and your chance for revenge, which is what you want, isn't it?"

Ifan's eyes narrow. He does not trust this deal. No man offers such terms without a catch, least of all a stranger with nothing to gain and a grudge against everyone for how they have treated his father. It makes no sense.

Callum's face is fraught with guilt. I know he will not be able to forgive himself if Adam should be hurt. But something else is happening. The others are looking decidedly uncomfortable. Apparently the people of Llandymna have warmed to Emrys's son. Where they saw a kind of old-fashioned appeal to bringing Callum to justice, turning on Adam is not something anyone is prepared to do. Hesitantly, they back off and Ifan gives a shout of fury and dismay as he realizes he is being abandoned. As he reaches around for new ways to convince them, other noises interrupt him. Behind them, I see the flashes of electric torches through the trees, and shouts of people fast approaching. Among the voices, I recognize that of Tom Davies.

"I did warn you," Adam says quietly, with an apologetic shrug.

Ifan turns his back on him and prepares to meet the approaching onslaught. "Hold your ground!" he orders the rest of them. "We've done nothing wrong here."

For once, however, Ifan's boldness is not enough to convince his followers, who scatter in all directions trying to avoid arrest.

CHAPTER FIVE

RHIANNON

What follows is chaos. Police officers and their dogs crash into the clearing as people run in all directions. One man is immediately pinned down by two officers, who put handcuffs on him.

One down, five more to go, I think. But they scatter, and the police have only come into these woods during the day when searching for me. Dyrys at night is another matter, and I'm not surprised to see Ifan disappear into the shadows while another man is being stopped. Adam, Callum, and I stand still in the clearing, waiting for someone to try to arrest or at least question us, but the police are more interested in stopping Ifan and his followers, and we find ourselves left standing alone.

"What do we do?"

"Stay out of trouble," Adam answers. "Let the police do their work here."

"Did Grace and Nia make it back OK?" I ask.

"I haven't seen them," he replies.

"You didn't pass them on the road out of Dyrys?"

"No."

"They must have gone to your house, like you told them to," says Callum.

"I hope so," I say, wondering if they really would be able to find the way there in poor light, with so many people running around in the woods, "but we should go and make sure."

If they aren't there, I don't know how we will find them. But if they are, then we can all shelter in the mill house until everything calms down. I have food and water for us to wait out the night if necessary.

"Oi!" A shout cuts into my thoughts. Through a gap in the trees, we see Ifan, with his burning branch still over his shoulder. The barking is distant and muffled, telling me there are no police officers nearby right now. It will be harder to lose him in the woods if he has a light source and we do not.

"Split up," Adam mutters as Ifan approaches.

"What? No!"

"Rhiannon, Ifan is after Callum. If we draw him away, you can get to your house and make sure Grace and Nia are OK. I can't do it: I don't know how to find the place – you've got that thicket all around it, remember? Please, go and find them. We'll distract Ifan until the police can catch up."

He is earnest, and I realize he must be worried for his sister, not knowing where she is. I look from one face to the other, silently praying for their safety tonight, and then I turn away and run out into the dark corridors of the forest. It is almost unbearably difficult to keep running and not look back.

It's too dark to see anything at all, and I navigate the woods with no more than a memory of the path and by feeling the slope of the ground beneath my feet. I've often walked through these places at night, but then there was time to spare, time to waste in pretensions of grandeur and formality, which left me the ordered control of mind with which to choose a direction. Now I have only a moment to guess the turn between the trees, darting between the jagged branches.

I fall straight into the thicket and clamber over it, tearing myself free from the thorns that pull at my clothes. Sliding down the bank towards the night-black stream, I call Grace and Nia's names, and soon footsteps hurry towards me. I pull myself up to my feet as they reach me.

"Rhiannon? What is it?"

"You're here. Thank goodness. In all the chaos, we weren't sure you'd have made it to safety."

"We're fine, but what are you doing here? Weren't you and Callum supposed to be a long way from here by now?" asks Grace.

"I know, I know. He wanted to go back."

My heart is beating so fast now, I am sure everyone else must be able to hear it. Then I remember that if I am frightened, it must be nothing compared to what Nia feels right now. She eluded Ifan to warn us, and anyone could predict that he will not thank her for that. What's more, she is in an unfamiliar place, with people she barely knows, unable to do anything else to help them.

"As long as you're not seen, you should be safe," I tell them, "and the forest is wide enough that they might well pass this place without even knowing it is here. Otherwise... I could try to get you back to the village unseen."

"We can't go out into the forest now," says Grace firmly. "With everything that's happening tonight, it would be a miracle to make it out unhurt."

Before she can continue, Grace spies something past my head that makes her stop our talking. I turn to see the glimmering torchlights approaching even now. I know I've nothing to fear from the police, but equally every moment they spend identifying us is a moment not spent finding Ifan and making sure he doesn't hurt anyone. The other two seem to have had the same thought. We drop to the ground silently so that the beams will not pick out our faces. I can hear them now, drawing nearer in a clash of confused shouts that I cannot discern.

The noise of the dogs is getting fainter all the time. I sigh with relief as one set of footfalls flees past the edge of the thicket and keeps on running. In the next instant all my relief vanishes as with a splintering crash someone falls straight through the boundary. He grunts, and curses the forest for being so dense and painful. He's lying right next to where Nia is hiding. If he turns his head just slightly, he will be able to see her pale form among the shadows. I can see her edging tentatively away, holding her breath as she tries to move out of sight.

Then he decides to pull himself back up to his feet, and at once he sees her. She springs backwards, but not quickly enough, as he grabs her by the arm and tries to pull her towards him so he can identify her. As they both step into a patch of light, we too can identify him. It's Ifan.

"You!" he says as he recognizes Nia, still gripping her wrist so that she cannot get away. The burning branch he carried is lying on the ground where he dropped it. I glance over to Grace, and then realize what I am about to do. I miss running away: it was so much easier. I stand up slowly, so as not to startle anyone.

"Ifan! All this has nothing to do with Nia," I call. He notices me, but says nothing. Around us, shadows flicker and I think I catch sight of other figures moving around beyond the boundary, but no torches to announce the presence of the police. The only light is where the flames of Ifan's torch have jumped to a patch of brambles and now dance over the thorns.

I walk slowly up to them. I do my very best to look calm and keep myself from shaking as I approach. My heart is racing, but I give him a level stare and reiterate, steadily, "Nothing to do with her."

He tries to hold my gaze, but maybe there is something too disconcerting about this runaway girl who looks so calm in the midst of fighting and chaos. Either way, he cannot meet my eyes for long, and he glances frantically from me to Nia and back again. Very slowly, so as not to startle anyone into a defensive reaction, I move closer to the two of them and reach out to the hand grasping her arm. I lift his hand away, the way you might separate a child from something valuable they should not have picked up. He puts up no resistance – he seems too surprised at my confidence, and almost relieved to have an excuse to let her go. Nia at once takes a step back, out of anyone's reach, and stands with her back to the house, her arms folded around herself. Her wide eyes dart from face to face in the gloom. We all follow her gaze to Ifan, wondering what he will do next. He stares at her for a while before he speaks.

"You took his side," he says, sounding childishly plaintive.

"No," she shakes her head. "I always know better than to take sides. You just wouldn't listen when I tried to explain it all to you. Hasn't this gone far enough now?"

Ifan looks surprised. I wonder if this is the most direct Nia has ever been towards him. He backs away so that he is once again outside the border of my land. I cannot guess which way he will go next: will he resume raging around the forest, or have an epiphany of self-awareness? As he takes the next step, his foot catches the burning branch and knocks it further into the thicket.

The wood that I spent many a day weaving together under the watchful eye of a hawk, fashioning a boundary to keep out the world, has withered and dried out with time, and it now goes up in flames in a matter of seconds. We are separated from Ifan by the fast-growing wall of fire.

"Ifan!" Tom's voice is accompanied by the barking of dogs. I see him and Callum lit up in the firelight now. Ifan takes in the sight as well, and then runs in the opposite direction.

"OK, I've got this," Tom says to Callum. "Thanks for your help." He starts to chase after Ifan. Callum stays behind.

"We tried to lead him back towards the police," he calls. "Are you able to get around this blaze?"

The fire is spreading fast, lapping up the dead wood in tongues that keep growing. It is only now that I see how blind I have been to the full danger we are in. If the thicket surrounds us, then so too will the fire.

I rush to the far end of the land I once called mine, but already the flames are eating away at the furthest part of the boundary. Shaking now, I go back to Grace and Nia, and tell them what I have seen. We are completely surrounded. The flames are creeping in from the fence, leaping onto the living trees now. I hear Callum shouting, and then Adam's voice joins in, but the fire itself makes too much noise for us to hear them.

"Get away from there!" Grace shouts. Nia and I are standing dangerously close to a tree that has caught light and is beginning to drop burning twigs and dried leaves on us, so that the fire seems to be falling from the sky, as well as drawing in on all sides. We stand in a more open space at the centre of my land, looking around and trying to quell any rising panic. Nia's eyes dart about for any sign of an escape route, while Grace says nothing as she assesses our situation. Smoke billows in, and though I try not to breathe it in, I start to choke and splutter as it surrounds me. There is a sudden crash and, whirling around, we see a silhouette break through the wall of flames, roll along the ground and then jump back up.

"Have you gone mad?" demands Grace, helping her brother to his feet and beating out the flames that have attached themselves to his arm.

"Callum said you were stuck, and I thought we'd best find a way out together," he answers, as if it were the most sensible idea in the world, "but I don't think we can leave the way I got in."

The flames have already filled the gap that he crashed through and are towering higher. I know what he has just done is irresponsible to the point of stupidity, and we should probably trust his judgment less for it, but I am glad to see him: I can feel myself smiling involuntarily. There are scrapes across his arms that suggest he has had trouble with one of the dogs, and now his clothes are singed, but he smiles as if we were all perfectly safe.

A shout from Callum catches my attention, as he calls our names through the fire.

"We're here!" I shout back, not daring to go any nearer the burning thicket. "Are you all right?"

"You need to get out of there!" he calls, sounding panicked. "But I can't see a way. Don't worry about Ifan – Tom caught up with him."

"Find Tom – he can send for help! We'll keep looking for a way out of this."

He shouts an agreement through the flames and then he leaves. We stand together with our backs to the mill house as the fire creeps closer. My eyes sting with the thick drifts of smoke that keep blowing this way. I never thought the fence around my land would do so much harm. It was supposed to keep danger away from me, not increase it.

"Rhiannon, is there any wide entrance through this fence of yours? Anywhere the fire couldn't have jumped across?" asks Grace.

I cannot even bring myself to shake my head as I think back on the repairs I made so carefully each day. I can think of nothing to say when I take in the damage I have done. Adam and Grace have done more good in my life than they can ever realize, and Nia has never done anything to hurt anybody, and these three will be the undeserving victims of my determination to keep the world out. It's unthinkable. I must not let this happen. Suddenly the decision takes hold of me that I am going to somehow find a way out of this, and I will get these friends of mine to safety, whatever the cost to myself. I look down at my feet, and suddenly the answer is before me.

"The stream!"

"What? You can't be planning to put out the fire?"

"No," I laugh, astonished that I'm able to find something funny right now. "The stream runs straight through this bit of land, and I couldn't build across it properly. There'll be a gap on either side where it meets the boundary. It might just be wide enough for a person to pass through."

"That's our way out then!" cries Adam, and we head in that direction. In the frantic dark, twigs scratch and stones catch at my feet. Nia stumbles once, but finds her feet again as I lead the way to what has to be our escape route. Between trees that will perhaps be nothing but ash by the morning, the four of us follow the stream as it curves around the stone house and leads away from it, eventually to the border of my land, now marked by turrets of flame. Sure enough, there is a gap in the fire where the stream cuts through it, just wide enough for someone to squeeze through, hopefully unharmed.

As I step towards the dark space between the leaping flames, I feel the heat of the fire against my face, the scorching smell that makes me fear my hair is burning. I shrink for a moment from the tongues of flame dancing so unpredictably, jumping out and latching on to anything that might ignite. However, I haven't forgotten that this was my idea, and the only hope to get us safely out of this blaze. Closing my eyes to the fire's hypnotic powers, I take a few strides forwards into the stream and between the crackling wood hissing its goodbye to me.

The noise of movement behind me says that the other three are nearby and following. A moment later they are drowned out by the roar in my ears of flames so close to my face. I try not to imagine that my hair or clothes are catching alight, and keep going. When I next dare to open my eyes, the air is just a fraction cooler. I look over my shoulder to where Nia and Grace have already followed me through, while Adam is emerging through the gap.

"We're out!"

The cry is heartfelt and filled with triumph and relief. With a smile that nobody else will be able to see through the heavy billows of smoke, I continue to walk through the ankle-deep waters while the fire rages on either side, where it has spread to more of the forest. It is still difficult to breathe, so we hurry towards the promise of clear air somewhere ahead of us. When eventually we come to a place beyond the range of the fire, we step out of the stream onto dry ground, shaking glistening drops from our feet, and turn towards the edge of the woods.

Without a word of explanation, I begin leading them through the dark maze riddled with overhanging boughs. There are cuts, bruises and burns to see to, and I cannot fix these things, so I take them towards a place where they can be healed. The walk is slow, but I am leading the way back to the village.

At some time after midnight we reach the end of our slow journey. Staggering up a hillside I never thought to set foot on again, we drag aching limbs that have only just realized how weary they are towards the quiet flickering lights of the village. Far above us, low voices speak distant and indiscernible words from the overlooking streets, but we are silent.

With a restless murmur, the sky lets its heavy burden slip from its grasp. Slowly at first, the raindrops dance over my skin and I laugh quietly to feel them fall onto my upturned face, trickling over dry lips into my mouth. They sting slightly against my parched throat and burned arms. We all stop as we realize we are safely out of the fire's reach. I fall to the ground with something like the silent laughter of relief, and lie on the grassy slope. Looking to my left and right, I see the others have done the same, and we all rest for a moment here, like driftwood washed up by the tide. The far-off blaze in the forest quivers beneath the rain, and I close my eyes so that I don't have to see it burn or be doused.

We are found some time later, still lying on the hillside in the rain. I open my eyes to see Callum and Tom standing over us. They help each one of us to our feet and we walk the last stretch together. There's an ambulance parked in the lane, police cars illuminating the hedgerow with their blue flashing lights. People in uniform march around. Somebody – I do not see who – wraps a blanket around my shoulders, and without quite knowing how I got here, I find myself sitting inside the Evanses' farmhouse. I remember this place as if from a dream rather than memory. The same kitchen chair wobbles if you lean back, the same Welsh proverb hangs over the door, and the safe smell of being within walls hangs in the air. There are other people in this room with me, some also draped in standard issue blankets, some with cuts bound in white cloth, but all quietly together in this one house.

"What happened?" I ask Callum. He is sitting on the chair opposite mine, his arm bandaged.

"They're just taking statements now to establish what exactly went on in Dyrys tonight. I've explained my part in it all – how I made Ifan angry in the first place."

"Where is he?" whispers Nia, who sits beside me, looking around the room for her husband. Her hair is drenched in rain so that it clings to her head and shoulders. As she speaks, Tom returns to the house, ducking as ever beneath the low wooden doorframe.

"I'm sorry, Nia," he says, sitting down near us, "we arrested him this evening, and he will be coming back to the station with us. I know that even after all he did, it will still be hard for you."

Nia closes her eyes. Tom watches her with concern before turning to me. I wonder what to expect from him: a lot has changed.

"Welcome back," he says quietly, with a smile. I smile back. Then he glances over to Adam and Grace, and says simply, "Thank you."

Adam gives a silent nod, and that is enough for now. He begins to get up, but seems unsteady on his legs, though whether through injury or exhaustion I cannot tell. Tom stops him, saying none of us should move until we have our strength back, so Adam asks that a message be taken to Maebh.

LLANDYMNA

Tom knocks gently on the door, not really expecting Maebh to still be awake. But the door is on the latch, and she is in her usual chair in the front room. He hears Maebh's harsh breathing before he sees her.

"You stayed up?"

"I hoped there might be some news."

Tom shifts uncomfortably, wondering whether he would have brought Maebh an update if no one had reminded him.

"Maebh, Adam asked me to bring you a message. He said to tell you that Callum and Rhiannon have come back to the village with everyone tonight. And something about history not repeating itself – he said you would understand that bit."

The old woman's frail face suddenly breaks into a beam of brilliant happiness; the sort she has not felt in years. All that she feared is washed away into contentment.

"Even after all this time, he can still make me smile," she murmurs.

"Who?" asks Tom, thinking she might mean Adam, or possibly even Callum.

"Emrys. Always Emrys."

She sighs, and marvels at her old friend. Then she drifts off into sleep, and dreams of the Sparrow Girl and the Boy Who Shone. In some other dream world, they run like the wind through the springtime forest, and laugh as the carefree children they hardly had the chance to be. The birds fly alongside them and join in their songs, and all that is young and green is their home.

CHAPTER SIX

RHIANNON

Something doesn't seem right. I wonder what can have made me sleep through the first grey strains of dawn. When I open my eyes, I can see that this isn't the house in which I am used to waking. Its walls are further apart, its ceiling high and painted instead of canopied in ivy and stone. Stranger still, I am lying in a warm bed, with no hard earth to make my bones ache. I realize this is the spare room in Nia's house. Then I remember.

I remember the fire that will by now have reduced to ash all my food supplies, my sleeping bag – everything I kept at the mill house. It will all be gone. And I am here, back in a house in Llandymna, where I swore I'd never be. I feel almost tricked into it: coming here was the price for leading my friends to safety. I would have liked more time to prepare myself for this. But now that I'm here, I wonder if I'm brave enough to try to stay.

I remember that my arms still have dark smudges all over them because when we reached Llandymna last night it seemed petty to request water with which to wash away the soot and smoke, when medics were rushing around tending to proper injuries, where people had fallen in the woods or had a couple of teeth knocked out by someone determined not to be brought in. I remember that my skin hurts and my clothes are scorched almost to rags. I remember a police officer approaching me and asking questions that made no sense, until Tom interrupted saying that it could all wait until the morning, and told me to go and get some sleep.

I raise myself now to sit upright, which takes some time, firstly because my arms ache so badly and secondly because of the weight of the blankets that are drawn across my legs. I cannot think when I last awoke feeling so warm or well cocooned. I wriggle out from under the pile of covers so that I am free to move around. Outside the animals are clearly awake. I hope Nia has slept in this morning. Maebh once told me that deep sleep can be a time when the body repairs itself, and I think the more restored she feels after yesterday, the better.

Birds are singing outside too. Most likely other people are out there, in the streets and lanes, unless everyone is still as weary from last night as I am. I think of the people who are beyond these walls: of Adam and Grace, of Callum, Tom, Maebh, and Diana. I imagine them wandering around in the morning light, breathing in the fresh air and trying to take in all that has happened, or waking slowly and groaning at their bruises and burns. Perhaps some of them are sitting together at a window, looking out across the charred forest, sharing breakfast and thinking about the day ahead. A jolt of excitement rises up through me as I realize I have only to leave this house to see my friends and family again. They are there, so nearby, and I can go to see them whenever I want!

But maybe not all of them will be glad to see me. After all, some may be angry with me still for the things I said before I left. What's more, if I had not led Callum back to Ifan last night, there might not have been so much fighting, and if I hadn't built that wall around my house no one would have been hurt by the fire. Perhaps people will blame me. It is almost enough to make me want to slip quietly out of the village before I'm seen and punished. But not quite, for I know I have to try to make amends somehow.

Slowly, carefully, I get to my feet and walk towards the white painted door. I step out onto the landing as Nia comes walking up the stairs.

"Good morning," she says.

The moment is so surreal and alien to me that I forget to reply.

I stand there on the carpeted floor and say nothing. Nia does not seem to mind.

"I have to go over to Bryndu this morning, to the police station. But I've put the hot water on if you want a shower, and there are some spare clothes in the bathroom if you'd like them. They should be about your size. Help yourself to anything from the kitchen."

Of course. There will be so much to think about this morning, to make myself presentable enough to see people. I start mentally listing the things people who live in houses do each morning, so that I will not forget anything.

Nia goes out and I spend a good hour washing. There is mud under my fingernails, soot on my arms, and bits of dead leaves in my tangled hair. I clean my teeth over the white porcelain sink and study my face in the bathroom mirror. It is a long time since I have seen my reflection, except for in the stream on days when the water was clear and quiet. I think I look different, but I can't be certain. Maybe I have just forgotten what I look like.

I cover the distance of the landing and the creaky staircase on faltering feet, and tell myself this is because of the tiredness weighing down on me, but I know the truth is I could stride with speed if I wanted to; I'm nervous of what I'll find when I set foot outside.

Don't be so silly, I tell myself. *If there was a difficult journey to make, surely it was leaving the woods last night and climbing the hill. You managed that. Now all you have to do is walk up to the front door and step out into the sun. In many ways, this is one of the easiest and best journeys you'll ever make.* But it is quiet and cool in here, and though it's technically part of the village, it still feels disconnected from the rest of Llandymna. In this empty house, I don't have to face up to anything. There are no consequences or retributions. In here, it doesn't matter who I am or what I have done. When I step outside, it will matter again.

I quickly scribble a note to Nia, letting her know where I have gone, then make the few paces to the door, not allowing myself to be deterred. This must be done. I open the door, then place my hand against the wooden beam that runs up the side of the doorway and rest against it, looking out.

I spy a shawl neatly folded on the hall chair next to me and decide to borrow it from Nia for this morning. It is a blue-green colour and looks homemade. I wrap it around my shoulders and feel immediately safer to venture out, as if the shawl makes me less exposed to prying glances.

This is as much as I can do, and I have delayed long enough now. It is time to go outside and face everyone.

With a deep breath, I step forwards. It is sunny, for an autumn morning. I can hear dogs yapping to one another somewhere close by. Smoke curls slowly from houses further up the hill, perfuming the crisp air with warmth.

I walk across the fields to the village rather than take the road and risk being seen. I make it to Diana's house without passing anyone. It looks exactly as I remember it. The front garden is neat, and the path swept clear of debris.

A tiny figure totters around on the grass in front of the house. I stare at this child who has merrily escaped his mother's sight, and am amazed at how much little Owen has grown. He picks up a stone, then drops it, gurgling merrily at the noise it makes on connecting with the ground. Then he notices me watching him, and looks up at me with wide eyes that show no trace of recognition.

"You don't remember me, do you?" I say sadly, thinking of all the times I protested at being expected to babysit for him.

"Owen! Come back here!" another voice calls, and the boy's mother emerges. Her eyes fix first on her son, whom she expects to see, and then on me. Her expression of relief transforms suddenly to something less readable.

Diana and I face one another in silence. Then, because someone has to speak eventually, I say, "I'm back."

She nods, still looking stunned. "I waited up last night for news. Someone said that Callum had come back, and that they thought they had seen you too, but I thought it was impossible. I never imagined…"

I suddenly understand that all this time my aunt has been forcing herself to come to terms with the idea that she may never see me again. No wonder Callum was able to report that she hated people talking about me. The hope of others can be unbearable when you have none left yourself.

"I'm sorry," I say, "for everything I said… before."

She nods again, awkwardly, as if acknowledging my apology but unsure what to do with it. At once I see in her face a nervous uncertainty that I never noticed before. Diana seems younger than when I left: less self-possessed, but not like a queen fallen from her proud pedestal; more like an ordinary woman weighing up how gracious to be in the midst of all her emotions.

"I was so rude to you, and so difficult," I continue, staring at the ground rather than make eye contact for this admission. Still she says nothing, so I look up and press on, "Can you forgive me?"

Finally she smiles. "Of course," she answers, and she steps forward to put her arms around my shoulders.

Does she know yet, does she see, how much I am changed from the anguished girl prepared to hurt anyone around her if it made life closer to the fairy tales she treasured? My best hope of being welcomed home, and the best reconciliatory gift I have to offer anyone, is that I am a little less cruel than I once was.

"Have you really been living in the forest all this time?" she asks.

"Yes."

"You're not quite as thin as I'd have expected, then."

It is hardly a tearful, joyful return. There is nothing dramatic or easy about this. Our conversation is stilted, as we each try to remember what we ought to say to one another.

"Owen has grown since I left."

"Yes. He was only just walking then. Now he runs away faster than I can keep track of him."

I don't know what I expected. Of course there are many hurts to heal now, and a great gulf between us to bridge. But I think that in time my aunt and I may well be friends.

We talk a while longer about all the various people who have played a part in our lives, how they fit in different ways. I tell Diana how much Callum is changed for the better, and she admits to me she thinks Tom may have some knack for leadership after all, given last night's events. It is impossible to avoid mentioning Ifan, though that is uncomfortable, as neither of us quite knows what we ought to feel with regard to him. All this talk of other names makes me mindful of the people I have yet to see.

"I came to see you as soon as I woke up. I don't think many people know I'm here yet."

Diana is gratified at the special attention paid to her, and this helps her to accept the idea that I must now pay some more visits, though she doesn't let me go until I have eaten some breakfast.

I approach the next house and rap against the wooden door. A wonderfully familiar voice rasps an invitation to enter and, as the door is unlocked already, I step inside.

"It's me," I say.

Maebh looks as though she has aged many years in my absence. Her face is more gaunt, and she looks as if she might not have the strength to stand. Yet at my words she breaks into a beaming smile and her blue eyes shine as they search for the speaker.

"Rhiannon, my child, you have come home!"

And yes, as she says those words, I really do feel as if I have come home. She reaches out a bony hand and I take it in mine quickly, sitting down on the footstool beside her chair. She is chuckling to herself with delight now, and I find it impossible not to join her in laughing gleefully.

"It's so good to see you again, Maebh!"

"Tom brought me the news last night. You and Callum: both back! How wonderful. It's good to have a homecoming to celebrate. And I expect we have Emrys's children to thank for much of that."

"Yes," I say, "they suggested to us we should come back. Neither of us liked the idea at first, but after a time it started to make sense – but that isn't really what you mean, is it?"

Maebh cackles appreciatively. She has always had an interest in people: in their minds, their hopes, their choices.

"You know me well, my girl. You have learned something out there, then."

She knows something must have changed and wants to hear my account of it. What can I tell her? That I have learned the necessary skills to sustain my own life with no help from anyone else? That I was independent for a time, but that soon lost all its charm? That I think maybe life can be beautiful enough, and full enough, that stories exist only to augment it, not to compensate for its failings? That unconditional friendship is not a mere fairy tale?

"I think people don't have to be perfect, do they? To still deserve love, I mean."

"Very good. Loving others in spite of their imperfections is not at all a child's game. You have grown older while you were away."

I feel older. The ground beneath my feet seems less shaky now. I think back to all the anger and disappointment I felt when I marched stubbornly into the forest, and wonder how I had the energy for it all, or why it seemed so important what everyone thought of me then.

Voices seem to be gathering outside, growing louder as they call their neighbours.

"Tom is going to make an announcement at the church hall, to explain to everyone what happened last night," says Maebh.

"I guess I'd better go and be there for it. I don't suppose you'll come?"

"No, dear. It needs something more urgent for these poor bones to deign to move. Besides, you know old Maebh always knows exactly what is being said out there."

She says the last part with a mischievous smile. She plays the role of the wise old woman so convincingly, which at times reassures and disconcerts people in equal measure, but always affords her a place in the village.

"I'm glad to be here again," I say, as I leave her house. She waves me away with an air of complete contentment.

A small crowd has gathered in the hall, where tables and chairs have been hastily rearranged from the party that happened here last night. I quietly join at the back of the group, afraid that if anyone were to see me unexpectedly it would cause too much of a stir. Tom will give the announcement in his own way. That said, he is doing a remarkably good job of keeping their attention. When I was last here, he was widely mocked for not being more practical or interesting. Men laughed at him because they were glad to think they commanded more respect than he did. Yet now all eyes are fixed on him.

"Friends," he begins, "thank you for coming. There will be a more formal statement from the Bryndu station later today, but I have been authorized to speak here this morning. The Dyfed-Powys police were called to respond to an incident that took place in and around Llandymna last night. I was part of that response. You'll have heard parts of what happened already. But incomplete knowledge can be a dangerous thing, so let me tell you all the full story."

Here we are, at the end of all the trouble, still needing stories. They are powerful things, because with words alone Tom is going to give this village back its peace. As he begins the account, I hear reminders in his voice that this is a man who grew up listening to Maebh's tales. But he is also a police officer, and everything he says is fair and balanced. He does not take sides.

"Ifan Evans is co-operating with the police as we fully investigate all the circumstances surrounding this event."

I think of what this will mean for Nia: will her husband go to prison? Or will he come home and rage further at how he has been treated by the police? But lately we've learned that Nia isn't as fragile as she looks, and I feel sure she'll face it well, whatever happens.

Tom moves on to tell how all those who followed Ifan last night will need to be questioned, as will many who attended the party here in the hall. So far I have not been mentioned. Perhaps I am one controversy too many on this morning when people are trying to return their lives to something that looks normal and predictable.

When Tom finishes talking about last night, he turns to a much older incident in this village which he himself has only just learned about, and so announces what has been rumoured all morning: that Adam and Grace are descended from one of our own people. All murmuring stops as people listen intently. He briefly tells the story of Emrys, and I see the discomfort on people's faces as they hear how this village treated him. They will not forget that easily.

"And finally," Tom says, "today is a day for many returns and reconciliations. We are welcoming back not just Callum Rees, but also Rhiannon Morgan."

As he says this, he looks straight at me and I realize that he has known all along that I am here. A few people audibly start at hearing my name, and everyone follows Tom's eyes to where I stand. It is intensely uncomfortable, having all these faces turned towards me. I do not know if I should speak, or smile, or do nothing.

Fortunately, Tom calls their attention back again and finishes his speech. When it's done, the crowd slowly disperses, and a few people murmur "welcome back" as they pass me. The rows gradually thin, like a mound of sand being carried off by sporadic gusts of wind. First to leave are those who had little to do with this affair; then those who were involved but not arrested thank Tom and hurry away, trying to forget what they have done. Soon the only ones remaining are those who were caught in the centre of the fight and the fire. I suppose we had the most invested, the most at risk, so it makes sense we should find it hardest simply to wander off and return to life as if it's another ordinary day.

Callum approaches Tom, and to my amazement they hug one another like brothers. Can it be that these rivals are now friends again? Near them, Adam says something to Grace which makes her smile. It also turns out that Nia is back from Bryndu already. They gesture to her to join the conversation, and they speak softly, as they would to someone in mourning. Adam's arm is bandaged, but he seems to keep forgetting this. He tries to pat Callum on the back encouragingly and then winces as he remembers his injury.

I want to walk up to the five of them, but I am transfixed for the moment, unsure what to say to anyone, so I stand at a slight distance, watching them and delighting in this sight of five of my favourite people finally all safe. I stay here until Grace glances over and notices me. At once they call me over to join them. As I cover the short distance between us, I wonder what I can possibly say to these people that will be appropriate to what has happened to us all.

"I hope you don't mind that I borrowed your shawl," I blurt out to Nia. These are my sensitive first words?

But she smiles. "Of course not. The colour suits you – it matches your eyes."

"I thought she had brown eyes," says Callum. Nia gives a short laugh at Callum's skills of observation.

"Was it right, to tell everyone you are back?" Tom asks. A police officer who just commanded the attention of the whole village is asking my opinion!

"Yes, it made perfect sense," I reply. "Is anyone badly hurt from last night?"

"Not badly," Grace reports. "A number of small injuries from running around in the woods, and some scuffles that broke out, of course. But nobody had their heart fully in it, so bruises and shallow cuts make up the most of it. Adam has some nasty burns from throwing himself through the fire, unsurprisingly, but that's entirely his own stupid fault."

Adam gives a rueful grin as he is once again reminded. As I think of how he stepped through the wall of fire rather than leave us there; how Grace trusted me enough to let me guide Callum without her help; how she and Nia risked so much to warn us; how Callum showed his newfound character when he stopped running; how Tom defied everyone's expectations to take charge of the village and lead them out of chaos and violence into a peaceful fresh start,

I feel as if I am overflowing with admiration for them all. I beam at each of them, and say, "Thank you for bringing me home."

And now everyone is smiling back at me, as if they are actually happy I'm here. I would not exchange all the forests and fairy tales in the world for this.

Callum wonders aloud what we should all do now. Tom, who is ready to take a short rest from being responsible for everyone, suggests we go and sit for a while by the old war memorial. I suspect he chooses it because it faces north out of the village, and you cannot see the forest from there. If it is burned and charred, I don't want to know just yet.

CHAPTER SEVEN

RHIANNON

We have begun to settle into this new shape of our lives: so like the old way of things and yet so different. Adam and Grace have been gone a few days, but we haven't said goodbye to them yet because we knew they'd be back today.

Diana and I take my cousins to meet them in the village when they arrive. They have brought their mother with them: a gentle-looking woman whose age I would never have been able to guess. As I see the way they help her from the car and walk with her across the road, I am struck by all the kindness I have yet to show Diana.

"Ooh, she's beautiful!" Eira whispers. "I like her dress."

I squeeze Eira's hand. "Shall we go and say hello to her then?"

She nods eagerly, and we walk over to them, while Diana follows with Owen. It has been less than a week since I saw Adam and Grace, but it feels much longer.

"Hello again, Rhiannon," says Grace. "We'd like you to meet our mother, Abenaa Trewent."

"You are Rhiannon?" she says in a strong, beautiful accent, and I can't help but wonder what she has heard about me. "Bless you, dear girl. I am glad to meet you."

She has such sparkling eyes; she reminds me of Maebh. And here, as if on cue, is Maebh herself. Tom is walking with her over from her house. I wonder what the two of them will make of each other: Emrys's widow and the woman who has been trying to tell his story for almost fifty years.

289

I stand back as the two of them meet. I do not hear what is spoken between them, but I see the moment when Abenaa hugs Maebh.

We are meeting the others at our destination, so we all get into the cars and set out. We drive out of Llandymna, past the farm. I imagine Adam and Grace in the car ahead of ours pointing out to their mother the house where they stayed.

We have to stop a short way from Dyrys, because the roads are in bad condition after several days of rain. We walk together up the slope, taking it slowly for the sake of those who find walking much harder. To my surprise, Diana deliberately relaxes her pace to walk level with Abenaa, while I go on ahead with Adam and Grace.

"May I ask you something about your husband?" Diana asks.

"Of course," Abenaa nods.

"Did you talk with him much, towards the end?"

"Oh, we talked about everything! Why do you ask?"

"It's just that when Edwin, my late husband, was ill, it took me so long to face up to what was happening that I never got to have that last conversation with him. I would have liked to say so much."

"How long were you two married?"

"Ten years."

"Ten years is good. You live with someone every day, care for them, laugh with them: that's your conversation. I'm certain you had already said everything that mattered – through your days together if not in your words."

"Yes," Diana says, looking a little more hopeful. "Yes, I think you're right."

Up ahead, Nia is waiting for us on a little corner of the farmland where the forest has strayed past its borders. I hear the sound of running behind us, and there is Callum, racing to catch up with the group after he set out too late.

Everything is ready for us: the spot of earth, the green sapling the Trewents have chosen, the plaque that will sit at its foot. Though Emrys's life came to an end far from where it began, Adam and

Grace decided they wanted to commemorate him here as well, as an act of reconciliation with the village. So we've gathered here today to remember someone many of us have never met but have all been affected by.

Adam starts the digging, but others step in and offer to take a turn, and he is happy to hand over the spade. When the hole is deep enough, he and Grace plant the young tree while their mother says a prayer of thanks for her husband's life. I notice that she is holding the pocket watch that I found in the woods. I'm glad they gave it to her. They set the plaque in front of the tree, and we all stand in silence for a while on the side of that hill. Over the shoulders of my friends and family, Dyrys stretches away, like an old friend with whom I share many secrets.

As we walk back down towards the road, I skip to catch up with Nia.

"Goodness, you can run fast these days, Rhiannon!" she remarks.

"I wanted to talk to you about something," I say. "Well, to ask you a question, really. I was wondering whether – what with Ifan being away for a bit – if it would be OK for me to come and help out on the farm. Because the thing is, I don't think I can go back to being indoors all the time, not straight away. I've talked to Diana, and we've agreed I won't go back to finish my A-levels just yet. I'm going to take some time off first and then maybe do my exams later. So I hoped I could maybe come and work for you for a while."

"Of course you can. I'd love to have your help. And I might even pay you in something better than a few sneaked vegetables."

My mouth drops open. "You knew it was me who stole them?"

Nia smiles. "I guessed eventually."

Callum joins us on the way back.

"She said yes then?" he says.

I nod.

"You'll get to keep living outside, more or less. You'll be good at that too."

We go back to the farmhouse and sit in the front room. After a while the solemnity of the memorial gives way to lighter talk, and suddenly we are our normal selves. Callum tells the story of how he once tried to push Adam into the stream and managed to miss and lose his balance. Then we move on to explaining how we built a house from scratch for Callum. Abenaa asks Maebh to tell her what Emrys was like as a child, and Maebh shares some stories from her school days that sound almost familiar, as if she has told them before in another way.

I want to keep on laughing and talking, but the moment I've been dreading is here. Adam, Grace, and Abenaa are getting ready to leave. I watch them say their goodbyes to each person, and part of me hopes that they'll forget me – that I won't have to say anything. I have no idea how to thank them enough for all they have done. Whatever I say will feel inadequate. They thank Nia for her hospitality and welcome, commend Tom for all he has handled in the last few weeks, tell Callum to keep out of trouble, and wish Diana the very best for herself and her family.

Abenaa reaches me first. She takes my hands in hers.

"You have lived in the woods, so you know part of Emrys's story better than anyone now," she says. "Thank you for finding the watch that was his. I will treasure it, and so will Kofi and Ayawa."

"You're welcome," I say. "Thank you for coming here today. I think it's done everyone so much good to meet you and say goodbye to Emrys."

She pats my hand and then looks to her right. "I think my children want to speak to you now."

They are walking towards me, and I still have no idea what to say to them.

"We wanted to thank you," says Grace.

"Wha– you did?" I stammer.

"We were saying to each other on the drive here," says Adam, "how much we've learned from you. You're one of the most resourceful and determined people we've ever met. I'm certain that whatever you decide to do with your life, you won't give up until you've done it."

"And we have a small gift for you," says Grace. "Well, Adam's responsible for it, really."

She hands me a square of tissue paper. I unfold it and instantly recognize what is inside. I often wondered what Adam was whittling out of the piece of wood he picked up that day in the forest. Now a small wooden sparrow nestles in my palm, with a small hook fixed in its back so that it could hang on a chain.

"It's a reminder," says Grace, "of what you said about sparrows that day in the woods. That even if they might not look like the most imposing or impressive birds, they are brave and they look after one another, and that's important."

"It's wonderful," I say, and I take out the pendant that hangs around my neck and attach the sparrow to the chain, so that it sits next to the other three charms. Then I look back up to their smiling faces and take a deep breath.

"I need to say thank you. I don't think you know the impact you've had. When I first met you, I was angry and scared, and I didn't trust anyone. I left this place as a ball of rage and resentment and rejection. But you always chose not to focus on that side of me, even though I'm sure you must have seen it. Thank you for believing in me enough to bring out the best in me. You gave me the chance to restore, to find out what I'm capable of. You trusted me more than I trusted myself. I won't ever forget that."

I know I will cry if I say another word. I hug them both, and we say goodbye. Then we wave from the farmhouse as the Trewents drive away.

Callum sighs as the car disappears out of sight.

"Well," he says, the way people do when they need to say something. We look around the yard at one another: the residents of Llandymna, returning to normal life.

"Rhiannon." Diana marches over to me, displaying her superhuman ability to avoid getting mud on her shoes without appearing to break her stride. "Nia tells me the others are going to the White Lion now. I'm taking the children home, and I'll drive Maebh back too, but don't worry about coming with us if you'd like to go to the pub with them."

"Thanks," I say. "I'll see you later then."

"Right. Come on, Eira; time to stop playing with the dog!"

Eira reluctantly leaves Megan the border collie and returns to the car.

"Is Rhiannon coming with us?" she asks.

"Not just yet," Diana answers.

"But she is coming home, isn't she?" Eira presses. "She isn't going away again?"

I pick her up and realize how much heavier she is now than the last time I did this. I hear Diana sigh crossly at the sight of Eira's muddy shoes leaving prints on my trousers, but she manages to stop herself saying anything about it.

"I'll be back in time to read you a bedtime story, I promise."

Eira's face lights up at once. "Can it be one about talking animals?" she asks.

"If you like."

Diana smiles appreciatively as Eira gets into the car without any further fuss.

"Right then," says Tom when they have gone, "are we going up to the White Lion now?"

"Go on ahead," I say. "I'll catch you up in a minute or two."

Tom, Nia, and Callum walk up the lane towards the village. I run in the opposite direction, up the hill to the oak sapling surrounded by freshly turned earth. I sit down next to it, in the shadow of the first trees of Dyrys.

In just a moment, I will run back down the hill to join my friends. I will spend an afternoon catching up with them on the last two months. We will swap stories, or tell the same one from our four different perspectives. If I can, I will find a chance to share my favourite memory: of the day we built a swing over the stream.

Before any of that, however, I want to take a moment to sit up here looking out over the village that is welcoming again. Up here, where the wind is a little fiercer than down in the valley, I am motionless for a moment next to this young tree. I trace my finger over the letters of the plaque near it.

In memory of Emrys Trewent
It is never too late to go home

I am looking forward to the low roar of conversation again. But up here the only sounds are the gentle sway of Dyrys's trees, the wind brushing the tops of the fireweed, and the bright chatter of sparrows singing again.

THE RUNAWAY
Reading Group Questions

1. What do you think is the main reason why Rhiannon ran away from home?

2. Which character did you most relate to? Did you sympathize with one more than others?

3. Fences and boundaries are a recurring image in *The Runaway*. Why do you think they are important to the characters?

4. What were your first impressions of Diana? Do you think her involvement in village life does more good or harm?

5. Who do you think has the biggest influence on Rhiannon's worldview?

6. Maebh believes in the power and importance of stories, but Rhiannon's experiences show that there can be a cost in too much escapism. How have stories affected your life?

7. How would events have played out differently if Adam and Grace had never decided to come to Llandymna?

Claire Wong

An interview with the author…

What first inspired you to write The Runaway?

Over the years I've seen a lot of people struggling with big questions about their identity and place in the world. I think *The Runaway* started out as a letter to all the Rhiannons out there who desperately need to hear that they are doing OK and that the world is better than it looks right now.

Do you have a particular writing routine?

I like to start writing early in the day, and have my desk set up with a notebook, laptop, and cup of peppermint tea. If I get stuck at any point, going outside for a walk has the effect of hitting the refresh button on my brain!

What is the writing habit that you rely on to get you through a first draft?

It's a constant reminder to myself that now is not the time to be a perfectionist! For me, the first draft is about telling the story, throwing the words onto the page and giving yourself permission for the prose to be rough around the edges.

Which living author(s) do you most admire?

I admire Margaret Atwood for her sheer cleverness and versatility, and I absolutely love Niall Williams' beautiful style of writing.

Which book would you take to a desert island?

Prince Caspian, or any of The Chronicles of Narnia. I find there's so much depth to C. S. Lewis' writing that I can happily keep re-reading his books and always find something new and wonderful in them.

How much of you is there in your characters?

There's quite a lot of tea and cake consumed in this book, and that is certainly a reflection of what I consider important in life!

Who would your fantasy dinner guests be?

I like to think that Jane Austen and I would get on very well, which is probably down to how much her books have influenced my sense of humour. I'd also invite Virgil (the Roman poet, not the character from Thunderbirds) as I think he'd bring an excellent bottle of wine as a gift, and Walter Raleigh for some good travel anecdotes over dessert.

Which book do you wish you had written?

The Princess Bride by William Goldman. It's such a fun, irreverent adventure in a genre that is often quite serious and dignified. And it's extremely quotable. I remember once sitting in an office where half the staff knew the book and half didn't. One woman looked around at us all and said, "OK, shall we do this?" and with no further prompting half of us chorused, "Hello, my name is Inigo Montoya. You killed my father. Prepare to die!"

Who is your favourite literary character?

Dr Watson. He's easily overlooked next to Sherlock Holmes, but he manages to maintain compassion and kindness, and he's not afraid to be amazed rather than cynical in response to the world.

Did any of the characters in your book surprise you while writing?

Definitely Diana. When I started writing from Rhiannon's perspective, I knew that this girl who loves fairy tales needed someone to take the role of the wicked stepmother, at least as far as she viewed her world. In creating Diana, I drew from some real life characters I had observed, who took charge in small communities and seemed to enjoy that sense of importance. I didn't expect to like Diana, but as I wrote about her I found myself sympathizing more and more with this woman who is under so much pressure, even if a lot of it is self-imposed. She's more complicated and interesting than I intended.

What would your superpower be?

I'd love to have the power to be able to instantly understand and speak every new language I hear!

What is the worst job you've done?

I briefly worked in a cemetery one summer, and it was actually really interesting. The trouble was that although I was fascinated by everything I was learning about environmentally-friendly burial options, it made for quite morbid after-work conversations and I think I scared some of my friends.

What is the most important lesson life has taught you?

I've learned that I value being kind more than being right.

Which book (not your own) do you wish everyone would read?

Winnie-the-Pooh by A. A. Milne. I quote it regularly, and it makes me sad when people respond with blank confusion.

Which book do you suspect most people claim to have read, but haven't?

The Three Musketeers by Alexandre Dumas. There are enough film and TV adaptations around to be able to pass quite convincingly for knowing the story, but when I finally got round to reading it earlier this year I couldn't believe that no one had ever mentioned the ending!

How do you feel about physical books versus e-books?

I know e-books are very convenient for reading while travelling or for saving limited shelf space, but personally I always prefer the feeling of holding a printed book in my hands.

Do you have any advice for an aspiring author?

Read a lot. Write a lot. Be wary of taking too much advice.

The Second Bride

"With stunning prose and deep emotion, Katharine Swartz weaves a powerful story of love and redemption."

Maisey Yates, New York Times bestselling author

Ellen Tyson is living the perfect village life in Goswell. But when her stepdaughter moves in, her fragile idyll is fractured. At seventeen, Annabelle is surly, withdrawn, and adamant that she isn't, and never will be, part of her father's second family. As Ellen battles with Annabelle, new tensions arise with her husband Alex, shattering the happiness she'd once so carelessly enjoyed.

Then Ellen finds a death certificate from the 1870s hidden under the floorboards, and its few stark lines awaken a curiosity in her. Ellen tries to involve Annabelle in her search for answers. But as they dig deeper into the circumstances of Sarah Mills' untimely death, truths both poignant and shocking come to light – about the present as well as the past.

Interlacing the lives of Ellen Tyson and Sarah Mills, *The Second Bride* is a captivating and moving story about what it means to be a family, and the lengths we will go to for the people we love.

"The Second Bride kept me turning the pages until the early hours!"

Kathleen McGurl, author of The Daughters of Red Hill Hall

ISBN 978 1 78264 212 1 | e-ISBN 978 1 78264 213 8